Praise for *The Inside Out Man*

"A page-burner of a psychological horror story unfolding with the style and intrigue of film noir, *The Inside Out Man* is a compelling, unsettling exploration of identity, desire, and the darkest regions of the human psyche."
—Jacqueline Baker, author of *The Broken Hours*

"Near pitch-perfect prose that will keep the reader spellbound. A finely wrought and twisty novel that dares to go where few authors would." —*Cape Times*

"A well-written page-turner that will have you looking over your shoulder, or perhaps in directions you didn't know existed, *The Inside Out Man* explores the inner depths of the mind and the soul as it races toward a climax as unexpected as it is satisfying." —Richard Cox, author of *The Boys of Summer*

"Astounding . . . a psychological thriller that feels familiar, and yet is unlike anything I've read." —*Africa in Words*

"Fred Strydom is back with yet another thrilling and genius book . . . [his] effortless use of language and imagination takes the reader on a psychological euphoria with every turn of the page." —*SABC Digital News*

"Multilayered, honest and, as promised, a hell of a trip."
—*Books LIVE: Sunday Times*

"Brilliantly sneaky—a story as darn and bent (cough cough) as the main character, *The Inside Out Man* is as unpredictable as it is macabre and thrilling. . . . without doubt the best South African fiction title of the year. Kudos to the author; he's a rock star."—*A Girl with a Book*

THE
INSIDE OUT
MAN

Also by Fred Strydom

The Raft

THE
INSIDE OUT
MAN

FRED STRYDOM

Talos Press
NEW YORK

First published by Umuzi, an imprint of Random House South Africa (Pty) Ltd, in 2017

Talos Press books may be purchased in bulk at special discounts for sales promotion, corporate gifts, fund-raising, or educational purposes. Special editions can also be created to specifications. For details, contact the Special Sales Department, Talos Press, 307 West 36th Street, 11th Floor, New York, NY 10018 or info@skyhorsepublishing.com.

Talos Press® is a registered trademark of Skyhorse Publishing, Inc.®, a Delaware corporation.

Visit our website at www.talospress.com.

10 9 8 7 6 5 4 3 2 1

Library of Congress Cataloging-in-Publication Data

Names: Strydom, Fred, author.
Title: The inside-out man / by Fred Strydom.
Description: New York : Talos Press, [2017]
Identifiers: LCCN 2017006609| ISBN 9781945863110 (softcover : acid-free
  paper) | ISBN 9781945863141 (ebook)
Subjects: LCSH: Psychological ficton. | GSAFD: Horror ficton.
Classification: LCC PR9369.4.S85 I57 2017 | DDC 823/.92--dc23
LC record available at https://lccn.loc.gov/2017006609

Cover artwork and design by Mujtaba Sayed

Printed in the United States of America

For my mother and Wytze, who showed me all the doors,
but taught me to get my own keys cut

*People know what they want because they
know what other people want.*
—Theodor W. Adorno

The piano ain't got no wrong notes.
—Thelonious Monk

One Year Later

There is a nightclub on the corner of Bree and Orphan that sits between a pretentious restaurant and a musty old bookstore.

The fine-dining restaurant does its best to make you forget where you are. It'll have you believe you're in a centuries-old landmark in France, which may never in fact have existed. It's always full of people more than happy to bolster the lie, all there to pretend for an evening they don't have to go home to lazy sex and laundry baskets in their charmless homes.

The bookstore, on the other hand, is stacked from floor to ceiling with a shabby assortment of abandoned works. It is an orphanage for bastards, the issue of dead authors' love affairs. Nobody goes in and nobody comes out, and I am probably not the first to wonder how the shop covers its rent.

Between these two establishments, there is a building with a red door. A gold-plated plaque is etched with the club's name: Ten To Twelve. Enter the red door and you'll climb a steep flight of rough wooden stairs. On the second-floor landing, an enormous woman sits on a stool. After handing her the entrance fee, she pulls your change from a vintage cookie tin. On its lid is a grinning fifties housewife on a dinky blue motorcycle, with the slogan THE NICEST PEOPLE RIDE A HONDA! Fat fingers rummage in the tin and then touch your own as she passes your change.

You can smell onions on her; she's been eating a boerewors roll from the greasy vendor up the street.

But that's only if *you* go to the club.

I just get a nod from the Onion Woman, and walk straight in. It's dark and warm inside. Not the good kind of warmth, mind you, the kind that hugs you in your bed in winter, but the warmth of sweaty bodies and backroom generators and things decaying in drains.

The place is full of people, but I can't see their faces. I walk between sets of floating teeth and make my way to the bar. The barman, he knows me, but he isn't friendly. He'd almost certainly ignore me if he saw me on the street, but he knows what I like to drink—whiskey and ginger ale on ice—and he pours one as soon as I arrive.

I turn and suss out the silhouettes in front of me. The tips of cigarettes flare orange, and smoke curls upwards to the ceiling.

This crowd looks no different from a crowd on any other night, and I know the lighting (or lack thereof) is arranged to accomplish precisely this: to keep the vibe of the venue consistent, night after night after night. More than most, I've seen clubs come and go, and I tell you, that's the key to longevity: predictability. People will tell you they want spontaneity and innovation, but they're only kidding themselves. As shitty and grotty as a place might be, what matters most is that it's consistently shitty and grotty, and believe me, it will then live to rot another day.

In about five minutes, the manager of Ten To Twelve will arrive and sit beside me and shake my hand and ask about my day. He's a short man in his early thirties. His hair's gelled up into spikes, and he's all smiles. He's the manager because he knows how to smile at people he dislikes, and he's a particularly good manager when smiling at me. He'll ask if I'm ready, if my vinnige vingers are feeling up to another good show, and I'll nod and sip my drink and joke that I got a manicure just for tonight, and he'll grab my shoulder and laugh.

Then he'll head to the small stage at the back of the club and introduce me to the crowd. He'll refer to me as the real deal, the man of the hour, the Jehovah of Jazz, and that'll be my cue to down my drink and walk up. Everyone will clap and the spotlight will fall on the piano that's been sitting in the darkness like a coffin at the altar. I'll take my seat, lift the lid, and lean in to the drooping mike to thank everyone for coming.

At that point I'll do what I do best, the only thing I know how to do. I'll play jazz. I'll stretch my fingers across the keys and move them faster than I'm even aware of doing. I'll sweat and I'll forget. I'll forget about the Onion Woman, the grinning manager, and the crowd of teeth.

I'll forget about the whole goddamned world.

And for a while, all conversations will be put on hold. Not a word. Cos they'll all be listening, you see—that shapeless mass of teeth and smoke out there—listening as I rant and scream and cry through the strings of the piano, furiously imploring them all to set me free.

I.

Scratch, scratch

1.

First things first.

My name is not Bentley Croud.

It's been so long since anyone's called me by my full name that I imagine it belonging to some smiling stranger at some dull party. Someone tanned and healthy and successful. Whites of the eyes admitting to few or no vices. Straight rows of pristine teeth that have taken no punches. Someone who looks like me, has my face, shares my birthday, but who's taken every road I didn't, said a no to each of my yesses and a yes to each of my nos. That would be your Bentley Croud, and that would not be me.

No. The *I* in the story I'm about to tell you is simply known as Bent.

Bent. The misshapen state.

2.

I lived on the second floor of a run-down building on Lower Main, Observatory. The ground floor offered nothing but a succession of undernourished businesses on a street that fared no better. There was a poorly stocked hardware store that opened and closed erratically, obliging itself to no one. Beside the hardware store stood a Korean mart that sold ramen noodles, big plastic bags of tiny dried fish, cheap feather dusters that moulted at first stroke, small remote-controlled cars, and ceramic ashtrays shaped like the Venus de Milo or the Arc de Triomphe. There was also a barbershop that, in the four years I'd been living there, hadn't fixed its broken front window, opting instead for planks from a wooden crate. It was run by a Nigerian who more than likely facilitated a far more lucrative back-alley business after dark.

These three stores held up two floors of single-room apartments. Mine sat second from the end of a narrow corridor with a nappy-green carpet. The ceiling globes were filled with dead moths. I knew little about the occupants of the other rooms on the floor. Their doors were always shut, and the only sounds were the gabbling of televisions and the flushing of toilets. Every now and again there were the roars and shrieks and thuds of an argument, but nobody dared intervene, or call the police. The doors stayed shut and the televisions got turned up until the guy yelling that his wife was a *cheating fuckin' whore* got his own canned laughter.

I did, however, once go into my neighbour's apartment. He'd knocked on my door to ask if I could help fix his radio. An old man with a balding head and long grey strands that fell to his shoulders, he was fidgety and frustrated, barely acknowledging me even as he asked his favour. I soon realised that his problems were graver than chronic restlessness. His apartment was like a demented version of my own—the identical layout, except that everything was blackening and rotting, seemingly from the inside out. The windows were boarded up, and the kitchen bin was a Vesuvius of waste running all the way into the living room.

The radio itself seemed to be working fine, and I turned the knob, switching from station to station, to show him. He insisted it wasn't. He said he needed the numbers from the voice on the radio, and they just weren't coming any more. He'd scrawled hundreds of these numbers on his walls, on his refrigerator, and even on the grubby brown upholstery of his couch. But he couldn't find the pattern if the numbers stopped coming. Without the numbers there was nothing, he said. No meaning behind any of it. Without the numbers, there was only chaos and madness and fear. I searched the stations for the supposed numbers, going back and forth, but found nothing. I told him I didn't think there *were* any numbers, that there *was* no voice. At that point he grabbed me by my collar and threw me out of his apartment, bawling his eyes out as he shut the door behind me.

It was only much later that I learnt he'd once been the Head of Applied Mathematics at the university—a genius in the field of graph theory. An agoraphobic schizophrenic, but a genius nonetheless. He'd been dismissed after child pornography had been discovered on his office computer, and the wife had left soon after. His children had stopped calling, and he'd somehow ended up next door to me on the second floor of the Crack

Radisson, waiting for a pattern to emerge from the mess of things.

But that was only one story. One among many of the people living on my floor. The rest of the stories remained behind those closed doors, like the stories in shelved books, revealing nothing but their dusty spines. Most of those stories I would never know—or probably want to know.

There was one thing we had in common, though, and for that we may have been smarter than everyone else: we were all paying the lowest rent in town to house our shame.

3.

On Mondays I played at The Bijou, on Tuesdays at Van Hunks, and on Saturdays at Ten To Twelve. Each venue had its own piano, and each piano its own personality. Sometimes I was offered a percentage on the door, other times I was paid a fixed amount for a set. Neither method concerned me much, as long as I was allowed partial custody of my three idiosyncratic pianos. The Bijou had the stubborn keys, Van Hunks the cleanest chords, and the piano at Ten To Twelve was so light to the touch, so ready to release its sounds, I often felt it would play itself if it could. Sometimes crowds would trickle in, other times they were already there, packed tight in a murk of smoke and waiting. Truth is, once I began it didn't really matter whether I was playing for the Sultan of Brunei or Shirley's Hen Do—the audience became faceless, featureless observers, like ghosts in a haunted house. Once I'd finished playing (though it was not so much *playing* as it was urgently digging a tunnel out of a prison cell), I'd come around with clammy hands, a pounding heart, and the dizzy sense my atoms were being slowly reassembled.

Afterwards, I'd be approached by members of the crowd. I had to shake their hands, answer their questions, and welcome their gratitude—and I casually accepted this as part of my profession. There might be a woman out there who thought I was worth sleeping with, or a man who considered me interesting enough to pull a stool up to mine, but I was too well acquainted with these gestures to exploit them guiltlessly. This was simply how things went at these things.

One particular Monday, I finished up at The Bijou around ten-thirty, skipped the usual courtesies, collected my pay, and headed straight out. The joint was only a few blocks from my apartment, so I walked it. The street was quiet and empty, and my footsteps echoed. A dog barked, a bottle rolled along the concrete, and trees shushed in the wind. By the time I reached my block, the cold had crept through my coat and my cardigan to the flesh beneath. I buzzed my card at the front gate, walked to the lobby, went inside, and took the rickety elevator to the top floor.

Open this door, dammit!

The elevator had just creaked open, and I could hear yelling from down the corridor. The culprit came into view. A big man was beating his fists against the door next to mine. I fumbled for my keys in my coat pocket and crossed the carpet, avoiding his eyes as if he were some wild animal.

I'm warning you, I'm warning you! Open this door!

His fists swung against the door, mercilessly pummelling it. His face was glowing red. His breath hissed through gritted teeth. A sweat-drenched fringe hung over his eyes like rats' tails.

I'll kick this door down, I swear it! And when I do, when I do—

He gave the door a low kick with the steel tip of his boot. Good for him. I grabbed at a key, stuck it in and turned. The wrong key.

A woman's voice: *Go away!*

Okay, you're asking for it. You hear me? I said you're asking for it! Julie! I'm going to count to three, and I swear to God!

I flicked to another key and stuck it in the door. For some reason I turned my head and caught his eye. Both raised fists were against the door, his chest heaving as he caught his breath.

He was sizing me up, calculating my height and width and whether there was the right amount of cocky disdain to pull his fists from the practice range and bring them to the pit.

And you? What you think you looking at? You fucking my wife too?

I gave a quick shake of my head, pushed open the door, and shut it behind me.

Next thing I was aware of were the theatrical sounds of rough sex. I was lying on my bed in the dark of my room, trying to get to sleep, but brought back to wakefulness by *thump-moan-thump-shriek-thump*. She'd clearly let him inside at some point (I hadn't heard a door being kicked in), though I couldn't tell whether they'd reconciled or were punishing each other. I climbed out of bed and went to the window. A crumpled box of Princeton cigarettes lay in a bin beside the dressing table. I reached in to fish it out, straightened the box, and pulled out the only cigarette among five that wasn't broken. I shoved my window open, lit up, and breathed a grey cloud into the night.

The lights of the city were yellow, like sickly stars beneath the moon, bright and full. I remembered reading about horses that drop dead for no apparent reason during a full moon, and spent a moment wondering why that might happen. No possible explanation came, so I let go of the whole thing. For a moment I even forgot about the couple next door bashing against my wall; there was nothing novel about this incursion, and it wouldn't last longer than another two or three minutes anyway.

I flicked the last quarter of the cigarette out the window, and in the darkness I walked to the kitchen. I opened the fridge and tried to figure out what combination of condiments and left-overs could be used to make a quick meal, but nothing came to me. By the time I closed the fridge door, the sounds of sex had ended, and I went back to bed.

That's when my phone rang.

My phone did not ring often and definitely not at that time of night. A wrong number, most likely. I answered. A man introduced himself. He said he was an uncle, one I hadn't seen or heard from in many years. Still, I wasn't sure he was who he claimed to be (at any point, I was expecting the imposter to request a deposit into his bank account). He told me he'd been struggling to find my number all day, that he'd finally got it from one of the clubs (which pissed me off), but I listened carefully anyway, the way one listens only when there is nothing else on one's mind. The way an insomniac puts up with the repetitive details of a TV infomercial at three in the morning—listening to it and through it.

Then the man finally got to his point. He was calling, he said, to tell me my father had died.

4.

I don't know much about my father. He left me and my mother when I was too young even to remember my age at the time. In the instant I was told of his death, what little I recalled loomed as a big figure with big hands and the scent of aftershave. This was all I had of him, though even these pathetic memories may have been of some other man, or a movie I'd watched, or a dream I'd had.

When I was young, my mother did occasionally speak of this nebulous man, whose existence could be proven only by the fact that I myself existed. Sometimes she'd say just a few words to keep my curiosity at bay: *Your father cared more about himself than other people. That's all. Some people just do.*

She made it sound as if she was talking about the difference between people who prefer rain over sunshine, Bovril over Marmite. What she meant was that after my father's ship-building career really took off, in the early years of their marriage, he'd decided settling down and being responsible for a wife and child wasn't quite what he'd wanted after all. He was an explorer, my mother said, a neophiliac—preferring a new experience over a tried and tired one. She'd always known this, she'd go on to say. Even before they were married. It was part of the reason she fell in love with him, of course. But for her, marrying such an insatiably curious man would always mean a cold side of the bed to make use of on hot summer nights.

My mother was a piano tutor, and we were forced to get by on what little she made. She's the one who taught me to play, and were it not for my admiration of the great American jazzmen, her tutoring would have put me off for good. She'd sit beside me and poke a pen into my leg when I needed to play a sharp, and tap a book on my head to play a flat. She'd sigh, then grab my hands and move my fingers, insisting that every movement was either clumsy or wrong—some kind of musical abomination. Fortunately, my Art Tatum and Oscar Peterson records were there to modify my contempt, a reminder that I needed to know the rules before I could break them—and boy, would breaking them be good.

At the time, we were living on a smallholding on the slope of the mountain. There's not much I remember about that tiny house. I *do* remember it smelling of stale cigarettes and wet wood. I also remember that there was very little natural light and almost no ventilation, as if we were in a nuclear bunker during some untelevised war. But that was it. I may have just blotted the rest from my mind, without being aware.

Of the many years we stayed in that house, however, there was one night that often comes to mind. I've told myself it is yet another memory of my father—but I can't, and probably won't, ever be sure.

I was in my room doing something or other. My mother was in the lounge, smoking her umpteenth cigarette, building a mountain of yellow butts, as usual, in the perlemoen-shell ashtray that balanced on the armrest of the couch. There was a knock at the door and she got up to answer it. We almost never had visitors, so I went to my bedroom door to see who it was. I couldn't see much, but I heard a man's voice. It was deep but calm. He spoke with my mother for a while, and her voice rose as his began to sink. Soon, she was screaming at him. He said something like, *Take it, just take it*—and she was yelling that she wouldn't, and said, *Go to hell, we don't want it. Go right on off to hell!*

Then the fight was over, the door was shut, and I closed my own door. There was never a follow-up to that night. As the years went on, that's all I had to work with—that one night— like a detective trying to solve something that may or may not have been a crime at all. All I can add is that the following day my mother took me shopping for new clothes, something she hadn't done in months. *Money can't buy you happiness,* she told me, even as she bitterly (or not so bitterly) picked through rows of shoes, racks of coats, and shelves of perfume for herself. *If you remember that one thing, you'll be smarter than most of the grown men of the world.*

What she failed to add was that, while money couldn't buy you happiness, no money couldn't buy you anything at all.

Things did not improve. We left the house and moved into an even smaller place, a flat in the industrial part of town. Our furniture was always layered in a thin film of black ash, as smoke drifted through crevices from the crematorium next door. Not that our furniture stuck around for long. Eventually, even the piano was sold.

It was around this time that my mother started drinking. So often, I'd find her slouched on the living-room couch, her cheeks shining with tears, a bottle of brandy in her dangling hand.

By then I was playing well enough to give lessons myself, mostly to others kids from my school. I'd walk to their houses, give a lesson, and walk back after dark. The parents paid me modestly, but I'd have to hide my earnings in a sock at the top of my cupboard; more than once I'd caught my mother clawing at every nook and cranny for cigarette and booze money.

She accused me of lying to her, of plotting to leave her, of being exactly like my father. This didn't so much alarm as intrigue me. I was so desperate for direction that I looked to myself to better know my father. How was I like him? Was it the way I spoke, or walked, or something else? But there was nothing to be deduced: most of the time, she just blurted out her curses in a drunken stupor. She'd have pointed to a hat rack and compared it to my father—that is, if we hadn't already sold the hat rack.

And I was beginning to resent him. He'd been gone for longer than I could remember, but the teenage me wouldn't stand for what the pre-adolescent me had had to endure. My mother hadn't always been the sweaty, stinking woman in the living room, refusing to eat or shower. She'd once been a woman of dignity and grace. Stern, but giving. *He* was off somewhere, screwing around, cavorting, and spending his way to hell. Surrounding himself with the finest of everything. Paying for smiles. Not giving half a shit to be split two ways. And we were *here*.

Until it wasn't *we*. It was I.

A songwriter would probably have said my mother died of broken-heart, but to hell with all that. She died because she had more booze in her veins than blood. She died because she hadn't eaten a proper meal in days, and whatever she did have in her stomach had come back up her throat as thick, throttling bile. The morning I walked into her bedroom to find her sprawled on her sheets, naked and twisted and bloated, her face caked in vomit and her eyes rolled up like a broken slot machine, there wasn't a single blues song that came to mind. Not one romantic chord or lyric that could help make sense of the filth and the shame. And that was the one thing I'd always been able to count on.

Sometimes, I guess, there's nothing but the horror.

5.

There's a girl named Coby who bartends at one of the venues where I used to gig every so often. It was my favourite place in town to have a drink, and the only bar I'd frequent even when I wasn't about to gig. Could it have been because of the hipster décor, the selection of microbrewery beers, or perhaps the fact that nobody ever seemed to recognise me? Unlikely. It was probably because of Coby, my saddest version of a soulmate in a city where real friends are about as hard to catch as a suntan on a rainy day.

Coby must have been in her late twenties, I reckon, though I'd never had the courage to ask. She was a pretty girl, no one could say otherwise, but made a helluva effort trying to mask all that with dark eyeshadow and a factory's worth of metal piercings. Her hair was short and pixie-like, and there was always a new tint, green one week, purple the next. Sometimes, watching as she worked, I imagined what she must have looked like as a schoolgirl: I invariably pictured one of those posed school portraits that usually ends up in some dumb frame on a mantelpiece. I imagined Coby virginal and freckled and smiley and a little awkward. No eyeshadow hiding her tiny eyes, no gel spiking her frizzy ginger-blonde hair, yet all the while suppressing a small inner voice—her parents had picked her hair, her maroon uniform, and the photographer her smile—that one day, one *goddamned* day, she'd show them who she truly was . . . chains, rings, tints, grotty bar job, and all.

After getting the call from the mysterious uncle about the death of a father I had never known, I couldn't get to sleep, so I snatched my coat and left to see if Coby was on shift. I entered the bar and took a seat, grudgingly allowing my order to be taken by a barman. Coby was at the far end of the counter, leaning and grinning at some tall, long-haired biker guy. He had a smirk stitched shut across his face, like the scar on Frankenstein's monster's forehead—the one that stopped its brains from falling out. He kept his calculating, dozy eyes on her, mumbling something witless, I imagined, and she seemed to be lapping it up. My drink arrived and I downed most of it. Eventually, she made her way to my side of the bar. She smiled and I smiled back, raising my glass. Was I just another one of these idiots, thinking her smiles meant anything more than a call to help pay her rent?

Hello stranger, she said. *I haven't seen you here in a while.*

I smiled and lifted my glass. She wiped the counter as she filled me in on her week: the leave her boss wouldn't allow her to take for her sister's graduation. Her cat's skin issue. The homeless woman who'd stumbled in the previous week and gone picking through the pots. The desperation of a starving woman hadn't even crossed Coby's mind: *It must be great being like that*, she said, *not giving two shits about anyone and just waltzing in to take whatever you want. Pretty free way of being, huh?*

I didn't say what I was thinking—freedom of that sort always ended up as no freedom at all. Instead, I nodded and sipped at my drink.

I asked about her sister's graduation; I figured it was the topic she'd be most willing to discuss. Also, the question made me seem sensitive and selfless. It worked. Coby's eyes widened and she dropped her flirty demeanour. She told me her sister had just finished her final year and would soon be an honest-to-god doctor, though in *her* eyes her sibling was still that twelve-year-old using a plastic stethoscope on a teddy bear.

Seriously, can you believe it? she asked, as if I too might only be able to imagine this medical student as a child.

I smiled and shook my head.

I know, right? Anyway, Bent, when you playing for us again?

I told her I didn't know. Her boss hadn't got in touch with me and I knew better than to ask. When he had the money, I'd have the gig.

Coby paused, smiled and nodded. She asked me about my week.

I shrugged and told her the apartment *was* getting colder, that's for sure. A ridiculous thing to say, but it was the truth: the apartment was getting chillier by the day—and with regard to lifestyle, winter is transformative in every way. It changes the way you sleep, the length and frequency of your showers, the colour of your skin, the amount of food you eat, and your levels of activity. This kind of issue bothers me, exhilarates me, alters my physical form, and gets me thinking in utterly new ways. My music changes. My interests change. My concepts of comfort and discomfort evolve. What could be bigger than that? To Coby, however, I was just talking about the weather.

You know what I like about you, Bent? she said.

What's that?

You're simple, she said. *Complicated as all hell, but simple.*

And then she turned to serve some other guy.

6.

I'd already found my grey suit jacket, the one I'd worn only twice some years ago. All I needed was a tie. The first time I'd worn the suit had been at an interview for a call-centre job (which lasted a week before my tiny cubicle and stack of weak leads plunged me into an existential quandary). The second occasion was a Halloween party I attended as a demonic lawyer. Good look, mind you—suit, briefcase, and flaming red face with horns. That had been the last time. Since then, the jacket had wrinkled at the collar and the shoulders had lost their shape. Also, it wouldn't button up without giving me the Heimlich manoeuvre.

Finally, I found a tie, one I'd probably borrowed from someone a very long time ago (I don't think I've ever actually bought a tie). I put it on, then grabbed my black shoes from the bottom of my bedroom wardrobe, and sat on the armchair near the window to polish them. I slipped them on, and did up the laces. Opening the wardrobe, I combed my hair in the full-length mirror on the inside of the door. I parted my hair to the right, created a neat path of white scalp, and combed the sides flat. I tightened the noose of my tie, and patted the front of my jacket.

For at least a minute, I stared at my own reflection, waiting for it to say something, explain itself, burst out laughing.

But the man in the mirror didn't move.

A man in a shabby suit with a hard and expressionless face in a shitty apartment, with nothing to say for himself. My eyes turned to the wall clock. I closed the wardrobe door. The funeral was in half an hour, and it'd take a good twenty minutes by car.

The taxi arrived. It hooted twice, waited a minute, and then hooted again. I didn't move. I stood in my apartment like a stranger in a foreign place. My suit was tight as a straitjacket and my hard shoes were cramping my feet. I leant against the wall, unable to breathe.

The walls began to warp, bulge and close in, as if to suffocate me. The mirror went mercurial in its frame, twisting the room. Twisting me. The car hooted again, and the walls and mirror flattened. Back to normal. My breath found its rhythm. I sat in the frayed corner armchair, stared at nothing for the longest while, dressed like the dead man himself. And then, finally, the hooting stopped.

7.

The attorney was a fat man with a head that looked as if it could be popped with a pin. His big office smelt like some kind of fast food, and an ashtray on his desk was filled with the yellow corpses of Dunhill cigarettes. The curved walls were lined with shelves of law books, endless volumes I could barely imagine being read in their entirety. Ornately framed certificates and photographs lined the walls: fat attorney in sunglasses on a catamaran. Fat attorney standing beside a prominent politician. Fat attorney on a ski slope—geared up and grinning like a snowman who'd magically come to life.

Just the day before, I'd received the call from his secretary regarding my father's last will and testament, and so here I was, sitting before him in a red leather chair, watching him as he fumbled and sweated and spoke between wheezing breaths.

Your father was a secretive man, he said. *I know. I was his attorney for almost twenty years, and rarely met with him face-to-face. I know you've never met him. But your father was your father.* He slapped a brown folder on his desk. *Neither God Almighty, nor the law of Man can deny that.*

I don't want anything from my father, I said.

My words didn't surprise him. He didn't even look up. I could only deduce that he'd heard it all before—that he'd heard a hundred stubborn sons make a hundred stubborn statements about the final hand-out of their dead and disowned fathers. The fact I meant it was immaterial to him.

That may be so, he continued, licking his thumb to open the folder. *But your father's dead, so what I have here for you isn't his to give any more. At this very moment you're the owner, so do with your inheritance what you will after leaving this office, but it'll be leaving this office in your hands. Sorry, son.*

He cleared his throat and wiped his forehead. It was cold outside, but the central heating had been turned up to a level of which only Dante and the devil would approve. The fat man paged through documents in his folder, pulled out one and placed it neatly on the desk, then closed the folder and moved it aside. He leant forward, fixed his eyes on me, put his elbows on his desk, and wove his fingers together.

Now, he said, fingers flapping as if he were playing a trumpet. *What I'm about to give you on his behalf may or may not make sense to you. I suppose that's what your father intended. Like I said. A secretive man.*

I didn't want to listen to him go on about my absconded father. A lifetime of absence had more than convinced me.

Until that moment in that office, I'd entertained the possibility that the will was a hoax. But there was *my* name on a document, specifying a hitherto unknown inheritance—some mysterious item or amount I was entitled to, now that my father was dead.

Before I go ahead, do you have any other questions? he asked. It was a professional reflex; I could tell he was hoping there'd be none.

Was my father a good man?

A good man? I'm not sure what you mean.

You knew my father.

We probably met with each other only two or three times over the years.

And in your opinion, was he a good man?

The attorney rubbed his hands together and diverted his eyes, looking over my shoulder.

He was rarely in trouble with anyone, he said, his eyes return-ing to me. *I can tell you that much. I didn't expect a Christmas card every year, if that's what you're asking.*

His patience was the only thing about him growing thin. I said nothing in response, though he'd waited just long enough to give me the opportunity. Then he moved on with the pro-ceedings.

As I've already said, if you're expecting this to come with any kind of clarification, I'll have to disappoint you. I know nothing about what I'm about to give you. I have no idea where it belongs or what it opens. For all I know, it has sentimental or metaphorical value—who knows?

The attorney leant sideways and opened a drawer. He pulled out a small antique box adorned with minute, detailed engrav-ings. The attorney slid the box across the table, gestured with his palm for me to open it. He coughed loudly, took a handker-chief from his top pocket, and dabbed at the phlegm on his lips.

I stared at the wooden box for a moment, then laid my hands on the lid. I ran my fingertips over the narrow band of carvings, deciphering its peculiar narrative: an eagle swooping down on a rabbit, which was chasing a carrot, which was being dragged by a bicycle ridden by a boy, chasing a winged girl who was ascending into the sky, in pursuit of an eagle.

Slowly, I lifted the lid. I glanced up at the attorney, but he just shrugged. There was no note, label, or tag to explain the fact that, inside the box, there was nothing but a long, rusty key.

8.

I can't claim to understand this city.

I've lived in it my entire life, and yet the older I get the less sense it makes. It's a city of good intentions, I can say that, but then a good intention isn't worth a thing. You only need a Friday night on the town to see everyone's good intentions go up in a blaze, like a Viking funeral on a boat, disappearing into nothing.

Sitting in the back of a taxi on the way home from a gig, I looked out the window. The usual lot of people were scurrying and scrambling in search of some sort of good time: teenage girls with too much make-up shivering in queues, cupping their elbows, their knees knocking under finger-me skirts. Brawny XL jocks squeezed into medium t-shirts cotching in alleys as their friends uploaded YouTube clips. Discarded blue train loaves clogging drains outside coffee bars where fifty-buck butterscotch lattes are served in recycled jam jars. A dealer lurching from behind a column: *Hey you, you want it, jus' come with me, up here, around the corner, we almost there, jus' a little further, you got money on you?*

Across the road, a prostitute wearing a gold dress was chatting up a dark-suited businessman looking for a cheap lay— and no doubt wondering if all the talk about the plague was just propaganda: *Surely this one, the one right here, in front of you, surely she's fine? She's carrying a healthy amount of weight in her cheeks.*

The taxi eased past St. George's Cathedral, its stained-glass Christ triumphing over darkness and evil as he sits on the broken backs and crushed skulls of the slaves that laid the stones. Behind, the Company's Garden, with the rose beds, aviary, and that very old pear tree, where people choose to feed bushy-tailed rodents rather than the men slumped on benches. Around the corner, the Castle with its five bastions, home of the ghost of Lady Anne Barnard, who runs through the halls with her hands covering her face, and Governor van Noodt, doomed for all eternity to shout and swear at the ceilings. Underneath lies Donker Gat dungeon, the torture chamber where rain water often rose high enough to drown prisoners. Such stories abound in that place. Outside its walls, the crevices between pawn shops and electronics stores are haunted by addicts, gangsters, and thieves. Not quite dead, not quite alive.

We turned into Main Road, and I asked the driver to stop so I could buy some smokes. Back in the car, I asked if I could light up. He said it was fine, so I wound down the window and took a drag.

Soon afterwards, I was home.

9.

I couldn't sleep for days. I just lay beneath my blankets and stared at the ceiling. The problem was that the darkness wasn't merely the absence of light, it was a heavy substance, filled with something I couldn't recognise, couldn't name. It was the *light* that was empty. Switching on the bedside lamp didn't help. I could still see the night, swirling out there, pressing against the windows. Occasionally, I drifted in and out of some watery version of sleep, only to discover that scarcely five minutes had gone by when I awoke.

On the third night of sleeplessness, I opened my eyes and saw someone sitting in the armchair in the corner of my room.

I blinked.

The figure kept disappearing and reappearing, until I made out the shape of a man. His faceless head leant back, and long arms were draped over the armrests.

I called out to him, feeling stupid as I did so. The shape didn't move. It seemed to be watching me, or waiting for me. It's not a bag or a coat, but it isn't a man either, I thought. You're dreaming. You haven't slept in days, and this is some ridiculous half-and-half, the product of a delirious, fatigued brain. That, or the curtain's hanging skew, blocking the light in a funny way.

Finally, I flicked on the bedside lamp. There was no coat and no bag. The curtain wasn't hanging funny. But there was also no man. Apart from the familiar tatty armchair, I saw nothing at all.

10.

You look like shit, Coby said as I walked up to the bar. *Hey, sorry,* she laughed—embarrassed or maybe surprised she'd reached this level of blunt familiarity. *It's just . . . God, you look like shit. Are you sick or something?*

I smiled, told her I was cool, just not getting much sleep.

A lot on your mind?

My response was a pair of raised eyebrows.

She shook her head and said she'd fix me a drink. But I'd have to trust her and turn my eyes away—the elixir was an age-old secret translated from a sacred scroll, entrusted to her by a bearded wanderer in Yemen, a potion wrested long ago from the hands of ancient, warring nations . . .

I smiled, looked away, and let her get on with it. There seemed to be a good crowd. Coby's boss had finally got round to calling (I like to think Coby had something to do with it), and a gig had been put in place. As usual, he'd done a good job of marketing it; the house was packed to the rafters with seemingly sober people, and sober was always a good start.

Coby gave me the drink, which turned out to be a blend of coffee, Kahlúa, vodka and pumpkin juice, dressed with whipped cream and cinnamon. She asked me what I thought, and I told her it was delicious. She spoke about some drunk who'd bothered her earlier that evening, and a bookshop that had opened next door, run by a man who looked like long-haired Riff Raff from *The*

Rocky Horror Picture Show. I asked if she'd seen any good books in there and she laughed and said, *Naaah;* there were mostly old text-books, business manuals, and tattered self-help guides—books that taught the etiquette of gentlemen's clubs, how to smooch your boss's arse, and make sure the little lady at home didn't get any wild ideas about having a life of her own.

The manager was already up on the stage, tapping the mike as he drew the attention of the room. He welcomed everybody, reminded them of a two-for-one drink special, as well as an upcoming motorcycle charity ride, and then he introduced me. I made my way along a narrow opening towards the stage. Heads turned in my direction, and there was faint applause. The manager stepped out of the pool of light, clapping like a circus seal as he walked away.

A piano sat just beyond the spotlight. I cleared my throat, and took my seat. I ran the tips of my fingers over the cold keys, across their smooth ivory surfaces.

I closed my eyes, took a breath, and began.

Now, most improvised jazz is simply the ability to mutate and deploy familiar patterns, the jazz licks. There's nothing truly improvised apart from the combinations, the timings and the patterns you're willing to pull from your repertoire. Don't get me wrong: there are choices to be made, a significant amount of creativity, but jazz sounds like jazz for a reason. Do it enough, *steal* enough, and you can convince even yourself that you're making it all up as you go along. You won't even have to think about what to use and when to use it, just as a literary specialist effortlessly quotes from a myriad of poems to illuminate any given argument, or a preacher summons pas-sages from the Bible to complement his convictions. In my experience, the less I consciously thought about what I was doing, the better I was playing.

But not that night.

That night, I didn't just lose myself to my music. I blacked out. When I finally came round, I realised that more than fifty minutes had passed, though I had no recollection of having played anything.

I rose from my seat to animated applause. Silhouettes whistled and whooped and clapped. In a daze, I made my way back down to the bar. People tapped my arm, commending me on my set as they grinned from their seats. I nodded and mumbled my thanks. My hands were trembling and my heart racing as I pulled out a stool at the bar.

What had happened up on stage?

I'd lost all sense of time and, were it not for the crowd, would have thought I'd fainted or had a stroke. But people don't applaud you for having a stroke. No, I'd *played* something up there, something that had lasted for almost an hour. Anyway, Coby could explain what had taken place from the crowd's perspective.

I gave a lazy wave of my hand, and she walked towards me, smiled quickly, and passed without a word to serve a customer at the other end of the bar. I waited my turn, thinking she'd compliment me, tell me how much she'd enjoyed it, or at the very least share some new anecdote or crack a joke to level me out. But she didn't. She moved from the customer to the kitchen door, preferring to have a laugh with one of the waiters. She guffawed at something he said, staring into his eyes with a girlish sort of admiration. Was she ignoring me? She *was* ignoring me. Something was wrong. I thought back to her fleeting smile. It had been odd and unsettling, devoid of the warmth, sincerity, the playfulness I'd come to expect of her. Between the piano and the bar, something had changed. But what had I played—and what had she heard?

I watched her over the rim of my glass, waiting for a look, a glance, but it didn't come. By now I was almost certain: there was some aspect of my playing she hadn't liked. She'd seen something in me, something she could no longer trust.

I ordered three tequilas and threw them back, one after the other. I lit up, finished the cigarette and twisted the butt in the ashtray. Coby moved from customer to customer, stopping and smiling at each in just the way they wished. The barman came up to me and I ordered a whiskey straight. He said something, but I didn't hear a word. I downed my drink: *This one's for you, Coby, cos why? Cos screw you, that's why.*

My next drink was for the Crack Radisson, for my paedophile neighbour and the quarrelling lovers. The tequila that followed was for my mother, who was probably having one (or two, or three) for me too. Some place dark and small, where there's no way left to pass the time apart from getting wasted, finding new ways to hate yourself with each tick towards eternity. I drank to the city, to the ghosts, and to dearest Dad. And then, raising my glass to the cloud of smoke, I drank to myself, because, to hell with it: I deserved it most of all.

The barman pushed a cup and saucer in front of me. A single sugar cube sat on a teaspoon. I stared down at it, taking a moment to register what I was seeing. Tea. Bloody tea. I looked up. The barman shrugged and said it was from a secret admirer. I sniffed at the cup. A strong herbal brew.

Drink it up, the barman said.

I lifted the cup and saw a small scrap of paper sitting on the saucer. I grabbed the paper and read: *turn around.*

I immediately did as the note instructed. My eyes swept the room. Many had already left, and a cleaner was busy in a corner. That's when I caught sight of a man sitting by himself at a table near the door. His face was hidden by shadow, but he was wearing a neat, well-fitting suit. He lifted a tea cup, held it up to me, and took a slow, deliberate sip. Steam from the cup twirled upwards.

I got up from my chair and walked across to him. The features of his face became apparent. A handsome man in his late thirties or early forties. A hard jaw. A perfect haircut. He was wearing a black jacket with a white shirt, collar unbuttoned, reminding me of a line from a Patsy Palatine song: this is how the upper side gets down, doncha' know.

Thanks for the tea, I said. *But I'm not much of a tea drinker.*

He smiled and said, *Well, I'm sure the alcohol will be waiting for you once you're done, chief. It doesn't hurt to give the liver a break, does it?*

What do you care?

I don't, he said. *But if we're going to chat, Bent, I'd like to make sure I get the most out of our time—and the booze, well, that's not going to help.*

Are we going to chat?

I hope so. If you're willing to make time for a fan, that is. He pointed to a chair. I pulled it out and sat down. He was clearly a man used to getting his way, and this was how he did it: making you think the choice was yours. Truth be told, I was intrigued by him.

He held out a hand. Hesitantly, I shook it. And then, leaning into the light, he introduced himself as Mr. Leonard Fry.

11.

Leonard poured a second cup of tea from a small ceramic pot. *I've seen you play a few times. Once at Ten To Twelve, a couple of times at The Dubliner. You're very good, but you know that already, don't you? Yes, I think you know precisely how good you are. A good thing*, he said, taking a sip. *Knowing your worth.*

Funny, I said. *I've never noticed you before.*

Oh, I usually arrive late and leave early, Leonard said. *I pop in and out of places. I do that. I'm afraid I suffer from a condition that prevents me from being able to stay in one place for very long. Acute restlessitus, perhaps.*

But you stayed tonight.

I did, he said, *and so did you. Fate still smiles, apparently.*

No, I thought. Fate doesn't smile; it smirks. He'd seen me lingering at the bar all night and had stayed with the specific intention of meeting me. There was no fate or coincidence involved at all, and he must have thought me an idiot to infer otherwise.

But let me get right to the point, he continued. *I like the way you play. I'm not going to get into why that is, but suffice to say I'm having a bit of a farewell at my house this weekend, out in the country-side, a get-together with a few close friends, and I'd very much like you to come up and play for us.*

This weekend?

Friday night till Sunday night.

I can't, I'm afraid, I said. *I'm booked up.*

Cancel. I can make it worth your while.

I don't play for the money, Mr. Fry.

Oh, I see, he said. *And would that be because of something you have against money?*

I've seen what money can do.

And what's that?

Corrupt.

Leonard Fry laughed. *Is that so?* he said. *Well, I say anyone who loses himself to money never really had much of a self to begin with. You say money corrupts? I disagree. I say it scrapes away the hypocrisy. Money digs the real you right up. And the reason people are wary of money, my friend, is that they're simply afraid of who they are. Only cowards are afraid of money. Cowards and posers. And I've heard you play; you're neither, so let's spare each other the trite little truisms. We're more interesting men than that.*

He took a notepad from his top pocket, and began to write something.

It's not just that, I said. *I don't have a car. I've got no way of getting to the countryside—*

Buy a car.

I chortled. *Buy a car? Just like that?*

With the first half of your pay.

He whipped the pen away, tore a sheet from the pad, and slid it across the table towards me. I curled over the corner and read it as if it were a poker hand: a one followed by six zeroes.

What's this? I asked.

That's what you get for saying yes. The other half I'll pay you at the end of the weekend.

Two million rand?

Well, half for now.

For one weekend?

Tell me you'll do it, and it'll be in your account by the morning.

This is ridiculous, I said, shaking my head. *You could get anyone you wanted with this kind of money.*

That's the plan.

I sat back in the chair, staring at the paper as if I was looking at it wrong somehow, misinterpreting the digits. It was far more money than I'd made in four years of doing the rounds, slinking in and out of local holes, often wrestling with broke owners to get paid. But I was far from being won over; the sheet of paper may as well have had *wrong* written all over it.

I'll think about it, I said, folding the paper and slipping it into my pocket.

Think about it? Leonard said, clearly baffled. *Think about what?*

You, I said. *Showing up like this. No disrespect, but I don't know you from a wrong note. I'm not sure I trust you.*

Trust? A question of trust. Hmm. I see. All right, then, well, tell me who you trust.

What?

It's a simple question. Who do you trust?

I'm not sure what you mean.

How about that bargirl over there?

Coby?

Yes, Coby. Do you trust Coby?

Coby was still behind the counter, emptying the tills and printing out the invoices for the night. She didn't notice us staring at her, or maybe she pretended not to notice. A couple of hours earlier I'd have been surer about that.

I gave a shrug and looked away.

If you're not sure, then you don't, Leonard said. *One minute she's joking, flirting, batting her fake eyelashes, and the next she's ignoring you. Acting like you're a ghost.*

I turned to Leonard as he cleared his throat and leant forward on his elbows. *Let me tell you something else you already know*, he continued. *Life, regular old life, will do just fine screwing you around on a daily basis without bothering to pay you for your time.*

I didn't actually believe any of it. I didn't expect the money to be in my account by the morning. But so what, life would go on as usual. I'd be okay with that. I was old enough to know these sorts of things don't happen in the real world, anyway. Nobody just calls you over and offers to change your life. There are no real surprises. The idea that something extraordinary will one day happen purely by chance is just wishful thinking. Most of us die with nothing more than the luck of having existed at all—our sole claim to fortune. Still, the art of getting by, of having some fun, is playing stupid and playing along.

I paused, sighed, and said, *One weekend?*

Leonard threw his hands up in the air: the old faux-surrender. *Friday night to Sunday night.*

I play piano. That's it?

He clapped his palms together and held them up to me. No weapon. No ace up the sleeve. No novelty buzzer to shock me. *Do we have ourselves a deal?*

I guess we'll know by the morning, I said, tapping the pocket that held the scrap of paper. Leonard's lips slowly stretched into a wide smile. I watched as it crept across his cheeks, that smile. It was like a living thing, a creature that sat on his lips making deals for him.

There is one thing, though, he said. He pulled out a box of cigarettes, shook one out, and put it between his lips. Then he held the box out, but I waved it away. In that instant I somehow knew I was done with smokes for good.

My friends have particular tastes, he said. *You'll need a suit.* He lit up and took a drag. *Black. Not navy, not grey, and definitely not beige. Black. You're there for the weekend, so you'll need three new white shirts, three pairs of new black socks, and new underwear. But most importantly, a good black suit. No tie necessary. We like it casual. Think you can handle that?*

Sure, I said.

Good.

At that point, things began to feel believable, his offer genuine. We're never sure there's a real deal being made until the fine print comes up—and right then, it was the print on the labels of my cheap and undesirable wardrobe. It was weird, the idea that it could all really be happening. Suddenly, I felt unprepared.

I used to play a bit, Leonard said, looking at his palms. *I have big hands, like Rachmaninov. They thought it might help, but it didn't. Big hands weren't enough, apparently. Go figure.*

I thought about my gig that night, the fugue, the shift in Coby's manner. Then I said, *Can I ask you something?*

Absolutely.

Tonight, I went on. *You were here all night?*

I was.

What did you think of my set?

Your set? Tonight, my friend, it wasn't you playing, Leonard said with a leer as he stabbed at the ashtray. *Just saying, chief. From down here, it sounded a lot more like the devil.*

12.

I woke up with only a vague recollection of the night before. The man in the suit was lost in a swirl of alcohol and smoke and darkness. Like the Cheshire cat, all that remained was that white grin. My head was pounding, my mouth was dry, and I felt the usual post-inebriation sense of guilt—but that all disappeared as soon as I checked my bank account at an ATM.

As promised, the money was there, a line of big fat digits sitting atop the few bedraggled bucks I already had. Even so, I could barely believe what I was seeing. Money's not money until it stinks up your hand. Any moment, I expected the screen to flicker, and the amount would be gone.

But that didn't happen.

The numbers remained.

I looked over my shoulder. An old woman was standing behind me, a big red perm mushrooming around her head as if somebody had hit a nuclear pause button. She was impatient to get to the machine, picking at her teeth with a long, red fingernail. She may have been standing there for all of five minutes.

I withdrew nothing from my account, snatched my card as the machine spat it out, apologised to the woman. Then I went into the shop next door to buy a small orange juice with the change in my pocket.

13.

The next time I went to the ATM, later that afternoon, I withdrew a couple of grand, more as a test than anything else. I rolled up the notes, looked over my shoulder, and shoved them into my back pocket. I scurried from the outside teller and went into The Drunken Sailor. I ordered three courses, and got through two bottles of wine. After that, stuffed and tipsy, I walked home.

There was no gig that night, which suited me fine. I wasn't in the right state to play, and the reality of a vast amount of available cash had begun to sink in. Once home, I called the two bars I'd been booked to play on the weekend, and told them I had to cancel. *A family emergency*, I said.

Neither bar made much of a fuss. Each manager wished me well, told me they'd see me the following week. After hanging up, I sat on my bed in the darkness and thought about the countryside gig. I'd committed myself, after all.

My stomach was in a tangle. I felt nerves I hadn't felt in years, possibly not since my first public performance. It was just a gig, I told myself. Nothing more. That's what I'd agreed to, right? Play piano for a private party. Ignoring the money for a moment, I'd played plenty private parties before.

I turned on the television.

A jewellery-store robbery had been caught on a security camera, which showed a man in black pulling out a gun. A clerk ducked behind the counter, the man leant over and emptied a round into his back, then grabbed handfuls of jewellery, filling his coat pockets as he did so. In stuttering slow-motion frames, the robber dashed for the door. The footage was replayed, with its gravelly voice-over and a detective's explanation. Gun, duck, shoot, grab, dash.

Gun, duck, shoot, grab, dash.

I switched off, and the screen was blank.

This was Monday.

After clearing the funds, I walked into a used-car dealership and spotted a white Cressida—an older box-shaped model I've always preferred. Every new car looks like a melon or a loaf of bread. No character. No class. The dealer agreed, of course. *This one's an oldie but a goodie*, he said, running his hand over the bonnet. Good tread on the tyres. A recently replaced radiator. No leaks.

I sat in the front seat and rolled my palms over the leather steering wheel. The inside smelt like stale petrol fumes, and the faded dashboard was peeling. The upholstery was mapped with mysterious stains and a weathered baby seat was fixed in the back. None of that mattered. I took it for a test and it ran fine. The dealer could tell I wasn't in the mood for fussing, and was prepared to knock off a couple of grand if I bought it cash. So, that's what I did.

This was Tuesday.

There's a barbershop on Buitengracht that has a twirling white-and-red pole outside. I wondered if the owners were aware of its symbolism: the blood and bandages of mediaeval surgeries, places where men could also get a shave and trim. Civilisation's constant rebranding of pain and death.

Three barbers were on duty, and I picked the one with the worst haircut, assuming it to be the substandard effort of one of his colleagues. Afterwards, the barber pointed me in the direction of a Turkish tailor a few doors down. He measured me up for the black jacket of my choice, and while he did the alterations, I hopped across the road. I bought three shirts and a new pair of shiny black shoes, as well as some black socks and underwear from a clothing store next door, one with so many CLOSING DOWN SALE signs one could swear it was the name of the shop.

This was Wednesday.

At the entrance to the Crack Radisson, a homeless man reached out to grab my coat. He'd appeared from nowhere, a filthy, bearded man of indeterminate age. His clothes were rags. A grubby green beanie hugged his head, and a few brown teeth jutted from grey gums. He wanted to speak to me, but I told him I didn't have the time. He said he was Jesus. I thought this was his name, or nickname, until I realised he was professing to be *the* Jesus.

I've come back, he said, *but nobody will believe me. Nobody will help me.* He'd even walked into a church to announce himself, but they'd thrown him out. He didn't understand the world any more. It was colder than he remembered, the sky without stars, and the buildings so tall he could hardly find his way around. Then the grimy, piss-reeking son of God asked if I could spare a few coins, and I said I was sorry, *So sorry, really*, as I pulled my coat from his grip and walked into the harsh light of the lobby.

This was Thursday.

14.

A thick mist swirled along the base of the mountains, in and out of valleys, and across the highway. Hidden by the dense whiteness, the sun was nowhere to be seen. Here and there the tip of a pylon, or the bulges of a dark hill, or the crumbling shell of an abandoned farmhouse came into view. I'd set out two hours earlier, after receiving the directions on my phone, with the only stipulation to arrive before sunset. I could be faulted on more things than I wished to admit, but punctuality would never be one of them. Punctuality is, after all, the best-kept secret to survival.

The Cressida climbed the mountainside, but the lights did little to improve visibility. The car heater was cranked up, though it seemed a wonder that the thermostat functioned at all; every other feature, from the windscreen wipers to the hazard lights, appeared to operate at the flip of some unseen coin.

Otherwise, everything was working out fine.

Everything but the goddamned mist.

The last petrol station was run down, and the pumps looked like rusty old refrigerators. The lone attendant hobbled from his cubicle and filled the car as I walked to the shoulder of the highway. The sun was low on the horizon, and sickly in the fog. Straining through the grey, it looked exhausted and defeated.

I paid the attendant and went on my way.

Signs marked the bumpy route, pointing the way to isolated towns up in the mountains: Angelico. Kuierkraal. Ouberg. Finally, the sign for Krymeer appeared, and I took the turnoff. No sooner had I done so than a large dark building appeared in the distance, tucked between the hills. Exuding an aura of extravagance and excess, it seemed out of place in the surrounding countryside.

This was Leonard Fry's Casa de Triomph.

I pulled up to an iron gate in the centre of a circular stone wall. As I leant over to push the intercom, the gate opened slowly, inviting me in. Weeping willow saplings stood at equal intervals in the garden. Hedges were trimmed to cubes, and the green lawns were immaculate. The stone manor itself was like something concocted over the course of an architect's bad trip, a cross between a parliament building and a cathedral. Spires of varying lengths jutted upwards, as if for protection against a sky that might fall at any minute.

Several luxury cars were parked in semi-circle around the front entrance. I pulled up alongside them, checked my reflection in the rear-view mirror, and took a deep breath. I reached into the back for my black jacket on its hanger, got out, put the jacket on, and grabbed my gym bag. The grey building towered over me as I went up the stone steps and stood between two columns framing a tall pair of doors. I stared at the black wrought-iron knocker, and just as I was about to grab it, the door opened—

A tall, attractive brunette stood before me. Nude. At first I thought I'd turned up at the wrong house (and was therefore somehow to blame for her nakedness), but her expression suggested otherwise—I was precisely where I needed to be. She scanned me from top to bottom with deep brown eyes as she leant against the door on a long slender forearm. A smile crept across her small mouth. Without permission, my eyes slid down: her breasts were firm and perfect. Her pubic hair was a narrow strip. She was a tanned, voluptuous fantasy—and I did my best to seem cool and unaffected.

The pianist, she said with a smile. *Just in time.* She turned, looked back and said, *This way,* swaying gently as she moved, as light on her feet as a cat. I went into the house and closed the door gently behind me.

Craning my neck, I studied the décor, and the golden, ribbed arch of the ceiling. The tiled floors were as white as a crime scene bleached of incriminating stains. Several paintings hung on the maroon walls in large, ornamental frames.

As I walked, my eyes strayed from the paintings to the woman's firm yet hypnotically undulant arse and back to the artworks: a faceless man in a hat, sitting on a wooden chair in an empty room without windows. In the next painting, a woman's delicate hands massaged the blubbery back of an obese man playing cards with headless men around a table. In another, a small dog licked at a bloody head-wound on a staring old man, presumably dead.

All the paintings seemed to have been done by the same artist. Each was skilfully rendered, but hooked on bad news. I wondered if it said more about the painter or the collector that such a sinister collection was so proudly and publicly exhibited. It was a painting at the end, however, that made me stop and peer closely.

In dark, disorderly strokes, there was a depiction of a woman lying on a rumpled bed, holding a bottle of whiskey. Her eyes had rolled back in her head, and foamy vomit lined her mouth. The silhouette of a boy stood in a doorway to the woman's right. My eyes darted from the whites of her eyes to her pale and twisted limbs. The bottle. The boy. The duvet dangling on the floor . . .

(Sometimes, I guess, there's nothing but the horror.)

Who did these? I asked. *These paintings.*

No questions, piano man, the brunette said, waving a finger, as if ignorance was the theme of the party and my probing was ruining the mood.

I nodded, gave the painting one last look, and continued after her. We passed doors that stood ajar. I did my best to catch a glimpse of what was going on. The party had clearly started, though the gaps didn't reveal much: men dressed in black, brief flashes of female flesh, champagne flutes, food platters. A laugh. A low moan. The clink of glasses.

Top of the stairs, the woman said with a suddenness that jolted me. *Third door on the left. That's where you'll be staying. End of the second-floor corridor. That's where you'll be playing. The only two places you need to know. Understand?*

I nodded, asked, *Is Leonard around?*

The woman laughed. *Leonard's a round. Leonard's a square,* she said, and then she slipped through one of the doors, disappearing as swiftly as she had appeared, abandoning me and my gym bag at the base of the staircase.

I followed her instructions and ended up in a plain little room with a single bed, a small television, and an old-fashioned phone. I put my bag on the bed and lifted the silver lid off a plate of food on my bedside table. Fish, green beans, potatoes, and gravy. The food was warm, as if it had been prepared at precisely the time I'd walked in the front door. I wasn't hungry, so I put the lid back on and ventured to the end of the second-floor corridor. A piano stood in a semi-circular glass enclosure, which was in the corner of the large room. Nobody had yet made their way up there, but it looked prepped for a helluva party. There were seven leather couches, three fireplaces, a number of mattresses scattered across the floor, and more ice buckets in iron stands than I cared to count. Another grander entrance to the room was positioned at the far side, a double door with large red knobs. Tables on either side of the doors held rows of empty glasses and silver trays laden with fruit. Beside the tables were vintage-style chests that seemed to be filled with props, masks, and other accessories.

I left the room the way I had come, through the back entrance, and entered the piano enclosure from an adjacent door in the outside corridor. A black piano stood in the centre of a raised platform, together with a lamp and an old-style telephone atop a small red table. The walls were made of mirrored one-way glass. My image bounced against the glass, which reflected the mirror behind me in a series of endless reflections, all moving in eerie unison with my infinite selves.

I sat down at the sleek black piano and lifted the cover. I ran my fingers over the keys and thought about the opening piece I'd play. One for the ladies, I thought. A little ditty I liked to call "Greedy Fry's Goodbye Orgy."

15.

The house filled with guests, though I didn't see a soul. I could hear them scuttling around, like large rats beneath the floor, but ask me who they were, what they looked like, or what they were all doing, and frankly, pal, guesses leave messes. Nobody used the corridor between the piano room and my own. When it came time to play, the phone would ring in my bedroom and a woman on the other end would say nothing but *Please make your way.*

I'd go and play for an hour or two before another phone rang in the piano room to sign me off with a cold and curt: *Thank you.* I'd then return to my room to find another meal and a bottle of water on my bedside table. There was a tiny window in my room, with a view of the hills. Once or twice I sat and stared and waited for something to move out there, a bird or small animal in the bushes, but nothing did. The outside world may as well have been a painting. So I'd watch bad television, go in and out of sleep, until I was brought back by a sound that seemed to creep from my dreams: *ring-ring—ring-ring.* Then, *Please make your way.*

The playing itself went fine. Without a visible crowd, a spotlight, or any guideline as to what to play, it flowed easily. The hours at the piano weren't anything like as long as the hours in my bedroom. Time passes quickly when I play. It's always been like that, and I've come to the realisation that nothing—not cigarettes or fast food or the city smog—brings me closer to death than a seat at the keys.

A peculiar thing was the way the lights would suddenly flicker, very briefly, at all times of the day and night. The ceiling light in my bedroom flickered (though without the TV being affected), as well as the gold-cupped wall lamps in the corridor, and the light in the piano room too. It almost seemed deliberate, as if someone was flipping a switch, though eventually my mind ceased to register the flickering at all. As for the party, I could only imagine what was going on in that room—the women, the mattresses, the panting and moaning . . .

But surely a weekend of group sex wasn't enough? So, what else? Drugs? Possibly. *Probably*. With each passing moment in the mansion, though, my curiosity waned. I grew certain that the walls, the one-way glass, and closed doors hid nothing more than just another bacchanal. Human pleasures stem from simple seeds. Rich, poor—we whore the same senses. We eat, we drink, we jerk off (alone, or with someone else), ingest our chemicals and bloat our egos. And that's about the sum of it.

16.

The second night, I had a dream.

I'm driving to the manor through the mountains, but there is no mist. The sun is shining and the sky is blue. I drive the Cressida up to the iron gates and they slowly swing open. My car creeps up the driveway, but instead of luxury cars outside the manor, I find an assortment of hatchbacks and station wagons and regular old sedans. I get out and make my way to the entrance. The door opens, but there is no beautiful naked woman waiting for me on the other side. Rather, I'm greeted by an old man in a smart black suit. He smiles, waves a hand for me to enter.

It takes a short while to realise that the man is in fact my neighbour at the Crack Radisson. His cheeks are full and rosy, and his grey hair is neatly cut and combed to the side. The crooked and neglected brown teeth are even and white.

"It's good to see you," he says, extending his arms to hug me. "Thank you for coming."

I say nothing as I step into his embrace. His arms wrap around me like tentacles. Staring over his shoulder, I become aware of something in the background. The black blubbery mass of living tissue is thick as an insomniac's night, sliding in and out of itself, filling the hallway, slithering up the stairs, pressing against the walls. It's like nothing I've ever seen before, yet at the same time I know it all too well. Primordial, grossly uncomfortable with itself, it groans in distress.

The old man at the door doesn't seem to have a problem with this thing behind him, which may even be some kind of house pet. The man pulls his head back and grips me by the shoulders to get a good look at my face. His eyes dart from feature to feature. "My, my. Yes," he says. "Remarkable. Unmistakable."

I walk inside.

He tells me he's an uncle I've never met, and that he was once a university professor. A specialist in graph theory.

Instead of grisly paintings, I see a collection of beautiful black-and-white photos showing famous musicians, a sleek trumpet—and an infinite line of piano keys. The doors of the rooms are partially closed, and I hear the wails and sobs of men and women, all dressed in black. But I can't take a closer look, not with that thing filling the house, swelling with every passing moment.

"The numbers," says this elegantly revised version of my neighbour, as he smiles beneath red eyes that well with tears. "The numbers have stopped coming, and oh, how we miss the numbers. We can't go on without the numbers. So, if you don't mind, of course, would *you* do us the favour?"

I nod.

That's when he leads me to the piano room.

And that's when I woke up.

17.

Sunday was difficult. I'd played so much my repertoire was running thin. The day before, the phone had rung every hour to give me a break, but on the Sunday, *nada*. Sweat poured from my forehead as I hammered the keys, as my eyes darted expectantly to the phone. The veins in my hands bulged like well-fed snakes. Any minute now, I told myself, they'd call, let me off the hook for a few minutes. Thank me for my time.

Any second now.

My wrists were straining. The walls of the room were shrinking. I gritted my teeth. I didn't care about the money in the bank account. I didn't care about whatever Fry was getting up to with his guests. I felt a sharp and intense hatred, like a knife to the gut. I'd been playing for hours, and I wanted out. Had enough. Each piano key was like a small closed door. Each finger, a pounding fist. Each note, a scream. And just before I was about to say fuck it, go to hell, Fry, I'm done—

Ring-ring.

I stopped playing, didn't answer the phone. I let it ring as I hung over the keys and looked at my swollen, trembling hands. Blisters and bruises. The phone continued to cry like a spoilt child, demanding of my attention. Then I picked up the receiver.

Thank you. That'll be all.

18.

I stood beside the bed, rolling my clothing and packing each item into my bag. After straightening the bedding, I shut the windows overlooking the bland wilderness. I headed out the door and took one last walk to the piano room to see if I'd left anything behind. On my way out, I peeked into the mattress room. Everyone had left. It was empty. All cleaned up, with no sign anyone had been there at all. It looked like nothing more than a large living room, with its crescent of brown sofas facing three empty fireplaces.

I stepped inside the room. The wooden floors creaked beneath my shoes. The room smelt of sweat and lavender. My eyes flitted from corner to corner, and I imagined that any moment I'd be ambushed by a Mardi Gras of masked characters—large feathered figures with their cocks and tits hanging out, incanting as they stripped me naked and strung me up in a ritual sacrifice.

I drew aside a thick velvet curtain and looked outside. The day was grey. Dull, shapeless clouds stretched on forever. Below, long black cars were making their way along the gravelly road to the main gate. The procession was slow, with cars following one another at consistent intervals. The party was done; the weekend pantomime was over.

The pantomime of regular life, however, was about to resume.

So, I take it you'll be off soon.

I spun round. Leonard was standing in the doorway, spinning a milky drink around in a tumbler.

That was the plan, I said, hoisting my bag.

He nodded, downing his drink as he moseyed across the shiny floor.

I can only imagine what you must think of all this, he said, waving the tumbler in the air. *Of what we've been getting up to.*

You didn't pay me to think. You paid me to play.

No, sure, you're right, he said, jutting out his bottom lip. *But that doesn't mean there weren't a few thoughts on the matter. And wouldn't it be fun, getting inside that head of yours. After all, it's the great and secret wish, yes?*

What is?

To know each other's innermost thoughts, free of all the niceties, the diplomacy, the manners, and the fear of rejection, of being misunderstood. Complete and utter openness. All our dirty little thoughts and deepest desires on open display. Imagine that. Then I suppose we'd have to make our way through it all, through each other's raw truth. He gestured to the window. *Like entering that thick, white mist out there.*

I said nothing in response. All I could think of was something I'd heard once, that philosophy is the pastime of the privileged. For the rest of us, it's all about survival.

Do you have any plans tonight? Leonard asked.

Not really.

Ah. And then he paused. But I could tell more was coming as he seemed to ready himself for his next proposition. (I already had a bold *No* waiting in the wings.) *Have you eaten recently?*

I'm okay, I replied.

In truth, I hadn't eaten in hours, and if pushed for a plan, that'd be it, to grab something greasy on the way home.

Well, I wonder if you wouldn't oblige a bored man a moment longer, he said. *Any chance I could convince you to stay for dinner?*

I looked at my watch but the time was irrelevant.

In fact, I insist, Leonard said, capitalising on my hesitation. *My chef is making your favourite.*

How would you know what that is? I asked.

I don't, he said, smiling. *But whatever it is, that's what he'll be making. Do we have a deal?*

Is that all you do?

What's that?

Make deals?

Leonard raised his empty glass. *Isn't that all any of us can do? Come. Put the bag down. Join me for dinner.*

I looked out the window again. The cars were gone, and the mist still hung heavy. It'd probably be better to wait until it cleared—and, even with my healthy new bank balance, it wasn't as if I'd be having dinner in a mansion again any time soon.

All right, I said. *Beef enchiladas and refried beans.*

Excuse me?

My favourite.

Of course it is, Leonard said, picking out an ice cube and crushing it between his teeth.

19.

L eonard took me on a tour of the manor. As we walked along its many corridors, in and out of its countless rooms, he related its convoluted history.

It had begun as a farm, he said—a stable, in fact—where a disillusioned soldier had retired long ago to breed horses. They were the healthiest and strongest in the region, and most were used in war. One day, the man got word that the enemy was stealing over the mountain to slaughter his horses. Upon hearing this, he led his finest stallion and two pregnant mares up to a cave, where he waited. The enemy arrived, and massacred his herd. Disembowelled, headless horses lay strewn across the grassland. In the aftermath of the killing, the stables were razed to the ground.

At the bottom of a winding staircase, we came to the east-wing conservatory. We walked inside, and Leonard continued with the story. At the start of the last century, the manor was built as a halfway house for travelling officials and politicians. *But even then, this place was filled with awfulness*, Leonard remarked. The cover-up of a murdered whore. The ambush of a Zulu leader. The signing away of future generations. *One could say the house is cursed*, he said. *It's like a filter. Anything that passes through here has its goodness removed, and the residue, what's left—the distilled evil of a person, of an ambition, of a plan— is spat out its doors and into the world.*

I found Leonard's account simultaneously fascinating and absurd. I watched him closely as he spoke, the way his hands rose and fell, pointing at this and that. Like a child speaking feverishly, caught up in some myth of his own making. Or like a madman, prophesying the end of the world with an intensity that made you look to the sky, just in case.

After the politicians, he went on, the manor was used as a hotel for almost thirty years. And then the owner hanged himself in his bedroom. *Debt management*, Leonard said firmly. He took me to the garage and showed me his cars. Six machines lined up like showgirls. An Aston Martin in British racing green. A gun-metal Jag. A black Lincoln, a yellow Mustang, a vintage Rolls-Royce, and, lastly, an elephantine SUV.

As we walked between the cars, the story continued. The house stood vacant for almost ten years before being converted into a rehab centre for rich crackheads, junkies, and drunks. Sometime later, a high-profile sex scandal put an end to that. The house passed through the hands of two private owners— one died of a stroke, while the other went head first through the windscreen of a speeding truck—and then there was Leonard and his millions, ready to have a go.

I asked what could possibly have drawn him to a house with such a history. He climbed into the driver's seat of the Mustang, stroked the wheel, and said, *A ludicrously fast car. A beautiful woman. There's nothing quite as alluring as the one you've been warned about, is there?*

20.

Leonard guided me through the rest of the house. At the back, I was surprised to find a pier jutting out over a lake. He continued to talk about the history and the architecture, but my interest was waning. I humoured him anyway. I tagged along as we passed between the poolside chairs, which were still draped in damp, crumpled towels. We walked the length of the long outside bar counter, overflowing with half-empty bottles and tiny pink umbrellas. Stepping back into the house through the reading room, I saw piles of books stacked like skyscrapers of a miniature metropolis. Scanning his library, I was reminded of the painting I'd seen in the lobby, the one of the boy standing in the doorway with the deathly pale woman sprawled on the bed. I wanted to know where Leonard had got it, but then what? Would I come right out, ask him why it reminded me of stumbling upon my mother's body in precisely that pose?

Leonard took a remote from his inside jacket pocket, pressed it, and the lights flickered three times.

And that? I asked, remembering how they had periodically flickered all weekend.

That's how I get the attention of Carl, he said. *He's gone completely deaf, but there's nobody who can do what he does. He cooks like a Michelin chef. Knows how I like to do things, and when I like to do them. And I trust him. That's the important thing. He's like family. So I had the lights fixed. Three flickers, I'm in the west wing; two, I'm in my room; and one, I'm in the east.*

This explained the flickering. But I was puzzled. I asked whether it wouldn't have made sense for Carl to receive his messages on a phone.

I tried, Leonard said. *But the man's eighty-three years old, tough as tripe. He wouldn't know what to do with a phone. Hates them. No, he prefers it this way. The lights. Pen and paper. And he manages just fine.*

Minutes later, Carl waddled into the room. He was a short, stocky old man with a bald head and skin like the grey sand of a shitty beach. One that got no sun. He handed Leonard a notepad and a pencil and Leonard scribbled his instructions. Then Carl left, and Leonard pointed at the doorway, ushering me into the next part of the house, the next part of the story.

21.

As promised, we were served beef enchiladas and refried beans for dinner. The luscious mess arrived on silver tableware that was clearly from a more elegant era. Carl had laid the table in the dining room, where he filled our bulbous glasses with red wine and left. Leonard held his glass to the light and voiced his appreciation of Chilean Cabernet. He professed to enjoy local wines, as well as those from Australia and New Zealand, but he wasn't really a fan of old-world varietals. He found French wine particularly boring. All those years of tradition and reputation had inhibited the French harvesters; they were reluctant to experiment, to try anything new, and you could taste their conservatism. Their fear. Chileans, on the other hand, had no reputation to uphold. No real legacy. They were free to do anything they wished, and thus, their wine was more surprising, more complex, and, most notably, delicious.

I nodded, gave the wine a swirl, then downed it like Coke. He asked me what I thought of the food, since it was my favourite, and I said it was pretty damn good. In truth, I was hardly a connoisseur of Mexican food, but Leonard deferred to me as if I'd combed the globe for the ultimate spicy wrap. Little did he know that most of my dinners came from hole-in-the-wall outlets in buildings scheduled to be demolished, or grimy grills near bars and clubs. Sandwiches marked with thumbprints.

Sausages fried into rubbery oblivion. And none of this ever bothered me much.

Tell me a bit about yourself, Leonard said.

What do you want to know?

Do you have any family?

I thought about my father in his grave, his flesh collapsing under his morgue make-up. I had no face to put to the corpse, so I conjured up an image of some generic dead guy. White wispy hair. Pale skin. Worm food.

In reply to Leonard's question, I shook my head and shovelled in another forkful.

Do you have a girlfriend? he persisted. *A wife?*

No.

With a glug of wine, I washed down my food. Leonard grabbed the bottle and refilled my glass. He stared at me for a moment, and then returned to his meal, cutting his wrap into several bite-sized portions. All perfectly equal in size.

Tell me, Bent, what is it that you want out of this life?

I'm not sure. To keep going, I suppose.

Keep going?

To survive.

Yes, survival. We do what we can, don't we?

I tore my eyes away from his gaze and said, *Looks like you've overshot the mark a bit.*

You could say that, chief. Leonard smiled. *I know people dream of having the things I have. Of doing the things I've done. After all, at one point, I dreamt about wanting it, and that's why I find myself here. In this big house. Surrounded by my things.* He sat back in his chair, paused. *In fact, there's very little I haven't done, very few places I haven't been. Of course, there are always new toys out there, but it seems I've lost my appetite. I've run the gauntlet on clichés, chief. Stayed at the finest hotels in the world, thrown parties in sky-high penthouses.* Leaning forward, he said, *I've slept with women, lots of women, every type.*

Again he paused, and again I said nothing.

I own houses on four continents. Don't mistake this for boasting. That's not my intention. I've lived my share of several lifetimes. I could probably live a few more. But it wouldn't matter, because all of it has been to attempt . . . well, the unattemptable.

And what would that be? I asked.

Leonard lay his knife and fork neatly on his plate, and forced a small smile. He took a breath and folded his arms across his chest.

I appreciate what you did for me this weekend, he said. *You were superbly professional. I've had musicians before. Things have got messy at times, but you, you did your part. You played wonderfully!*

Just did what you paid me to do, I said.

Sure, sure. But aren't you curious about what was going on here?

I was at first, I said.

And now?

Not so much.

Because you already know the answer, he said. *I mean, what else could it be? Sex and drugs and food and drink. Right? Right.* His voice dropped as he continued, *The same as always. It's unimaginative. That, and there's also the one conundrum none of us can ever solve, no matter how hard we try . . .*

I asked, *What conundrum?*

That no matter what we do, where we go, or who we're with, we can't escape ourselves. Our own physical presence in every moment. I can't sleep with a woman as someone else, can I? I can't travel somewhere without me being there.

He looked up, a forlorn look on his face. *There are cheats; there are drugs, but still, it's not the kind of solution I'm talking about. It's quick and it's easy and superficial. There's no depth to it because it isn't earned, it isn't permanent, and after a while, well, the drugs don't work in quite the same way. So, what's left? Me. Just me. Always. Wherever I go. It's a cruel joke. And like I said, I've lost my appetite.*

I had finished my meal and my glass was empty. Leonard suddenly seemed very small in his gigantic dining room. The shadows around us obscured old lamps and books and various antique ornaments. The walls loomed high, and my eye caught an enormous painting of people having a picnic in a park. For a moment I imagined Leonard sitting alone in that cavernous room, eating dinner and staring into that painting, imagining himself there, in it, together with the group. The little girl with the kite. The man with the hat, reading a book under a tree. The two boys with paper boats at the water's edge. And in the background, a man in a coat, out of place and solitary, standing with his hands in his pockets. His face hidden—

Right then, something odd occurred: the man on his own—the man I'd just looked at—was now standing alongside a woman. Whether I'd initially missed her, or she'd suddenly, somehow, materialised, I couldn't say. Whatever the case, there she stood, scarf around her neck, looking out towards the lake at a third boy in a striped beanie at the water's edge, who was pointing to some geese.

Leonard, oblivious to my long, dumb gazing, went on: *Don't get me wrong, please. I'm not interested in sympathy or pity. This is my problem and my problem alone. I expect no one to understand, and that's just fine. The reason I'm telling you, however, is to prep you for what I'm going to say next . . . because I need to make one more deal. Perhaps the last one I'll be making for a while. You see, I'm hoping to take a kind of . . . trip.*

At that point I remembered Leonard telling me that the weekend gathering would be a farewell party. But after the attack he'd just made on the limited offerings of the world, I found it hard to imagine the type of trip he had in mind.

Where are you going? I asked.

My guests believe I'm moving to another country, and that I won't be back for a very long time. It's easier that way. There won't be any questions. Well, not for a while, anyway. Everyone is under the impression I've decided to, well, take a sabbatical, so that should make things easy for you.

I sat upright. *For me?*

Ever since I first heard you play, I knew you were the one. I can't say why, but I knew. You see, Bent, that's the real reason I called you here this weekend. *That's why you're still here and the rest of my guests have gone home.*

Something sparked in my head. An alert button had activated: I'd been tricked. Manipulated. I instinctively sprang from my chair.

Please, he said, *please. Have a seat. I don't mean to scare you. Please, just*—and he pointed to my chair.

I paused for a moment, and then slowly sat down.

Leonard rested his elbows on the table. He rubbed his palms together. *I'd appreciate it if I could talk openly with you. There's no reason to be alarmed. We're just two men talking. So, can we speak freely?*

On guard, I mumbled, *Okay.*

Good. Now, tell me, what are your feelings on madness?

Madness?

Madness. Does it ever scare you, the idea of going mad?

I haven't really thought about it, I said. *Don't they say the mad don't know they're mad?*

Leonard smiled. *Maybe that's true. In which case, everything we do in our regular lives, the way we talk to people, the way we dress and act, the things we aspire to, is madness?*

I wasn't sure if I was supposed to respond.

He emptied what was left of the bottle into my glass. Then he sat up, cleared his throat, and dropped the smile. *Okay. I've kept you here for a while already, so let's cut to the chase. Here's the thing. I'd like to propose something. And I'd like you to think carefully about what I'm about to say. I've practised this conversation in my head many times.* He looked up, as if through the ceiling into the room above.

Then he took a deep breath, exhaled, and began: *There is a room in this house. There's only one way in and one way out. There's virtually nothing inside. No furniture apart from a bed and a bedside table. No clocks. No calendars. There's a toilet and a basin. There are twelve boxes of soap. Four toothbrushes. About two dozen tubes of toothpaste. A hundred rolls of shitting paper. A blanket. Two changes of pants, ten pairs of underwear, and four* shirts. *That's it. There's one lock on the door, and only one key to that lock. Now, what I'm going to ask may seem strange to you. I don't necessarily need you to understand, but what I do need is for you to agree to help me.*

Help you with what?

Well, Bent, my friend, you see, in a few days' time I'm going to enter that room. The door will be locked behind me, and that's where I'll stay, by myself, for exactly one year. He took a big swig of his wine. *I'd very much appreciate it if you would . . . how shall I put it . . .* facilitate *this by staying here.*

Staying where?

In this house, he said, waving his arms about. *Which will be your house for a year. This house and everything in it. The cars, the toys, the lifestyle—*

Wait. I was lost for words. *I'm sorry. What exactly are you asking?*

Let's call it an experiment. One year for each of us to do things differently. What's a year in a lifetime? The rest of our years will get mashed together, vanish in a blur, but if we do this, well, we can die with the knowledge that we did what we could to swim out from the islands of our own little lives. Proving we're not cowards like everyone else.

Look, maybe I'm missing something, I said.

He gave me an indulgent half-smile.

You're saying you want to stay in a room—a bedroom—for a year?

Leonard opened another bottle, poured a glass, and took a sip. Then he said, *Twelve months. Three hundred and sixty-five days. And all I'd like you to do is pass food through a slot in the door. Three times a day. Every day. Nothing else, and no speaking. Not a word.*

He put a finger to his lips. Then he looked at me hard.

I'll probably beg you to let me out at some point, tell you it was all a mistake, but it is important you ignore me. No matter what I tell you to do. Do you understand? Just leave me be. Don't answer my questions. And of course, don't tell anyone I'm in that room. No one. *That's crucial. Not even Carl will know. Like I said, I've had my farewell and nobody will come looking for me. It'll just be me in that room, and you in this house.*

I laughed. *This is ludicrous.*

Leonard seemed not to hear me. *Of course, I wouldn't expect you to do this for nothing. I'm happy to make an additional arrangement, on top of your weekend's earnings, guaranteeing you'll never need to work again. A hefty living allowance will be deposited into your account every month. Along with full access to everything I own. But I'm quite certain the money won't persuade you. Not completely. Though the experience might. The challenge.*

You're joking, I blurted. *This must be a joke.*

No joke.

And once the year is up?

I walk out, we go our separate ways.

But why? I don't—I shrugged my shoulders—*why would you put yourself through something like that?*

For a moment, he seemed nonplussed.

Why? Hmm. I suppose I do need a why. Something to assure you I've given this real thought. Well, okay. Fair enough. Let's see, now.

He pulled a cigarette from his top pocket, smoothed it with his fingers. Then he stuck it in his mouth, leant forward, and lit it with the flame of the candle placed between us. He took a drag, exhaled. The smoke rose into the darkness like a mushroom cloud. As if the planet had just blown up.

Leonard calmly continued: *I suppose I could elaborate on my endless desire to have the world entertain me, reducing life to a parade for my own pleasure. But I'll spare you the bored-rich-man's lament and break it down like this.* He flicked some ash, went on: *Take away the things we own. The houses. The clothes. The cars. Etcetera. Take away the people. All the jabbering and the dinner dates and the handshakes. The schmoozing. The bills. The noise. The media. The preachers. Image after image. The fucking slideshow of life. Take away the traffic and the weekend retreats and the jet-setting and the events and occasions and traditions on top of traditions. Take away the things we've convinced ourselves are* important. *Our little responsibilities to each other. Our mundane habits. Our rituals. What to wear. What to eat. Where to go next, what to do next, on and on and on. Take away this entire swirling hurricane of existence, and then take away our ability to control any of it.*

The cigarette drooped on his bottom lip as he unbuttoned his cuffs and rolled them up. *Now ask yourself,* he said. *What remains of us? Who are we without any of that stuff? What do we think about? Cut off from the world, what do we hold on to, what do we let go of? Do you know, Bent? Because I don't. I don't know the answer to any of those questions. But I do know this: I know that when I look in the mirror I see a copy of a copy of a copy. I also know that the idea of being locked in that room for a year, well, just the thought of it makes my stomach turn. Terrifies the shit out of me.* He gave a nervous chuckle. *But really, why should it? Hmm? I mean, why should being in a room by myself make me feel that way? What harm could there be? And yet, I can't shake the fact that the prospect makes me feel more scared—more* intrigued—*than I've felt in a long while.* He stubbed out his cigarette; it was only half-smoked. Then he turned to me. *And in the end, isn't that the point, Bent? To face that secret, voiceless something inside ourselves?*

He stopped, and I took it as my cue. *Well, maybe there's nothing waiting for you. Just boredom.* I slumped in my chair. *A year of the worst boredom you've ever experienced.*

Leonard guffawed. I still couldn't tell how serious he was about it all. Was he high? Had he just cooked up this plot now, over dinner, or had he been stewing in it for weeks? With every word he'd become more dishevelled; as he ran his hand over his head strands of hair rebelled. *Oh, there'll be boredom, I'm sure. But nothing like this.* He flicked his eyes around the room. *Think of it as a whole new level of boredom. And fear. And frustration. But here's the kicker. No release. No shortcuts. No diversions. No channel-hopping my way out of it. There'll be nowhere to go, except straight through the muck and the mist. No, Bent. I'm quite sure. For at least the next twelve months, what I'm interested in isn't out there. Not any more. It's right here,* he said, tapping the side of his head. *What I really want to know is this: after everything is gone, after everything I've spent my life obsessing over has disappeared, what's left of me? How deep is my rabbit hole? What will I find in the company of nothing and no one but myself and my own thoughts? And if I go in that room and it's madness*—his eyes glinted—*if there's nothing in my stripped mind but eat-my-own-shit insanity, well, hell, won't that be a trip?*

II.

Knock, knock

22.

It's my first day of being eleven years old.

Earlier in the week, my mother decided she wanted to throw a birthday party for me. She said I could invite a few kids from school. Not the whole class, just a few, because she had no intention of running a circus. A cake. A couple of games, two hips, one hooray, and everyone out the door by four in the afternoon. The trouble was, she said it five days before my birthday, in one of her better moods. At the time, I'd thought, Don't get excited, Bent. Five days is a long way away. That's at least four or five yells, a couple of door slams and more blames and bloody klutzes than I can count. By the time my birthday actually arrives, there's a big chance she'll call the whole thing off.

But today's the day, and she's been up since eight. Three clumps of balloons are dangling from corners of the ceiling. One's flying from the postbox so my friends can find the house. I've invited four boys. I gave them my handmade invitations earlier in the week. On each card I'd drawn a picture of myself standing next to the boy I'd invited—my arm over his shoulder and his arm over mine. None of them seemed excited to get it. Two of them said the drawing was lame. One asked if he'd be the only person at the party because I'd drawn only the two of us. I laughed and said, "No way," but I wasn't sure he believed me. The other said he'd be there, and then stuffed the invitation into his bag and ran off. I watched him blitz to catch up with the gang and thought about my invite, crumpled under his tatty exercise books and Twinkie wrappers.

That was two days ago.

Today, my mother steps out of her room wearing a floral dress. She pats herself down and twirls on bare toes. I'm sitting on the edge of the couch near the front window. She asks me what I think of her dress. I think she looks nice in her dress. Her hair is brushed, which is nice, but her lipstick is very red. Her skin looks like the top of my lemon-meringue birthday cake, the one sweating on the table over there, between the stack of side plates and the packets of chips and the polystyrene cups. I end up telling her only half of what I think, that she looks nice. "Really nice, Mom." She looks at the clock on the wall; there are only ten minutes left before they turn up. She runs into the room to fetch her shoes. I turn to look out the window, waiting for that first car to pull up, my stomach turning with every passing second.

But there's no point.

My friends, they don't come.

It's already three o'clock. They're two hours late, and I'm still sitting at the window. I haven't touched any of the eats—I'm not very hungry—but my mom's already had a glass of wine. After a while, she puts the glass down and comes over to me. She says, "Never mind them. Come. You and me. Let's do our own thing." She tells me to get in the car. We reverse out hurriedly. The lone blue balloon is still hanging from the postbox, like a flag on the moon.

We drive to the mall and my mother says we're going to watch a movie—"Hey, just you and me, when last have we done that?" It's a good question, because I really don't remember. My mother knows nothing about movies but she sees a poster of a man in a black suit and sunglasses, and there's also a dragon, and a pretty Chinese girl with angel wings.

My mother says, "That looks good, something you'd like, hmm?" and she gets us tickets, sending me to the snack counter with a couple of coins. She doesn't realise she hasn't given me enough for much more than a small popcorn. Not even a Coke, but I don't have the heart to tell her. Instead, I say that I don't feel like anything else. "And you just decided to forget about your mother, then? Okay, well, keep the change, Scrooge. The movie's starting, let's go in."

We take our seats in the front row, and I pick up that there are no other kids in the cinema. The screen stretches up in front of us and I lift my chin to see; as soon as the trailers start, I start feeling dizzy.

The movie begins. It seems like everything happens at night, and it's always raining. I try to follow the story but everybody uses big words. I can't figure out the good guys or the bad guys. But I do work out that there's a gangster who's died. He goes to hell and meets the devil. But this devil isn't a red monster with horns; he's just some old man in a coat. The devil tells this dead gangster he's going to send the gangster back to earth, and he'll have special powers, and guns strapped to his arms (I don't know why). There's a lot of talking in the movie, and the story, well, I don't get it. I feel myself nodding off.

I start to think about those four boys I invited to my party, wondering why they didn't turn up. Maybe they wanted to come but their parents wouldn't let them. Maybe they went right past that blue balloon without seeing it. I'm sure there's some good reason; they're my friends, after all. I'm always with them during break. I make them laugh a lot. It doesn't make sense. As my eyes begin to close, the sounds from the movie start to mix with my dreams. I hear the boys from my class, talking to each other—*where is she? i don't know! last chance, pal. i seriously don't know (click, click) but i know a guy who does! you know a guy? i know a guy. then start talking. okay, okay! take it easy, man!*

Then the voices stop. I feel myself slipping away, out of the grip of this difficult day. Suddenly, I'm jerked awake by a tug on my wrist. I turn to see my mother beside me, and I know that face of hers. Even in this dim cinema, I know that face. She's furious. She grabs me by the wrist and pulls me out of my chair.

"That's it!" she yells, in front of everyone. "That's it!"

Everyone in the cinema is looking at us, watching, as I'm dragged up the staircase by my angry mother. I'm too confused to be embarrassed just yet, but the embarrassment is just around the corner. I can feel it coming. For now, it's just a dopey strangeness. We burst out of the cinema and the ticket collector hops to the side as my mother yells for the manager. The attendants try to calm her down. She doesn't want to be calmed down, she tells them. She wants the manager. "Now!"

An attendant runs off into a back room and the mall security guy in the corner seems nervous. The manager strolls out, a bony young man, about half my mother's age, I think. He's got pimples around his mouth and his forehead is glistening like a frosted doughnut. He holds out his hands and asks my mother what the problem is—which I'd also like to know.

"It's my son's birthday!" she yells. "Did you know that? He's eleven! Today! And I've just been with him, watching the biggest load of shit—the biggest load of absolute rubbish! There's no warning on your poster! Nothing!"

"Ma'am, what poster?"

"The poster in front of the bloody—"

She points, though not at the poster, and says, "There's no warning, none of you could be bothered to mention, even when I bought tickets from you—yes, *you*, missy!—you said nothing about all the sex and the swearing and the killing!" She is shouting. "So what kind of sick racket are you people running here?"

The manager turns to look at the short woman behind him, the one my mother called missy. He says, "Did you mention to the lady that this movie's restricted?"

She lifts her shoulders, and says, "No."

"No, *exactly*!" says my mother. "Exactly."

"She was alone," the woman says. "Her son wasn't with her. She was alone. I didn't—I would have . . ."

Everyone's looking at my mother, who's just realised this is true; I was at the popcorn counter. The manager wants to put an end to this.

"Okay, well, ma'am. I'm terribly sorry. And what I *can* do is refund your tickets. That's what I can do—"

"Refund?" By now a crowd has formed around us. "My son has already seen these things, these lurid, awful, horrible things. Right, now you tell me, how's he expected to un-see them? Eleven years old. On his birthday. Killing and sex. Fuck this, fuck that, every second word—tell me, now! How does he un-see and un-hear these things? Can you refund him on that?"

Sometimes my mother doesn't know how to stop, and this is one of those times. The security guard has come over and passersby are sniggering and I hear them call my mother a kook, a psycho, a bitch. I start to say I didn't see anything—that I was asleep the whole time—but nobody is listening to me. Instead, it seems as if the whole place is crowding around my mother, who's screaming to the devil about sex and killing— fuck this and fuck that—and how there was no reason for me to be exposed to all of that, for a boy my age to have to see and hear those things. Then she yells again, "And on his *birthday*, of all days!"

23.

Leonard instructed me to go home, to take a few days and think the whole thing over. I left after dinner and was soon back on the mountain pass, chugging along in my Cressida. Friday's misty white world had morphed into a starless black night. As I drove behind the odd tail light, Leonard's words were like a cold draft blowing through the swing-doors of my mind: *There is a room in this house. There's only one way in and one way out . . . One year for each of us to do things differently . . . We can die with the knowledge that we did what we could to swim out from the islands of our own little lives. Proving we're not cowards like everyone else . . .*

So, would I play the rich man for a year, stay in a mansion with the owner locked in a room, hoping to go mad—all just for kicks? This bored and wealthy man, desperate for the one thing his money couldn't buy—a bit of *perspective?*

I wasn't sure. My initial urge was to scrap the offer entirely, tell Fry to go to hell, and slink back into my life. I'd write the weekend off one bottle and gig and blanket-tossing night at a time. He was just another man with too much money. That was it. He couldn't be serious. Playing a game. Testing me. With no intention of doing anything remotely so ludicrous. But the longer I drove, the more I felt there was something else. Sensed it in the dark part of my mind. A curious little hum. Not even a whisper yet. Just the *idea* of a whisper, the thought of a thought of a thought, and it went like this:

What. If.

I drove on through the dark countryside, thinking about my dream—and that big black thing behind the old man. That abomination, struggling to fit inside that hallway, growing larger and slimier with each passing moment, sliding up the walls, suffering in the prison of its own existence.

Leonard was right about that mansion.

There was something wrong there. I could feel it. I couldn't say what it was, exactly, but somehow it had got inside my head. Added that dead woman to the painting in the hallway. Turned Leonard into a raving, unhinged madman. I turned off, onto the highway, and before me lay the glowing orange embers of the city. I drove on—*chug, chug, chug, splutter*—as if crawling my way out of a deep sleep.

24.

After those rooms with their high ceilings and all the paintings and fancy things, my apartment seemed small and dark, filled with broken toys. I threw my laundry in the hamper and packed my toiletries into the bathroom cabinet. It was a little after ten when I climbed into bed, but I struggled to get to sleep. I wasn't tired. I'd felt exhausted earlier in the day, but the tiredness had evaporated. My senses were charged. My eyes were wide as moons. I could smell the steaming shit of the street. I could hear every skitter through the walls—*kitta-kitta-kitta-kit-kit*. The fridge, mumbling to itself. The wall clock, ticking incessantly, counting down to its eventual end.

That, and the end of everything else.

I retraced recent events all the way to the moment I'd met Leonard in the bar. I sifted through our opening chat for anything I may have missed. The winks. The nudges. The way that smile moved around his face. And how could I forget the condescension? *I say anyone who loses himself to money never really had much of a self to begin with.* Over dinner, he'd claimed the opposite, that his money had led him from one dead end to another, and after all that *spending* he was barely able to recognise himself in the mirror.

I turned my pillow around and dropped my head on the puffed-out cold side. It felt like a new pillow for about a minute and then the feeling was gone. The same old pillow and the same old bed and the same old me. Pushing the blanket down to my waist, I turned on my side. There was nothing outside the window. Just darkness. No moon, no stars, just the endless black of night, as if I were in some rusty lunar module drifting through space.

I needed to get out of that apartment. After all, there was no reason for me to stay. I had money now—more money than I'd ever dreamt of having in my bank account—and in the morning there'd be more, the remainder of my payment. So, what would I do with it? I could put down a deposit on a small house in the suburbs. Furnish it with the perfect sofa and the perfect curtains. The perfect closet full of big-brand clothing. Adorn the walls with stretched-canvas prints of mountains, buy a matching set of seashell towels and a TV the size of a highway billboard. That was one way to go about it. Then again, I could forget the future and blow it all, splurge on a few months in a five-star suite and grow accustomed to being pampered just in time to run out of money and return to this shitty life, none the wiser.

How about *travel?* I could travel. People travel—they're always going on about its pleasures, its benefits. Leonard had become disillusioned with travelling, but only because he'd done so much of it. I was a long way off from that—I'd barely been out of the city for longer than a few days at a time.

Then again, I could go nowhere at all, stay right where I was, keep tossing and turning with the *tick-tick-tick* and *mumble-mumble-mumble* and *thump-moan-thump* against my walls.

Or . . .

I turned over, lay on my other side.

I could take Leonard up on his offer. I could put off spending my two mill and try on his life—like a kid in his dad's oversized shoes trying to see if he can cross the room without tripping. A trial run at a way of life most people will never get to experience. One year, and then he'd walk out the room, and we'd go our separate ways, right? That's what he'd said. A chance to do things differently, to see things differently.

A chance, he'd said, to flip our lives and be new again.

Like the cold side of my pillow.

25.

The following day was peppered with several baffling moments.

The first bout began with my weekend fee paid out in full. There they were, all those noughts on the screen, and yet I couldn't think of a damn thing to do. It was an amount that gets noticed in bank accounts, so it was only a matter of time before the tax people turned up, forks and knives in the air, ready to feast. For now, though, the money was there, and I didn't even take myself out for a fancy lunch somewhere to celebrate. I left every digit in its place, and went about my regular mundane business.

The second baffling thing: I ended up having lunch in the last place a newly minted millionaire might find himself—a modest nook at the bottom of a run-down block of flats. A local dive where the old man who made savoury pancakes stood every day behind his counter. Even "modest" seems a generous description of his joint, with its two small tables, mismatched cutlery, and at the entrance, its shabby stack of magazines sticking out tattered tongues of gossip. Inevitably, the old Sicilian would approach with a smile and ask what you wanted as he wiped his hands down on his apron. Then he'd nod thoughtfully, and say, *You know what, I'm waiting for delivery, so I can't get you that, but*—darting behind the counter, rummaging in his fridge, whipping out old Tupperware containers—*I've got some avocaaaado here, some peppadews, the feta cheese . . . no, the goat's cheese . . . and what's this back here*—rummage, rummage, rummage—*olives! I've got olives. I make you this kind of pancake, yes? I promise, you eat this pancake I make, and you forget that one you think you want!* And you'd say, Yes, sure, sounds good, because that's how the guy rolled in his pancake nook—and all the locals knew it. That's why anyone went there at all. It was like a restaurant run by a man who'd never been to a restaurant in his life.

The only difference that particular afternoon was that the old man didn't seem to recognise me. We'd never been on first-name terms, but I visited often enough to be singled out with: *Long time, my old friend. How you been, where you been hiding? Keeping well? What you want today?*

For some reason, that afternoon there was no hint of recognition in his eyes, none of the usual welcoming comments, *You just sit here, you tell me what you want—I make!*

I ate the pancake he prepared for me, waiting for a familiar quip, but it never came. Instead, he gave me my bill and said, *You enjoy? Yes, of course you enjoy! You tell your friends, your family! You tell them this place you find! I put a big table out for all you! You come back! Now you know my home and you come back, yes? My new friend!*

The third baffling moment: that afternoon, I got a call from the manager at Van Hunks, asking if I was up for a gig. The pay wasn't great, he added, and he knew it was last-minute, but he'd make it up. I told him not to worry about the pay, and agreed for no other reason than the chance to feel normal, if only for an hour or two.

I turned up around six-thirty, downed a drink, and by seven, I was seated at the piano. The place was packed, but something was wrong. I never expect anyone to stop what they're doing, to turn off their conversations and devote themselves to my playing (I've had my fair share of gigs where nobody's bothered to look my way, and good for them, really), but there was something grotesque about the scene before me. It was like the scrambling, tormented mass of winged demons in Signorelli's depiction of Dante's hell, revised for the happy-hour generation. A twisted orgy of rib-munching gluttons and drunken kids.

At one table, a twenty-something in a t-shirt emblazoned with a severed hand giving the finger stood up before his friends and began a showy story. The friends threw their heads back and laughed as he seemed to give a crude and exaggerated impersonation of some poor sod. Spit flew from his mouth as he yelled his punchlines. His eyes bulged in his head. The friends guffawed. One fell backwards on his chair. The entertainer climbed onto his own chair, arms flailing as he pretended to jerk off. I looked around. The manager was nowhere to be seen. Carrying plates, the waiters rushed in and out of the kitchen doors as if refilling buckets to put out a fire. I turned my eyes to the kid in the t-shirt, my fingers on the keys. His eye caught mine. Ice-water ran through my veins. His eyes tapered into two slits, his smile curling into a vicious hook. His friends kept laughing, beating the table with their fists, chugging their drinks. Everyone else in the restaurant kept ladling food into their mouths—deaf, blind, or without two shits to give, who could say for sure?

Yet, all the while, standing on a table in the middle of a dim room, the kid directed his eyes my way, his t-shirt giving me the bloody middle finger. Despite the raucous restaurant, I could somehow hear his thoughts: *You're going to die here. No one can hear you, piano man. So pound it. Pound the shit out of it. You're going to die here. Alone.*

That's when I stopped playing, right in the middle of my piece. I walked off the stage. I'd never before stopped midway through a gig—and never with the intention of abandoning my post—but it didn't make a difference. Nobody seemed to see me dash for the door, apart from that arsehole who turned to watch me as I headed for the exit. He was applauding, too— *clap, clap, clap, clap, whistle!*

I burst out into the street like a drowning man coming to the surface of a dark, impossibly deep lake.

26.

I arrived at the mansion late on Wednesday afternoon, half-expecting Leonard to turn me away, to laugh at me for having taken his bizarre joke seriously. Maybe he'd tell me the idea was due to all the drugs he'd taken, and that he was sorry for leading me on. (*Pay you to lock me in a room for a year? Did I really say that? I must have been off my rocker. But wait . . . no . . . you* believed *me? Jesus, man.*)

I'd prepared myself for the embarrassing possibility. I thought about how I'd laugh with him, shrug and smile, and so keep my dignity from flying off. But I wasn't at all prepared for what greeted me: a giddy kid about to take a ride on a roller-coaster. He could barely contain his excitement.

Dinner had been prepared for us. We took our seats at the dining table, and shortly afterwards Carl entered with a large tray. He laid out a mosaic of small dishes between us, in the middle of the table. Leonard had ordered his favourite foods, though only a small portion of each. Twenty different dishes on twenty tiny plates, so that he could taste them all without rolling off the chair in a coma afterwards. I watched as he tucked a white napkin into the top of his shirt, grabbed a fork and danced it over one dish, then another, and another, making up his mind about which he'd enjoy first. He speared a chilli sardine, then scooped a mussel from a shell. He took a forkful of biryani. There was a small caprese, just two slices of tomato and mozzarella, and a small block of lasagne in a balsamic reduction, two simple lamb chops, two tempura prawns, and two slices of grilled aubergine. Leonard systematically savoured them all. As an accompaniment, he sipped twenty different wines. I sat at the other end of the table, nibbling a bit, but mostly watching as Leonard worked his way around his elaborate last supper.

I didn't entirely understand the fuss. It wouldn't be his final meal, not like a prisoner's supper the night before the electric chair. When I asked Leonard, he said it wasn't about the food; it was about the choice. The power to select, he said, to say he wants to taste paella now, a spoonful of miso now, a bit of crispy duck *now*—and have the power to order it just like that, in the sequence he desired. Once he went into the room, he said, there'd be no choices at all.

But tonight—he held up his glass, winking—*tonight is not tomorrow. It's not next week. And it's not eight months from now. It's tonight—so we indulge in choice. We make love to this bitch of a life we've been living, and then kick her out of bed. So eat up, Bent.*

Throughout the twenty courses of Leonard's dinner, I hardly said a word. Lost in his own delight, Leonard Fry didn't seem to care. There were a couple of details he felt it necessary to mention—mostly about where to find certain things, and what to do if such and such happened. In a few days, Carl would be travelling home to be with his family. As far as Carl was concerned, Leonard would be flying off to another country and leaving me to house-sit. A groundsman would come by every two weeks to tend the gardens, but he need not enter the house. He, too, had been paid in advance. As far as housekeeping went, I needn't worry about basic supplies or groceries: there was a walk-in freezer at the back of the kitchen with enough shanks, turkeys, steaks, lamb chops, and pork sausages to feed us both for the year. The pantry was packed with pasta, rice, and canned foods. There was a vegetable garden the size of a small parking lot out behind the kitchen. Since Carl wouldn't be around, whatever I decided to cook should be enough for Leonard too.

There would be no written contract, if I didn't mind—it would have to be a gentleman's agreement. Could I accept that? I nodded, and he made it clear that no one but me would know of his presence in that room. While his lawyer was in possession of a sealed document explaining the deal, it wasn't to be opened unless I instructed the lawyer to do so. My copy was on the desk in the upstairs study. It had been drafted in the event he popped a blood vessel while in that room, only to have someone later accuse me of having kidnapped him—a scenario I hadn't considered at all. The notion sent an icy ripple up the back of my neck. It did, however, raise an interesting question: what was I supposed to do if he suffered some kind of physical problem—a seizure or a stroke?

Leonard smiled and shook his head.

Simple. You leave me, Bent. You do not open that door. Basically, I suck it up or I bite the big one. I can't have any reason to trick you into opening that door early. Soon enough, I'll be trying everything to convince you to open it. I expect to reach an extremely low point in that room. The mind doesn't give up its poisons easily. But I need that to happen. I need to charge on through, whatever that might mean for my mental state. You understand what I'm saying?

I nodded, darkly thrilled by it all.

I wanted to ask why he thought he could trust me in the first place, but I didn't. His answer wouldn't mean much—and he had already placed his bet on the table, with the wheel now well in motion. What really fascinated me was the fact that everything had already been organised. Carl. The groundsman. The explanatory document. The food. He knew I'd come back. Either that, or he had some alternative plan, regardless of whether or not I turned up at his door.

But no.

He knew I'd be coming back.

Leonard took his napkin from his lap and dabbed at his mouth. Then he pushed his hand into his pocket and the lights of the room flashed twice. A moment later, Carl entered and cleared the plates in a single go, with effortless panache. He returned to fill our wine glasses, and Leonard grabbed the note-pad hanging from his neck, took his pen and jotted something down, then gave them both back to him. Carl gave a quick bow, and left.

Leonard quickly stood up, untucking his shirt from his trousers as he led me out of the dining room and up the stairs. *The date is April the seventeenth*, he said, looking at his watch. *The time is ten after ten. Which means that, precisely one year from now, April the seventeenth, at ten-fifteen p.m., you will let me out. It's all in the document. There's a calendar on your bedroom wall to help you. I suggest you tick off the days.*

He'd timed this all to eerie perfection. Somehow, my return had been factored in. The length of our dinner. Every last detail, each moment. We passed along corridors until we stopped at a wooden door. Leonard pointed to a slot cut into the bottom, the size of a dog flap.

I asked if I could take a look inside the room, but he refused. *Think of the room as having been disinfected*, he said.

Disinfected?

Disinfected of thought. Nobody has been inside but me. Any ideas about the room—what it is, what's in it, what it signifies—these are mine, and mine alone. I can't have any of your projections floating around in there, chief. Do you get that?

Strangely, I did understand, but had the same thing been said by anyone else, at any other time in my life, I wouldn't have understood at all. I knew what Leonard meant, but only because I was beginning to understand Leonard himself. I was being pulled into his orbit, and in a manner so sly, so measured, that I barely knew it was happening—the way we spin around the sun with no sense of motion.

So this is it, he said with a smile. *Are you ready?*

Now?

I didn't expect it all to be so sudden. I still had questions. Right then, I couldn't think what they were, but there are *always* questions. Questions go on long after the answers run out, and maybe that's why he wouldn't give me an opportunity. He dipped into his pocket, pulled out a key, and handed it to me. I don't know what else I expected, but it all seemed so unceremonious. No farewell speech. No valedictory gesture. Just a man about to enter a room.

I began to feel nervous. I needed to say something, or ask something, but all I could manage was, *Are you sure about this?*

Leonard smiled, bent down, took off his shoes, and handed them to me.

There is nothing more offensive or repulsive in this world than a sure thing, he said, and shook my hand. Then he thanked me, wished me luck, opened the door and went inside. I strained to see something through the gap, but I could see nothing; it was too dark.

The door closed behind him. *Slam.*

Then silence.

I stood alone in the corridor, staring at a closed door. I could barely register the gravity of what had just occurred. I glanced over my shoulders, looked at the door. Finally, it clicked: it was all over. Or beginning? I didn't know. I couldn't profess to know much of anything in that empty moment. But there was *one* thing left to do, a final signing on the dotted line. And it was up to me.

I stuck the key in the door, then locked it.

27.

Exploring the contents of a man's house is like exploring the contents of his mind. There are images and objects, patterns and textures, things organised in a clear system—forming part of some design—and then there are other things that are in a mess. You know each of the things is connected to a past, if only in some vague and tenuous way. Some of the things you see are impressive, some heart-breaking, but most are bits of junk that seem unworthy of consideration at all, so there they stay. You can go through drawers, stare at the man's paintings, admire his collections, turn your nose up at his lack of taste—but the one thing you won't find is *meaning*. There's no meaning behind any of it, just endless loose ends. Nothing more than hoarding, this is a disguise, one that projects a complex interpretation of himself and his place in the world.

And if Leonard Fry's house was in any way a measure of his mind, then there was plenty of stuff furnishing it—lots of fascinating, shiny, dusty, arbitrary and vulgar things. Ancient artefacts and new mechanical toys. Tribal sculptures. Four-hundred-year-old maps in golden frames. A Japanese deep-sea diving suit from World War Two (which looked to weigh about three hundred kilograms). A genuine nineteenth-century zoetrope, with flickering images of a man galloping on a horse. There was a collection of what seemed to be centuries-old vases, all decorated with chrysanthemums. Hundreds of books stacked in piles reached upwards, like the forest of trees they'd once been. Curious hand-crafted musical instruments I'd never seen before, and rooms and rooms and rooms filled to the ceiling with more and more of Leonard's shit.

I went down to the kitchen, where gleaming pots and pans hung from a beam above a marble counter. Carl was nowhere to be seen—retired for the night, I guessed. After exiting through a door at the opposite end of the kitchen, I climbed yet another unfamiliar flight of stairs.

I found my way back to the main bedroom. There was nothing exceptional about the room—not when compared to the rest of the house. A king-size bed faced a large window overlooking nothing. A plain wardrobe stood alongside a dressing table with a mirror. There were no pictures on the walls, nothing but a large white calendar that began with that day's date, 17 April, and ended on the same date the following year. My travel bag was on the bed (probably brought up by Carl). Opening it, I realised I had clothes for only a few days, though I'd be in the house for a whole bloody year. I'd packed in complete denial of the reason I was packing at all. That was suddenly obvious. I undressed and climbed under the blanket. I'd never felt such a comfortable mattress. I stared at the ceiling, thought about Leonard in his locked room, and for the first time, it all felt as if it were actually happening. He was there. I was here. The game had begun. The weight of our agreement plummeted down on me, like a piano falling from a five-storey building.

On night one, I hardly slept a wink.

28.

Next morning, I thought I'd go downstairs, where I'd find Leonard at the kitchen table, drinking an espresso and reading a newspaper. He'd drop the paper, revealing a smirk, and I'd realise the whole thing had been a gag.

But Leonard wasn't in the kitchen. Carl was there, poaching eggs and frying bacon. Without so much as a smile, he pointed to a table on the patio outside. The morning was a country stunner, everything crisp and glistening under a mild sun. A goose skimmed across the lake and flapped off, skywards. Carl exited the house and laid the food out in front me. My juice was poured, slices of toast were fanned out across a silver platter, and then I was left to eat my breakfast. Afterwards, I got up and walked back into the kitchen. Carl was gone, but on the counter I saw a tray with a covered dish and a bottle of juice.

Had Carl prepared this for Leonard? I lifted the cover and saw scrambled eggs and three strips of crispy bacon. I took the tray and went upstairs to Leonard's locked room. There, I stood and stared at the door, wondering if there was anything I may have missed, some ritual I'd forgotten to enact. I got down on my haunches, carefully pushed the plate through the slot, then slipped the bottle through. I quickly stood up, and, remembering that I wasn't to say a word—no matter what—I took two steps away, turned, and went back to the bedroom.

29.

From the get-go, I had this idea of just enjoying a rich man's life, doing whatever I wanted in that outrageously large space, with all kinds of props and gadgets at hand— but I soon found there was little that kept me occupied for long. There were certainly novel features that piqued my interest. For one, there was a waterproof touchscreen jukebox in the shower. Also, an impressive entertainment theatre with three rows of leather armchairs facing an enormous curved television on the wall. The walls held shelves filled with movies, all untitled in uniform black boxes. I picked out two, and sat through three thirty-minute enigmas, dreamlike black-and-white films in foreign languages, devoid of plot or coherence. I watched naked women running around in a desert landscape, an old man flailing around in an enormous industrial vat filled with raw chicken breasts, a suited man wandering aimlessly with a giant button attached to his forehead, which was pushed by passersby. Rather than conventional movies, they were grisly pieces of performance art, like random clips from nightmares—shock-fodder that straddles the line between genuine profundity and pretentious crap. The whole time I sat there, I imagined Leonard watching by himself, all dressed up, sipping whiskey, no expression on his face, absorbing it all. Waiting to feel some-thing. Even if the feeling was merely disgust.

I found a snooker table, had two tots of whiskey, and sank a few balls. I played a round of one-man darts. I joylessly played the piano. An hour or so on, I sat outside and paged through some reading material I'd found—mostly yellowing *Reader's Digest* magazines. I skimmed through some outdated scientific stuff, and then got stuck into supposedly true stories about extraordinary individuals (such as the Austrian explorer trapped in a cavern for nine days before beginning to eat expendable parts of his own body—if such a thing is at all possible).

On the third floor, at the far end of the building, I found a gymnasium. It was a bright room complete with a punching bag, an assortment of weights, and a couple of complex cardio machines. I changed into shorts and a t-shirt and did forty minutes on a treadmill. Not being an exercise type, I thought I'd at least try it out. Being cooped up for a year provided a good opportunity to adopt some kind of fitness regimen.

As I ran to nowhere, I watched the news on a flat-screen in the top corner of the room. I don't often watch the news. The same tired old tunes. A missing schoolteacher. An overturned bus with seven dead and four in critical condition. A new Chinese entrant into the energy market. A railway strike. A rapper in rehab. Something about Syria. Macedonia. Making biodegradable electronics out of corn.

With a click, I switched the world off.

30.

Next day, only two noteworthy things took place. First, I watched from a top window as Carl hobbled out the front door to grab a taxi to take him home. He was wearing a grey hat and coat and carrying a briefcase in each hand. He didn't once turn to look at the house. He slid his briefcases in the boot and climbed into the back of the black car. His eyes didn't so much as glance my way as the taxi glided out of sight, leaving me alone in the house.

Well, almost alone.

Soon afterwards, I had my first glimpse of the groundsman. He entered the property—a big, pear-shaped man wearing blue overalls—and got started right away. For a long while, I stood and watched as he mowed the lawns, trimmed the hedges, and turned the soil in the beds. I didn't have much else planned, so I stared out from the upstairs window, somehow expecting that the more I watched, the more interested I'd become in what I was looking at. Leonard had been right: the grounds-man brought his own lunch and made use of an outhouse, so he didn't need to knock on the door. I didn't even bother to go down and introduce myself to him. By the end of the day, he had packed up and left.

Apart from this, I occupied myself for a while by looking for clues to Leonard's life, to work out how he'd earned his wealth. But lacking the audacity to rummage through his drawers or sift through his documents, I didn't come up with much. I wandered the house, peering at pictures on the walls, hoping to find something of interest. No picture gave me any clearer idea of anything: unrecognisable faces at a fancy party, a black-and-white photograph of a docked yacht called *Britomartis*, and a man riding a majestic black Friesian horse.

That night I slept okay, though I did wake once or twice thinking I was at the Crack Radisson. And like the previous nights, this one was dense and dreamless.

As the days rolled by, I did occasionally wonder what Leonard was doing in his room. Was he sitting on the floor with his legs crossed, eyes closed, facing a corner in deep meditation? Was he lying on his back, hands behind his head, counting imperfections in the ceiling? I couldn't rest on an image. Sometimes I'd put my ear close to his door, hoping to catch a hint, but nothing came my way, not the sound of a tap or the flushing of a toilet.

One morning, I took a walk outside to find his window— but no luck: from the outside, it was hard to tell where his room was. Perhaps he didn't have a window at all. Maybe a view would provide too much sensory stimulus. As I circled the manor, however, I became aware of the sound of my shoes on the cobbled stone, and then I felt eyes on me, as if he was watching from somewhere, from a small window I'd possibly missed. I picked up a stone, rubbed it between my fingers, dropped it, stuck my hands in my pockets, looked around once more, and then I went back inside.

31.

Things go well until they don't go well. At all.

You wake up and the day looks like any other. There's no reason to suspect you're about to have it tough. You're precisely where you laid your head the night before, but you've somehow awoken somewhere else, in a world that doesn't quite play by the rules you thought you knew. This day has surprises in store for you. Plans to shake things up a bit.

The day was a Tuesday—that much I knew—though it'd become hard to keep track without checking the calendar (little point in doing this, anyway). With nowhere else to be, I found the actual day didn't matter much. I'd had a few calls from the city, a manager here and there asking if I'd be up for a gig, if I'd be back any time soon, but I said no. I stuck with the family-emergency story, though I had no reason to lie. Each time they called, I was reminded that there wasn't much to miss about the city. No matter how many pangs of dumb longing I felt (for one particular greasy food on some grotty street, for one particular tatty bar stool in the corner of one particular bar), a single call would do the trick, turn me off going back, as if I could somehow smell the city over the line.

But I digress. On the Tuesday in question, I went about my chores. I emptied my laundry into the washing machine. While it spun, I had a ramble around the house, feeling satisfied that, however mundane, I'd done something constructive with my day. I went downstairs, and landed up in the large garage where Leonard kept his cars.

At the flick of a switch, a row of fluorescent beams came alive, revealing a series of pristine machines. I sauntered between the cars, ran my fingers along their sides, peeking through the windows as I did so. Without thinking, I opened the door of a green Aston Martin and sat in the driver's seat. Voices warned that I should leave before something bad happened, but I tuned them out, as if I were switching to a different radio station.

The scent of the car was the first thing to hit me: brand-new leather and fragrant wood. I rolled my hands over the dimpled steering wheel. The key with remote was dangling from the rear-view mirror and I grabbed it. For a second I stared at it in my hand, then I stuck it in the ignition and turned it. The engine woke with a roar. The sound went through my bones, stirring some long-dormant thing inside me—the primeval thing that had enabled man's discovery of fire, sent a rocket to the moon, and levelled cities with a single bomb. The thing that scares and defines us in equal measure. I pressed the remote, and the garage door lifted with a whirr. Sunlight poured inside and I narrowed my eyes. Outside, the world sat quietly minding its business. I adjusted the mirror and revved the engine.

A low growl, the gears smoothly engaged, and I was off.

Brown veld rolled out before me endlessly. It felt like I was on an uninhabited planet, with shadows lurking on hillsides, and clouds materialising and vanishing like unsure thoughts. That was it—as much commotion as you might expect in the countryside. Time isn't its normal ravenous self out in the middle of nowhere. Not like in the city, where it's gluttonous and insatiable. No, in the countryside, time savours, sipping slowly.

And nothing ever changes.

Not really.

A fairy of light danced along the gleaming bonnet as I switched to third and sped up the pass. I shaved each corner, swung to the left, then the right, shot out from under an arch of trees, and burst into the sunlight. The engine screamed, and I floored the pedal. Soaring down the south side of the mountain, I turned onto an open stretch of highway, and the needle climbed from one-twenty to one-forty, one-sixty, one-seventy, one-seventy-five, quivered around one-eighty, and then, because things go oh-so-well until they bloody well don't—

Fromp!

A dull and sickly *fromp*.

I wrenched the wheel, but the car skidded, ripping up grass and dirt and growling to a halt. The rear-view mirror revealed nothing. A cloud of dust swirled up. *You've hit something.* I fought to catch my breath and shuddered with the delayed realisation: *You've hit something, you idiot.* But what?

Slowly, I opened the door and stepped out. No other cars, though all around the long, thick grass waved silently. The sun had baked the land. There was the din of a thousand heat-stirred cicadas, and beyond that the sound of panting, faint whining.

A dog.

A coal-grey, not-quite-fully-grown cross between a Labrador and some stockier breed. A township mongrel probably bred for fighting, it lay on its side, head against the hot tar. Its chest was heaving unnaturally, and its fur was caked with blood. I got down on my haunches, and lowered my hand to touch the dog, but it snapped, its mouth a spring-loaded trap with teeth.

I stood and looked around. No hint of help from anyone at all. The highway stretched out in both directions, to the tips of its hot grey daggers. I grabbed my phone from my pocket and saw the signal was low, but managed to locate a clinic some thirty minutes away. I unbuckled my belt, slid it out, and edged the loop towards the head of the animal. The dog snarled, gave a yelp. In a single swift movement, I pinned its head to the ground and tightened the belt around its jaws. I carried the animal to the car, warm blood dripping from my elbows. I placed it on the seat, then slammed the door shut and ran to the driver's side. The car thundered back to life, shooting up dust and dirt as I got back on the road.

Tearing along the highway, I turned to the heaving animal, urging it to stay alive, to hang in there, to not give up on me now, for Christ's sake. Blood dripped from the seat, pooling on the carpet. The dog's eyes were opening and closing like broken shutters. Back and forth, with every blink, alive . . . dead . . . alive . . . dead . . . dead . . . *dead* . . . alive . . . alive . . . *still alive* . . .

And the blood. All that blood.

I couldn't just *see* the dog, I could smell it too: not only the rich, sweet smell of blood, but also the pungent stench of piss. The combination made me want to puke—adding my bile and half-digested breakfast to the waves of nauseating smells. I suppressed the retching. By now we were only ten minutes away. I glanced at the dog. Its eyes were closed.

Hey! I yelled. *Hey, you!* I hooted and leant over, screaming into its ear, *Wake up! Wake up!* And then, in desperation, I started barking, barking and growling like a big dog, loudly and viciously.

Buildings appeared in the distance, cream-coloured prefabs surrounded by high barbed-wire fences. Ahead, three scrawny kids were sitting on the edge of the road. They turned as I raced towards them, hopped up and scampered away. I looked at the dog; with each breath, it made a gurgling sound as more blood dribbled from its maw. My eyes darted back to the buildings, to the entrance gate.

To the dog again.

We were so close. So bloody close.

Just another minute and we'd be there.

The day bled away. Not a bird in sight. No murmur of a breeze. Nothing but a heavy mugginess in the air, left over from another season.

The sun was going down, burning out, and in the last of the light, I dug a hole next to the lake at the back of the house. As I did so, I hardly thought of anything. I didn't even think about the dog, which was now lying in a sack beside the hole. I didn't think about how I must have looked right then, a crazed killer, shirt and pants spattered with dark stains. I simply dug that hole; it was all that mattered.

My hole was close to two metres deep. When my spade hit stone, I wiped my forehead and decided it was enough. The hole was as deep as it needed to be. I lifted the sack of dead dog, carried it to the edge of the hole, and threw it in. It landed with a dumb thud, the sound of a dead thing. Then I grabbed the shovel.

As the soil rose and the sack vanished from view, I buried the day. It seemed to work. I felt the events of the morning slowly *un*-happen to me. It made me think—right there on that spot—of Leonard's slain horses, the ones in his war story, and how time worked the same way as my spade: every year, one mound of dirt piled on another, until nobody could safely say anything had occurred at all.

I finished up and patted the soil down with the back of the spade. I took the spade back to the shed, then went to have a closer look at the car, which I'd parked in the garage. The dull metal of a dent. A damaged bit of bumper. Dark patches of fur on the seat, making my stomach flip. These creative touches of mine were complemented by a long smear of coagulated blood. Grabbing some cleaning products, I frantically wiped at the blood and piss on the carpet, then moved on to the upholstery, even polishing the handles and the windows.

Pointless.

That once-beloved car was now not a car at all. It had devolved to something else: from an Aston Martin to a dog-eating Death Machine. Like some ghastly mechanical processor that turns live cows into hamburgers. I tossed the sponge in the bucket and left the doors open to let the interior dry out. Then I switched off the lights (leaving all the other cars alone in the dark with their murderous companion), found my way back to the front door, and locked it.

The hot shower I took wasn't very helpful in getting rid of all the dirt. Most stubborn of all was the blood under my fingernails. I tried to scrape it out but achieved nothing; somehow, the red had got really deep inside.

After the shower, I changed into fresh clothes and went downstairs to heat up Leonard's dinner, which had been dished up earlier that day: creamy chicken pasta speckled with green flecks of herbs. I took the meal to his door and fed it through the flap. The bowl disappeared, and a plate was pushed towards me, with the breakfast cutlery all rinsed and clean.

You've had quite a day, haven't you?

For a moment or two, I squatted in silence before the hatch. I was about to respond, when I remembered I wasn't supposed to say a thing in reply.

Leonard continued: *I could smell you passing by earlier, before your shower, chief. Funny, hmm? I could actually smell you. I'm not sure I'd have been able to before, you know? In the outside world, there's no way of keeping up with every new smell that comes your way. But in here*—I could hear him inhale—*well, you grow so accustomed to the smell of the place that every subtle new whiff, it just . . . well, it explodes in your nostrils. I could really smell it, you know? All the shit you've been getting up to out there. The sourness, the sweat.* Then he snickered. *But hey, whatever it was, was it fun?*

I moved back, still squatting, and froze, not daring even to breathe.

Leonard chortled. *Good, good,* he sighed. *No response. No answer. No matter what I say, right? No matter what I say—for a full year. You're worth every cent, Bent.* He gave a loud guffaw. *Every cent I spent, Bent. Cent. Bent.*

He played with his little rhyme, paused, and then went on: *You know something? I remember the day I bought my first sports car. It was a limited-edition gun-metal-grey Lamborghini Diablo . . .*

I shuddered. Did he know about the Aston? Highly unlikely. Even if his room had a window, it wouldn't be facing the front of the house. But I was getting ahead of myself—this was simple coincidence. I tuned in to his voice again.

Beautiful car. I remember seeing it in the showroom, immaculate. Gleaming. Glorious. And now, looking back, that was still my favourite moment with it, the moment just before buying it. Because as soon as I signed the papers and it was mine, truthfully, it scared the shit out of me. I idolised that machine. I wouldn't let anything come near it. I wiped off every smudge, lived in a state of ridiculous despair, knowing with every passing moment my magnificent machine was deteriorating in some microscopic way. Rust already growing on its underside somewhere. I knew I'd never be able to maintain its perfection, and this bugged me no end.

There was a long pause, and I shifted in my squatting position.

I suppose you're thinking that was stupid of me. But what can I say? Yes, it was irrational. A kind of compulsion. A sickness. But it took hold. So you know what I did? I walked up to the car, pulled out a key, and scratched the paintwork. I ran that key right across its side. One long scratch along the door. And whoosh! There was this sudden sense of relief. That's the best way to describe it. Because that's all I needed, you see. One nick. Just one imperfection. And I was free of it. Now I owned the car instead of it owning me. Isn't that funny? I had to taint the thing to make it mine. I had to fuck it up to assert myself over it. A car! You know what I mean?

I swallowed. My throat felt dry.

Yes, you know, don't you? he said lightly. *You've been asserting yourself all day, haven't you?* I could hear him chewing and slurping, and then he said, *This pasta is fantastic. So much flavour. Just wonderful.*

Then he was done. The story was over. The corridor once again filled with silence, as if the sound had been sucked from the room. The sound and the oxygen.

Slowly I stood up, turned on my heels, frowned at my fingernails, and walked to the bedroom.

III.

Knock, knock,
knock, knock

32.

In the middle of the night I woke up with a new memory. A slap of a memory that forced my eyes wide open, and made me sit up in the dark. I knew it wasn't a regular dream. A dream is like discovering a new species of animal, while a memory is like seeing an extinct one come back to life.

In this memory, I'm walking on a pavement on a clear sunny day. I don't know exactly how old I am, about seven, I think. My left arm is raised so high it hurts my shoulder, and someone's holding my hand. The hand holding my own is big and powerful. Hard and calloused. And as we walk, this big hand connected to my arm, it swings and pulls me. I can't see the rest of the body though, even if I turn my face upwards. There's just that strong arm, all the way up, not connected to anyone, and yet somehow I know it belongs to my father.

We're stepping off the pavement, crossing the road, but there's a gap in the memory, a brief intermission. Then it picks up again. We're in a stranger's living room. It smells like mothballs and ointment and tomato soup. I'm sitting on an old couch drinking flat Fanta from a plastic cup. I look out the window and see our own house across the road. But all I'm really thinking about is the fact that our neighbour who owns this house—this smelly living room, this old plastic cup—has a monstrously swollen left leg. It's so puffed up he's had to cut his pants off at the thigh. There's no shoe on the left foot, which bulges in places like a cauliflower head.

I can't make out his face.

From the leg up, everything is blurry. His outline keeps changing shape, like flares on the surface of the sun. On a crutch, he hobbles across the room, sits down at a piano. Clears the phlegm from his throat.

And then he begins to play.

The song he plays, it's a song I carry with me through my life, without being aware of it. Always playing in the background of everything I do. But it's not just a song. It's a song that shapes me, fuses with my genes, turns me from a dribbling mammal into a bona fide human being, one with ambition and desire and an illusory sense of purpose. I've never heard anything like this. I've never seen fingers move so fast. Eventually, the man's voice creeps in, a glorious drawl, a drone, and then he's singing along. The words to this song, I have them too, in this new memory.

But not all of them.

Just a few fragments, a few lines.

> *She throws a helluva shindig*
> *Knows jus' how to get the drinks in,*
> *And them all singin',*
> *Til it sudd'nly sinks in,*
> *That we ain't never met her before.*

The meaning of these words is lost on me, but I'm hooked on the sound, the way it merges with the music, dips and soars, sets me spinning.

> *She jabs like she knows us,*
> *Keeps toppin' glasses,*
> *And it's clear to us all,*
> *She throws a helluva shindig*

For every stranger she meets, see?
So we 'n she ain't ever alone.

Those were the only lyrics I could recall at the time. I didn't even know the name of the song. But there's more in this memory, because sitting alongside me is my father—bodiless, headless—and he says to me: *Remember, Bentley, some of the most gifted people in this world aren't necessarily the richest or most famous. Some love playing, but have no interest in the rest of it all. So they might be the best in the world at what they do, but nobody would ever know . . .*

I hear him, but I can't help thinking about that leg, that big swollen cauliflower leg the piano man carries around with him, and the phlegm when he coughs, and the fact he lives there by himself. I see my father tapping his foot to the beat. The piano man keeps playing for us, note upon note, layering that sound onto my mind like an ancient piece of cave art, a mystery that'll be there for millennia.

And then, my seven-year-old self, he takes that experience, and he pushes it down—way, way down—out of sight, and hearing, and mind.

Until the night, decades later, when I awoke in another man's bed, in another man's mansion, and it all came back to me as I sweated and stared out the window at the big blue face of the moon.

33.

The sky was grey. Rain fell like shards of glass, clattering and clanking on the roof tiles. Inside, the sound rumbled through the bleach-white lobby, along the winding balustrade of the staircase, to the steel-and-marble kitchen and the carpeted halls, filling each and every musty room in the house.

Even the locked ones, I'm sure.

My first few weeks in the mansion had been the hardest—or the easiest. It's difficult to say. Terrible things happened later, things I'll never forget, but in the beginning, what seemed worse than anything was the overwhelming and persistent dullness of it all.

I made meals. I cleaned my clothes. I pottered and slouched and napped. I failed to read any book beyond a few opening pages, and only ever sank half the balls I set up on the pool table. Nothing motivated me, and the prospect of making it through the year seemed increasingly and maddeningly undoable.

It was three nights since I'd woken from the dream/memory of my father and the mystery pianist, and this, I'd decided, would be my puzzle project. In time, more details surfaced, like images materialising through a dirty window that was slowly being cleaned. A faded yellow lampshade. A newspaper cutting in a frame on the wall. Tufts of white fur clinging to the carpet.

But no additional details emerged regarding the pianist or my father—two blurs in an ever-sharpening image of the living room—and all I had of the song was a scrap of the lyrics and the ghost of a tune.

Earlier that rainy day, I'd sat at the piano and tried to recreate the tune from memory. After an hour or two of mindless tinkering, arriving at nothing, I gave up. After taking a shower, I got dressed, went to the bar, lit the fire, and poured myself a drink.

Outside, the thunder bellowed.

Downing the last of my drink, I went back to the bar, where I popped in a few more ice cubes, free-poured a shot or three of Johnnie Blue, and topped it off with a slug of ale. I swivelled my glass, clinked the ice—a ritualistic start to my very own booze-lit ceremony—and took a long sip. My eyes peered over the rim, through the misted-up window pane—

There was someone out there, in the rain.

I wiped the window with my hand. A lone figure. I was projecting him, I told myself, cutting and pasting shadows and rain. But I knew that wasn't true; there was a man in a coat and hat standing between two trees. Motionless. Head tilted upwards, staring back at me from a distance.

At first I thought it was either Carl or the groundsman, but no; he wasn't either of them. He was thinner and taller, and with good posture. I couldn't see his face, but I could tell he was younger, somehow. The rain kept coming, beating down on him, spilling over the rim of his black hat and drenching his big coat.

Then he moved. Raised an arm as high as his shoulder and waved his hand. A slow open-palmed side-to-side, like a wind-up toy, just for me. Misjudging the distance as I put my glass down on the counter, I sent it to the floor with a crash. Splinters of crystal shot off in all directions.

I looked out the window again.

Gone.

The rain had crushed the flower beds. The drooping willows swayed like drugged-up hula girls. My eyes searched far to the left, far to the right, scrutinising every hedge and tattered tree, peering along the muddied road, all the way to the high wall that encircled the vast private property.

Greyness. Wetness.

Nothing. No one.

The second-hand of the wall clock behind me went on and on and on, an endless succession of tiny thuds. From where I was standing at the window, I could hear it go round and round, until the end of the world, until the sun burnt out and every one of us was dust, and every conceivable question was cannibalised by its answer, and every mystery was written off like a bad debt.

After seeing the mystery man, I went downstairs and stepped out of the front door, into the rain. There really was no one out there, so I went back upstairs. I grabbed my drink. Why was he there? Had he been sent to keep an eye on me? Leonard hadn't mentioned a third party. And if the man had been sent to spy, he hadn't exactly been discreet about it. He'd stood there in plain view, even waved at me. An icy breath passed over my skin as a new possibility struck me: what if it was Leonard I'd seen out there? What if he'd somehow exited his room and climbed down the wall?

Unlikely, but not impossible for a nut. I went down the corridor, put my ear to Leonard's door, held my breath, and strained for a sound, anything at all—when I heard the faint clearing of a throat. Leonard was still in his room. Back at the bar, I looked out the window; the rain had slowed to a fine drizzle.

So, if it hadn't been Leonard out there, who *had* it been?

I'd missed something.

This house. This man in his room. This plan.

Leonard's proposal had been bizarre, certainly, but I'd accepted the premise without question. After all, he'd given such a rousing speech, about how shitty and dull the world was, that I'd also felt the need to shut it all out. What I hadn't considered, however, was the likelihood he'd held something back. A few key details I'd have done well to know.

I poured myself another drink and tossed it back. Thoughts stacked one upon the other, crushing those at the bottom, with more piling up: I'd been hired as a glorified house-sitter, a sort of passive observer to Leonard's grand plan. But what if I wasn't just the sitter, but the actual subject? How could I be sure I wasn't being observed? Being studied? Tested? What if all of it, the whole deal, was a game, a way for Leonard and his rich bored pals to exploit a guy like me, someone with no friends or family, allowing them to pull off one shit-stirring prank after another, just to see if I'd break?

I stopped. Took a breath.

Just a little paranoid, even I admitted—but was it really impossible? Leonard himself hadn't been too coy: these plea-sure-seeking arseholes—these high rollers and big spenders— they got *bored*, didn't they? They needed *more*. More thrills. New and dangerous games. Hell, I might not even be the first. Maybe Leonard and his cronies met up annually, selected their nobody, trapped him like a rat in a maze, and then placed their bets . . .

All that talk about the *terrible filter*. The pictures in the hall-way of faceless men playing poker. The dog licking a hole in the head of a corpse. A drug-fuelled orgy in a house whose previous owner had hanged himself, on land where a hundred horses had had their heads chopped off. And now, a playboy locked in a room for a whole year, to do things differently— swim out, far away from the lonely uninhabitable islands of our lives . . .

Jesus.

I poured another drink, stiffer and taller this time.

My watch alarm buzzed twice.

One p.m. Leonard's lunch.

34.

I had another dream.

It went just as dreams tend to go, both entirely impossible and inarguably real. Also, it felt like something that had already happened, or was about to happen, or maybe both.

In the dream, I know I'm asleep in the master bedroom of the house, but I'm also outside, hovering above the garden like a cameraman rigged to an invisible high-wire. It's the middle of the night. The moon is so big and bright that everything is perfectly clear. Everything throws its own shadow.

The man in the hat and coat, he's there too.

He's got a spade in his hand, and he's digging. I know the place he's digging; it's the spot where I buried the dog. The stranger, he wastes no time, going about his business with a focused, rhythmic stab-lift-toss . . . stab-lift-toss . . . stab-lift-toss. The hole grows wider and deeper. In accelerated dream time the man's able to get to the dog in just a few brief, deliberate moves. My floating eye, it circles over the hole, and I can see the dog in the centre of the deep pit, no longer in the sack, but lying uncovered on its side in the loamy dirt—dead, dead, dead—until it isn't . . . and its head twitches, and its front legs move, and it's getting up clumsily, like a newborn foal. The man drops the spade and steps away from the hole.

The dog—thin, decayed, broken-boned—scrambles up the slope. It joins the man, standing at his side. The man pats the dog on the head. They turn and walk together, under the bright yellow moon, towards the house, and I know where they're going. They're headed to my bedroom, calmly and silently, one hesitant step at a time. The way the dog's walking, it's clear its back is broken in several places: it's like a moth-eaten piano accordion.

They enter through the back door of the house, tracking mud across the floor; then up the staircase, down the carpeted corridor, and past Leonard's door—he's laughing and laughing his head off.

Eventually, the man and the dead dog reach the entrance to the master bedroom. The door squeals open, and they come inside. The floorboards creak. The moon beams through the window. This duo, they approach my bed, where I'm sleeping, and I can see myself sleeping. The dog scratches at the base, trying to rouse me.

Scratch, scratch, scratch.

This dream-me, he opens his eyes, and he looks to the side of the bed, and my perspective switches to the him/me in the bed, with the dog at the bedside, missing one of its eyes and panting with a split tongue.

The man in the coat is beside the dog, tall and stiff, looming like a stone statue. He has no face, as if the sculptor couldn't care to finish him, unable perhaps to fashion the expression he wanted.

I ask what they want, both of them, but neither responds. They stare at me as I scramble pathetically in my sheets. I'm begging for them to explain themselves, to leave me alone, but I can barely contain my fear. My internal organs are mashed up. I'm going to spill out of myself and never be solid or contained again. The dog puts its paw against the bed, and *scratch, scratch, scratch.*

It goes on and on and on—

It doesn't stop.

Scratch, scratch, scratch.

And then I opened my eyes for real.

Awake. Sweating, cold, dry-mouthed, quivering—but awake. It took a while to figure out where I was, and if anyone was at the bedroom door. But the door didn't move. The moon beamed in through the window. And I wondered why, if it all really had been a dream, I could smell the faintest metallic whiff of blood on my hands.

35.

The next day, I decided I needed to know more about my man at the window. After giving Leonard his breakfast, I began my search for answers by rummaging through cupboards and drawers. I didn't know what I expected to find, but there had to be something.

I threw open Leonard's wardrobes, peeked into shelves, and pried open the sticky drawers in his desk. But I found little: a few invoices, ticket stubs. A loose photograph of a man who looked like Leonard—but it was too old to be him: a fuzzy Polaroid from the seventies or early eighties. At a guess, it was Leonard's old man, with the big sideburns and black sunglasses. He was sitting on a brown checked couch, with a baby on his knee whom I took to be Leonard. I homed in on little Lenny's face: a normal-looking, chubby-cheeked kid with no clue of all the shit to come. I turned the photograph over; in black ink was written: *7th June 1983. Happy burp-day daddyo!*

I put the photo back in the drawer. I wandered through rooms on a quest for clues, hoping for a bust that would out the whole spiel. The books on his shelves didn't reveal much, just Leonard's penchant for tough reading material: books on mechanical engineering. Advanced mathematics. Astronomy. Nautical navigation. I returned to his bedroom, and dug through the drawers of his bedside table.

I was just about to give up when it caught my eye, something white against the dark floorboards. A small square of paper, no bigger than a Post-it, lay beside the bed. I bent down to grab it, and my eyes ran over the handwritten words:

> *Here's an idea, arsehole.*
> *Pick up the phone sometime*
> *And call me.*
> *Jolene*

A phone number was scrawled at the bottom.

For a while I did nothing but stare at the words, wondering what the note could mean. I studied each swirl and loop, like some graphologist, arriving finally at a wise amount of nothing. I did, however, concoct a story: this was a morning-after note. This Jolene, whoever she was, had enjoyed a fun night with Leonard, he'd left her to let herself out in the morning, and she'd written in the hope that their casual fucking equated to something more.

Then again, if they did actually know each other, she wouldn't have put her number on the note, would she? Unless to say something like, *Hey Don Juan, let me make this reeeeal easy for you—cos clearly, you're not getting the message.*

Had Leonard ever seen this note? Had it slipped off the bedside table before he'd had the chance to read it? Whatever, it did seem to indicate that Leonard was in some kind of relationship with another human being (for some reason, none of the guests on my first visit seemed to count).

But maybe she was just a family member. A concerned sister. An old friend. Or an obsessive ex who'd climbed through the window while he was in the shower. Perhaps the mystery man out in the rain was really a missus, and this was *her* doing (okay, that seemed a stretch).

The fact remained: I didn't have a clue. Not that I was going to pass up an opportunity to delve deeper, especially with all that time to kill and curiosity to quell.

No, I needed to speak to this woman.

I wasn't sure about *what* exactly, but that would come.

Sitting on the edge of the bed with the note in my hand, I read the name over and over again: Jolene. Jolene. Jolene. Then I dialled the number using Leonard's bedside landline. I had no idea why I was calling her, but I felt compelled to, and with no explicit aim in mind. Perhaps, after the man at the window, I just needed to believe she was real.

The phone rang six times. When I was about to hang up, I heard a voice. *Ha! No, can this really be? After all this time?*

The words rushed out like a flash flood across desert terrain. I almost dropped the receiver. She sounded youngish, in her thirties, I guessed. Sharp. Confident. I said nothing as she continued: *So, you finally find your phone in that overpriced heap of rubble you call a home—and nothing to say?* There was a sexy playfulness in her voice as she addressed her locked-up Lothario.

I'm sorry, I said. *You see, well, I'm not actually . . .*

She paused, then groaned. *Oh, God! It's not Leonard, is it? Right, that'll teach me. You see, his number came up on my phone.*

My mistake, I mumbled, *I should have realised . . .*

Okay, let's get this clear. You're not Leonard.

No.

But you're using Leonard's phone. At his bedside table . . .

That's right.

I see. Aaaand . . . I should know who this is, should I?

No, we haven't met.

Ah. Did you dial the wrong number?

No. I fumbled for words. *Well, I found a piece of paper . . .*

A piece of paper?

With your name on it.

So you know my name.

Jolene.

Right. That's not terrifying at all. And you are?

Bent.

Bent?

That's my name.

Bent it is. Good. Now tell me, what are you doing in Leonard's bedroom, Bent?

I'm, uh, taking care of Leonard's house while he's away.

You're Leonard's house-sitter?

Sort of.

Sort of? And you got my number . . . how, exactly?

Well, I found it on the floor, actually.

Ha, yes, of course. In Leonard's house that's probably the best place to look for a woman's number. A chortle. *So, you found my number, and you just thought you'd call?*

Something like that.

I see. And—let me guess. You're hoping I'm a hooker, right? Or one of Leonard's cheap lays?

No!

Yeeesss . . .

Jolene's laugh made me doubt myself, even though I knew this wasn't true. And she sure didn't strike me as just another orgy room filler. The two of them were probably attracted because they challenged each other. She didn't sound like every other dullard out there, with only half a new thing ever to say.

Sitting on that bed with the phone, having wedged myself into their story, I suddenly felt like an amateur. A stupid fly stuck in a web made by two wily spiders. *Don't worry,* she laughed. *I'm messing with you. Any friend of Leonard's is a friend of mine—besides his actual friends, of course. Because even Leonard would know better than to let one of them take care of his house. So, you're not his friend, but you are someone he trusts in some way?*

I said nothing, didn't know what to say.

Hmm . . . okay, now I'm really curious. Right. Let's see. You're the shy type, but you've got some guts at least for making this call. So that means . . . well, I suppose that means you're curious too, right? Maybe about me, but I'm guessing it's mostly about Leonard. Right? So, how's my aim, Bent?

An arrow splitting an arrow that's dead centre of a bullseye, was what I thought, but all I said was: *Pretty good.*

Yeah, sure, pretty good. She'd done damn well, and she clearly knew it, but she changed the subject. *So, how long are you staying there?*

For a year. While he's away.

Uh-huh. And what do you do?

I'm a pianist.

A pianist! Wow. Classical?

Jazz.

Jazz! Do people still listen to jazz?

I'm not sure.

I've always thought it's one of those things too cool to be actually liked.

Well, I like jazz.

Of course you do. Never mind me, I'm in a funny mood.

Had I caught her at a bad time, I wondered. You call someone and you throw yourself into a moment in their lives, without invitation. It could be any old moment, but that's what you have to deal with. Life, in the background—like static.

So, a mysterious, monosyllabic jazz man. You know what, to hell with it. Against all odds, your stalker call's actually paid off. Look, since you're Leonard's new friend, I'm going to take a chance. There's a group of people coming over. For drinks, maybe some dinner if they're lucky. Just a few close friends. Nothing extravagant. I've got a feeling it'd do you some good to join us. Get you out of Dracula's castle for a bit. How's that?

Sounds lovely.

Oh, dear. Lovely? Try not to use words like "lovely" in front of my guests. They'll tear your eyes out if you talk like that.

Ah.

I'm kidding. After a pause, she said, *Bent, you aren't crooked, are you?*

Very clever, I thought, but said, *Nope.*

I'm not making a mistake by inviting some stranger, am I?

I gave a dry little laugh, said I was looking forward to it. She said, *Okay, then*, and gave me the date and address, which I jotted down with a pencil from Leonard's drawer. I should wear something smart, she said, it would make things easier on me—whatever that meant.

Then she hung up.

My heart did a drum solo. A double-time bridge. I got up from the bed and just stood there. The house was hollower than ever. Silent as a ransacked tomb. It had all happened so quickly: from seeing the man outside the window to finding the note to receiving the invitation to a party.

And the biggest surprise was the feeling that flooded through me.

Attraction.

I didn't even know what this woman looked like, but I knew I wanted her. My imagination went wild, giving her a physical shape, colouring that in, then breathing warm sexual life into this being, like God with Eve. I did feel fairly ridiculous about it, though: me, rocking on my heels in the centre of this room like a mental patient and growing horny.

So I considered rubbing the whole thing out.

Instead, though, I went to pour myself another drink.

36.

Days passed, though without further incident. The man in the garden didn't reappear, and with every passing moment the memory retreated to the back of my mind, to that place where the compounds of thoughts and ideas are broken down into harmless, non-reactive elements. The possibility that I was being scammed remained in my mind, and I spent an absurd amount of time checking for hidden cameras, and whether wall mirrors were one-way or not.

But I didn't find a thing.

I soon began to feel like a bored kid playing detective. Each time I *didn't* find a camera, or failed to expose a one-way mirror, I felt an acute, infantile sense of disappointment. That's when I knew I had to stop looking for clues, to quit worrying—and to stop thinking it was a scam. And that's when apathy crept back in. But when the day of Jolene's dinner finally arrived, an uneasiness grumbled in my gut, and my new concern became what I'd be wearing for the occasion.

Something new, I thought. To make an impression.

I opened a door and flipped a switch. Bright white overhead lights buzzed to life, revealing a wood-panelled walk-in wardrobe, almost as big as the bedroom itself. A hundred pairs of shoes sat waiting against the back wall. A row of dinner jackets and waistcoats hung neatly on the left, while a rail to the right was filled with an assortment of multicoloured motorcycle leathers, all covered in badges and emblems. A dozen helmets were lined up like robotic heads. In the glass-fronted drawers below, there were enough overpriced accessories to carry into the afterlife, as well as an assortment of watches with legendary names: Bulgari. Jaeger-LeCoultre. Vacheron Constantin. But I wasn't interested in the extravagant stuff. I picked out a turquoise shirt and a pair of trousers, the plainest and simplest I could find, both of which fitted perfectly. I selected a belt. Thin brown leather with a small silver buckle. Nothing too showy.

I couldn't remember ever wearing another man's clothes. I'd once tried on a pair of men's horn-rimmed spectacles lying in my mother's bedside drawer (my father's, possibly, but I never asked), and maybe a jumper I'd borrowed from a school friend one winter's day. But this was different. It was as if I could somehow *feel* Leonard, the time he'd spent in those clothes, his accumulated memories and experiences—the mnemonic sillage of old moments in every stitch and thread—all at awkward once. Or maybe, more than our houses, it's our clothes that end up haunted after we're gone.

I searched through rows of small elegant bottles arranged on a white shelf. Most of the brands I didn't recognise, but I grabbed one anyway and gave myself two liberal squirts. I threw on a black jacket, adjusted my cuffs, and turned to suss out my look in a full-length mirror.

I looked surprisingly good, though a haircut wouldn't have been a bad idea. A bit more sun might have helped too. My appearance was passable, I reckoned. Except—I was alarmed to discover—for my fingernails, which I'd tried so hard to scrub clean that day.

It had been more than a couple of weeks since the accident, but for some reason there was still blood under each of my fingernails—which were also somehow torn and broken. I held out my hands and ran my eyes across my fingertips. There was actually *more* blood than before. The carmine colour had spread almost as far as the cuticles. I studied my right-hand index finger from all angles, as if to identify a strange new insect, then pressed down on each fingertip to test for pain. They all felt fine. No discomfort at all. I was, however, reminded of having woken a few nights earlier to the smell of blood—on my hands. But that made no sense. The blood under the nails wasn't mine at all.

No reason to panic, a voice kicked in. It was nothing. A simple explanation lay just out of reach. I buffed my nails against the front of my jacket (gently at first, but then harder and faster), and used my index fingernails to scrape the others clean, but to no avail. Then I gave up, inhaled, and looked in the mirror.

I looked good. I smelt good. I felt good.

I turned out the lights and shut the closet door.

Ha, yes, finally . . .

Leonard.

I was passing along the corridor, on my way out for the night, when his voice came through the door. I wanted to ignore it, to keep going, but something, a stubborn thing with claws, held me in my spot.

I was beginning to worry about you. Starting to think I'd picked a prude. Someone without imagination. Good for you. Smelling so good. He sniffed deeply, loudly. *Oh, yeah. I know that one. That's for a night of action, I know. Since you've felt free to grab my toiletries, I bet you've tried on a couple of my clothes too, huh? Shirts. Trousers. Oh, yeah. Bet you're looking slicker than the inside of an oil tanker! So, what's the plan? Where you going? Who's the lucky woman? Or is it a man . . . I didn't really ask you that, did I? Huh. Can't really assume any more, can we? It's okay, hey, we're all equal in the eyes of the Lord, no matter what we do in the bedroom, right? Here's to inviting everyone to the party! We are who we are! And you, my friend, smelling so good, you are who you are—a bright and beauuutiful butterfly. Out of his chrysalis of convictions and judgement and disgust for us sad, privileged folk—ready to fly off* into the world. Oh, and please—I know you're not supposed to say anything to me—yes, yes, it's the deal. But you've just got to tell me how it all went, yeah? What she thought of that super slick outfit of yours. How she tasted. Whether you'll be seeing each other again, and whether next time . . . next time, he gave a loud, scornful snigger, you'll have the guts to go there as yourself, chief.

37.

I turned up around seven. I was about fifteen minutes late. Entering Jolene's front garden, everywhere I looked I saw some odd thing, as if a theatre company had had a yard sale and Jolene had got there last. Under a curtain of creepers, a lazy-looking stone satyr stood smoking a pipe. Old teapots hung from the branches of trees, reflecting the glow of hundreds of hanging fairy lights. In one corner, a patchwork couch slumped beside a mirror-mosaic table holding a half-filled glass of wine and a lumpy Joseph Merrick–like candle. Colourful and busy and cluttered, it all seemed a tad overworked, I thought.

A woman floated across the garden towards me, like a figure in a painting who'd stepped out of a frame. She was wearing a white dress and holding a glass of red wine in each hand.

My cryptic caller, she said. *You came.*

She was attractive, but not in the way I'd imagined. On the phone I'd thought she'd have a sleeker, more sophisticated look. But no: she was baby-faced, with wide curious eyes and a small but voluptuous mouth. She gave me a kiss on each cheek.

Thanks for the invite. You have a beautiful home, I said blandly, like a machine having just figured out how to feel. Politeness, I thought, the dull cousin of charm.

Jolene pushed on: *You don't look like one of Leonard's regular cronies. Nope. You haven't had enough sun on you. And your shoulders are up, your neck's too stiff, Lurch Addams. Loosen up!*

Here. She handed me a glass of wine. *Take two before meals. Now, come. We've got guests to entertain, you and me.*

She took me by the hand and led me to the house. The physical contact set something off in me. We swooped inside. The décor reflected the outside look, a mix of handmade objects and shiny hi-tech toys. A big backlit fish tank formed the bottom of the bar counter. An assortment of liquors and liqueurs were lined up, their trendy bottles making the contents look like milkshakes or glow-in-the-dark radioactive waste.

Heads turned to us, and Jolene extravagantly introduced me as the greatest bloody jazz musician she'd ever known—*Seriously, you've just got to hear him play, a musical genius, people, you've never heard anything like it!*—which resulted in a round of handshakes, murmured hulloes, pleased-to-meet-yous, how'd-you-dos, and a couple of kisses on my cheeks.

Faces swam in and out of focus. There was a woman with a black bob and too much eyeshadow who raised her glass to me with a wink. A balding man eyed me with distrust from behind round lenses. Two others slunk into the circle: a lanky guy with a long face, narrow eyes, and greasy hair who felt the need to mention he was a literary critic, and another acne-scarred man who looked like a seventies porn star—complete with ponytail, gold chain, and a nest of black chest hair on display.

Not a single one of their names stuck. It was nothing personal. Names just fall out of my head sometimes. The one thing I couldn't help thinking, however, was how different we all were—and not just different, but mismatched, as if we were a cross-section of people off the street who'd been roped into some kind of social experiment. That, or the cast of a gritty *Snow White* remake, featuring all-new Disney dwarves: Smiley. Sleazy. Pervy. Boasty. Misanthropy.

I was surprised to learn that nobody seemed to know their hostess very well. None of them had been to Jolene's house before. I didn't really get it, but I didn't dwell on it either.

For whatever reason, there we all were, Jolene's collection of strange new curios, hanging out with her, like the teapots in her trees.

We sat around the dinner table, and course after course was brought out by two smiling young women. Throughout, the guests talked about anything and everything that came to mind. For me, silence worked better than the bullshit. I opened a bottle of Blood River Shiraz and made friends with it. Two glasses in, Jolene leant over and grabbed the bottle, doing me the favour of topping up my drink.

What can I say, I said as she poured, *I'm a drinking composer with a music problem.*

She laughed. *So, are you glad you came?*

Everyone else was in their own bubble of conversation.

I am, I said.

She grabbed an empty chair and sat down beside me, looked around the room, pushed her hair behind her ears, and then turned to me with a smile that seemed to flick on with a switch. She crossed her legs, and her knee caught my eye, rousing me. I remembered how I'd felt after my call in Leonard's bedroom.

You know what, I'm sorry, she said. *It wasn't fair of me.*

What, exactly?

Inviting you. I'm not sure now it was the right thing to do. She stopped, put her hand to her mouth, tried again: *No! God. I mean, you're lovely. Really. It's been great meeting you. It's just, well, I think when the phone rang, and that number showed up, I needed to . . . I don't know . . .*

Feel closer to him? I ventured.

She gave a sigh, then smiled. I felt myself shrink before her eyes. Nothing nudges you out the playground quite like a woman who pities you.

You know, Bent, he's what you'd call . . . an enigma, she said. *The problem is, "enigma" isn't good. It isn't bad. It isn't anything. You can't fall in love with an enigma. It's more of a whirlpool. Or a black hole, sucking you in and then crushing the light. That's what an enigma is, and that's what Leonard is.*

Wow, I said. *That's pretty brutal.*

She jutted out her bottom lip. *Ah, he's already got to you.*

I immediately thought about Leonard, wondering what he might be doing right then. Sleeping? Writing his memoirs on the wall in blood and shit? Playing the world's longest game of 99 Bottles of Beer on the Wall? My mind swerved to the image of the man outside the window, waving at me, watching me, then vanishing without a trace.

I asked, *Have you known each other long?*

Yes and no, she said. *When it comes to Leonard, things don't really work that way.*

What do you mean?

She paused, looked up, tried again. *It's like the longer you've known him, the less you in fact know him. The closer you think you are to getting to the bottom of him, the further you actually are. Take you, for example.*

Me?

Ja, you, bright eyes. You're probably closer to him than I am. Yet here you are, trying to find out about him from me. And that's the thing. Like I said, an enigma. But you know that already, don't you?

With a shrug, I said, *I hate to disappoint, but I have no idea what you're talking about.* I folded my napkin tightly (six times, all together). As I did so, I noticed my blood-stained fingernails, and quickly unfolded it, sliding my hands under it. It took me a moment to pick up where we'd left off. *I don't know Leonard very well. We're not friends, really.*

No? she said, cocking her head.

I shook my head. *We're actually strangers. I water his plants.*

Water his plants. Hmm. Right. Important job.

Someone has to do it.

Sure, she said, with a gentle tug at my collar. *Well, I guess he must be pretty grateful since he was kind enough to let you wear one of his favourite shirts, hmm?* One last smile, and she stood up.

I've always liked him in this colour, she said. Then she kissed a forefinger, and traced it along the length of my nose.

Dessert arrived. A towering croquembouche drew oohs and aahs and predictable gags about guilt-trips and compromised dietary plans.

I'd tried small talk, but the banality hurt my head, and in the end nobody bought that I cared anyway. But the booze went down and a familiar haze blurred everything. Like Vaseline smeared on an old camera lens, it created the mistiness of a low-budget movie dream sequence. I couldn't shake it off, so I tucked in my tongue, and left it at that.

The only other person who refrained from yakking was Jolene. She danced by herself to Ella Fitzgerald and Louis Armstrong's "Dream a Little Dream of Me." As she swayed, I tried to imagine her with Leonard. How did they see each other? What did they talk about? What kind of people did they pretend to be with each other? Or was the issue that they simply couldn't help being themselves? And how much could Leonard possibly have cared for her if he'd chosen to lock himself away for a year without telling her?

Heels off, hair down, and eyes closed, she danced tipsily, twirling in slow circles, a beautiful ghost conjured up in a séance. She was soon joined by Eyeshadow Girl, with her awkward yet innocent sexual moves. The two women were simply letting go, I reminded myself. That's all. Remember letting loose, *Lurch?*

Porn Star was next to join, followed by Baldy and the Critic. By now Jolene had emerged from her mesmerising, solitary trance. The new dance to some recent pop song was a cheaper performance, without nuance, without any kind of truth, I thought. She slid her back up against one of them playfully, then threw her head back with a laugh—

Something in the corner of the room caught my eye.

Partially veiled by the fold of a curtain, a patch of fog appeared at the dining-room window. I did nothing but stare at it for a long while, wondering if there was anyone out there. My mind jumped once more to the man in the garden. I considered getting up to take a closer look, but didn't, afraid my guess might be correct. Then, as if there was indeed someone out there, the patch of fog shrank, expanded, shrank and expanded—

Hey, Mr. Cool!

My head flicked sideways, and I looked at Jolene.

She was on the makeshift dance floor, and as she came over, I quickly told her I didn't dance. But she just grabbed my hand and said, *Of course you don't, you've got another job.* She pulled me to a piano in the corner of the room.

I threw one more glance at the window.

The white breath was gone.

I shrugged it off, sat down, fingered a few of the yellowing keys. The piano was slightly out of tune, but the crowd was drunk and easy. So I played—a piece I hadn't played in years, some rockabilly number from a long-gone phase of my life. It came easily. The crowd whooped and cheered, and soon they were hovering over me. They were impressed—gasping and cheering—which made me play faster and harder. I riffed on the song, fingers doing a quick crab-walk from one end of the keyboard to the other. The crowd cried out for me to let the piano have it, to play faster and faster, and then they were back on the floor, in full arm-swinging, head-swivelling glory. For a moment the whole thing was almost fun, more fun than I'd had at the piano in a helluva long while—

But no.

Something inside me refused to let me grab the moment. The feeling grew. I couldn't say what it was, exactly. Not at first, though it began as a tingling, a low, arrhythmic something in my stomach. Around me, the room stretched and warped, and when I looked up—

Bulge.

That's the word that came to mind. The world began to expand, swelling and ballooning. I turned to look over my shoulder, but Jolene and the guests were no more. There were no longer five people on the floor, but only one—one fleshy mass with flailing arms and legs, like the rough draft of a new Hindu god, moving in and out of itself, and holes were opening, and the holes had teeth and pink tongues, and laughter poured out of these holes.

Panic. Panic. *Panic.*

I shut my eyes, opened them, and for a fuzzy instant they were all individual people again, as they'd been all evening—people whose names I still couldn't remember, but who were individuals nonetheless—until an arm slipped into another arm, and a pair of shoulders had two heads, and then this restless, sexless mass had one big head and many mouths, and one of them opened wide and yelled at me to keep playing, to *Pound it! Pound the hell out'f it, piano man!*

I looked down at my feverish hands. They were no longer connected to my arms, but detached and independent, doing their own mad thing. The walls began to bend, the piano softened and slumped, and I felt the darkness soak into me, reminding me of the night I'd first met Leonard. The fingers kept playing and pounding and playing, and the fleshy, bulbous chimera behind me kept laughing and singing and dancing—a human croquembouche.

And then everything dissolved and disappeared.

38.

Two paramedics wheel my mother out of her apartment block on a metal gurney—"One step, two step, easy does it."

Her dead body is covered by a baby-blue sheet. There's a wet patch in the middle, but I don't know what it is. A bit of piss? Sweat? Booze from the bottle that had slid to the floor when I'd found her? The rickety gurney bounces across the pavement and a hand flops out. Her fingers are fat and white, like raw pork sausages. As the paramedics pass by, the whole rig reminds me of a grisly buffet tray being rolled out for some big creature somewhere—something that just loves a cut of dead drunk mother. The paramedics, they don't even look at me as they wheel her across the pavement, as if *I'm* the ghost, as if that's actually *me* under that sheet.

I'm sitting on the steps outside my block. I'm not saying a word and there isn't even a sad lump in my throat. I don't feel much beyond a vague sense of curiosity. All I do is dimly wonder how many people have died in that very same spot over the entire history of time. Hundreds, perhaps even thousands.

I watch as the buffet tray is lined up with the back of the ambulance. The doors are already open—a low-rent version of the Pearly Gates. A man descends the steps behind me and stands at my side. He's wearing neat brown trousers. They stretch all the way up to the bottom of his black leather jacket, like a tree trunk disappearing into a dark cloud. Above that, a big thick moustache twitches, looking like a scared dumb animal clinging to his face. A hand disappears into a pocket, and out comes a box of smokes. He lights up, looks down at me.

"I'm sorry about your mother," the man says.

"Thanks," I say—as if I've just been praised for something.

The man, he pauses, then he says, "It was probably a heart attack. But I don't want to say just yet."

I think about how it doesn't matter at all whether it was a heart attack, an embolism, or an extraterrestrial brain parasite. Dead is dead.

"How old are you?" he asks.

"Eighteen in three weeks."

"You have a father?"

I jut out my bottom lip and shrug, indicating I couldn't care less.

"You earn money?"

I nod at this because, yes, I do earn money. I'm the only one who's been earning money for months now. But he doesn't need to know my business. And he respects that I don't tell him; I can see it on his face. Adults don't share personal details. It's the first step towards self-preservation in a world where no one gives a shit till you've got something they want.

The man smiles and takes a drag. The smoke jets out of him.

"Good," he says. "That's good. You gonna be all right here? You want—"

"No," I say. "I'll be fine."

"You're gonna have to come down . . . to the station, of course. There's paperwork. Stuff to sign. Nothing serious. Think you can handle that?"

"Sure."

"I'm sorry you had to see your mother go like that." He shakes his head. "You shouldn't have had to be the one."

I consider what he's just said, hold myself back from saying that if it wasn't me, it wouldn't have been anyone else. My mother and I were somewhat short on witnesses to our lives.

At times I thought that, for her, I was the only proof that she existed at all.

And maybe that went both ways. Maybe she was my proof, too.

The man—I assume he's some kind of cop—bends down and offers his pack of cigarettes to me. He gives it a shake and a single pops out. I've never smoked in my life, and I gingerly take it from him. He must know I'm not a smoker by the way I'm holding the cigarette, like I'm about to write something down, but he says nothing. He just flicks his lighter in front of my face. I stick the cigarette between my lips and lean forward. I take a deep pull, the smoke goes into my lungs, but I don't cough. I've seen new smokers cough on their first—but not me. I inhale, embrace a slight wave of dizziness, and take another pull. Then I sit on the stairs, puffing away and watching as the ambulance doors are shut and the paramedics amble to the front of the van. They're in no rush. They don't even switch on the lights, or the siren.

I really wish they'd put on the lights—just for a bit, if for no other reason than to alert the world to the fact that my mother's just died, to have the event of her death turn at least one or two last heads. But the way they drive down the street—so casually—there's no sign that they're carrying anyone at all. Even now, as she's being ferried out the world by her boatmen, no one gives a crap.

"And that's that," the plainclothes cop remarks. I think he's slipped up by saying this; he was only supposed to think it. He looks down at me to see how I react—his moustache does a nervous samba on his lip—but there's no need to worry; I'm in complete agreement with him.

"Yes. That's that," I say. And I finish my first cigarette.

39.

I woke up in Leonard's bed, in the master bedroom. I was still in my turquoise shirt and pants, feeling rough, with no recollection of how the party had ended, or how I'd got home. I climbed out of bed and went downstairs to the fridge. I drank almost a litre of orange juice, straight from the carton, and took two aspirin. Then I mustered the pluck to call Jolene—I needed to know what had happened the previous night. But no one picked up. I tried again a few hours later, without success, and then wrote it off, did my best to forget the whole thing. The warping walls. The flesh. The teeth and the tongues . . .

What was it all about? Whatever was happening, it was getting worse. The blackout in the bar. The hyper-lucid dreams of blubbery creatures and undead dogs. People popping in and out of paintings. Hell, maybe even the man outside the window . . . and now *this*, this surreal Jarosław Kukowski painting, followed by a full-blown fugue. My mind jumped from the likelihood of stress to a brain tumour to lead in the wall paint, before squashing the thought altogether.

I got stuck in to some chores.

There are always jobs to be done in a big house. Things seem to come apart at twice the rate of a normal house, as if they're protesting at being there. I found tools in the shed and refitted a hanging gutter. I replaced a broken window. I picked ripe vegetables and herbs in the garden, and rearranged food-stuffs in the pantry so that anything soon-to-expire could be used first.

I'd just about put the previous night out of my mind, when the phone rang in the downstairs kitchen.

It was Jolene.

She asked if I'd be interested in meeting with her the following day. No small talk, just a curt little question. I'd have said she didn't sound like herself, that there was something off—but of course I didn't know her well enough. No explanation for the call, but I agreed to meet anyway.

She'd suggested a public park where there was a broad, rolling stretch of lawn with big evergreen trees and a lake. An assortment of people were enjoying the sun, or sitting in the shade, in a fresh space, apparently with nowhere else to be. A little girl with a kite. A man reading a book under a tree. Two boys pushing paper boats at the water's edge. I noticed then that I was dressed wrongly, my big thick coat ten degrees out of place. Everyone else, in their shorts and skirts, had apparently got the note that a single spring day would be coming by a few months early, as a rehearsal.

Within a few minutes, I met up with Jolene. She looked somehow more natural than she had at the dinner, lovely in a more honest way, her hair straight and hanging loose, her lips pink enough without the paint. She was with a kid. A scrawny boy in a striped beanie, maybe seven or eight years old, eyes deep and dark as drains. Her son Edgar, she explained. He greeted me shyly, ran off, and kept himself busy with the world as the two of us walked along the lake, under awnings of leaves. Before we got into anything else, I was determined to find out exactly what had happened at her house the previous night.

Nothing, she said. *There's nothing to explain. You played the piano and we danced. I mean, you said you were a pianist, but wow, you play so well. There's so much energy in you. And talent.*

We were lucky to have you. But then, right after playing, you just stood, told us you had to go, and that was it. You went home. It was a little sudden, and you seemed so serious, but it wasn't the kookiest thing ever. I was worried you'd had too much to drink, but you insisted, and then you headed off. She turned to look at me. *You okay? You look pale.*

I nodded, left it at that, not mentioning my total memory blank. I also skipped the fact that just before I'd slipped out of consciousness, she and her guests had congealed into some kind of unreal flesh-show.

But then she had to ask: *You* really *don't remember?*

It's not that, exactly, just that I've been having these . . . I don't know what you'd call them. Episodes?

Episodes?

Sometimes I black out for a bit. Or see things that aren't really as they are. I thought I might be scaring her, especially so early in our first private meeting, so I just smiled and brought it all to the realm of the real. *Pretty sure it's nothing serious, though,* I said. *A bit of stress, maybe. My father passed away a couple of months ago.*

I was certain that had almost nothing to do with any of it, but cleverly took care of two birds: reasonableness and sympathy.

Oh, God, I'm sorry.

I guess you don't always realise how much things affect you.

No, I guess not.

She pushed her hair behind her ears—a familiar gesture. Edgar called to her from across a stretch of grass, pointing to a duck on the lake, and she acknowledged him: *I see, I see, be careful.* There was affection in her voice, but tiredness, too. I thought back to her as she'd started dancing, twirling by herself, before the rest joined in and things took a sharp turn for the twisted. There was that same vulnerability in her now. That same inner dance going on, just with a slower, sadder rhythm.

I'm sorry I called you, she said to me, staring down at her boots as they took steps across the grass.

Are you? I said.

Not sorry, but you know what I mean. I'm not even sure why I called you. I think I just needed to see someone. To talk to someone, share a couple of words with an adult. Things aren't always easy— raising her voice, she called, *Edgar, away from the edge!—Like you said, we all have our problems. But we're not always so ready to admit them to ourselves, are we? Instead, we lug around this constant weight, and then get so used to it, the feeling becomes normal, a part of us. The way life is supposed to feel. Heavy and shitty.*

We passed a family sitting on a picnic blanket, buttering crackers and handing around cool drinks, when two children detached like erratic electrons and chased each other around the nucleus, laughing and teasing.

Jolene, is there something I can do for you? I said.

No, she said, turning her eyes to her son again. *I just wanted to see you. I don't have any real reason right now, if that's okay.*

What about your friends? I asked. *The ones from the other night?*

Friends? Yeah, well, I don't actually know *any of those people. They're strangers. It's this thing I do. Probably not the safest thing, not these days, and certainly not with a young son in the house.*

I'm not following.

She sighed, looked down at her hands. *One day, out of the blue, I invited a strange woman in a parking lot to dinner at my house. This was after helping her with some shopping bags. The idea just popped into my head and I went with it. And it felt really good. So I did it again. I invited another stranger, an old man waiting at a bus stop. He said yes too. And then there was another and another and another . . . until one evening I had a full table. They all turned up, and we had a great night, the best I'd had in years. No tired old stories or expectations or politics or awkward histories. Drinking and eating and dancing with random strangers . . . it seemed to be, I don't know, a purer way of keeping company. So it became a regular thing, these dinner parties for strays.*

Strays like me.

Jolene looked at me and laughed. *Exactly like you. What can I say, it's more interesting than being on one of those online chatrooms.*

We watched the little girl's kite somersault down, abandoned by the breeze.

What about Leonard? I asked.

What about him?

Is that how you met him?

She stopped, knitted her brows. Then she said, *Nope. For Leonard it was the other way round. He found me.* She picked a leaf off a branch and folded it into a tiny piece. *I don't really know what to say to you, Bent. It'd be good to hear from him. Good for me and good for Edgar. He owes us that, at least, especially after everything he has—and hasn't—done. I'm not talking about charity. I'm not even talking about financial help. I'm talking about accountability. God, I can hear myself—and I sound so weak.*

You don't, I said, though I hadn't quite made up my mind.

She stopped, spun round, and put a hand on my shoulder. Her eyes were a deep blue, her pupils edged with pale sawdust-brown. The colours of the Earth from outer space, I imagined.

I have to ask, Bent. Do you know where he is?

I slowly shook my head.

She paused, gave a sad smile, then flipped an end of her light summer scarf over her shoulder.

We stood and watched as Edgar and a group of other children scattered bits of bread across the water, without any apparent strategy, losing half to the mud at the edge of the lake. A thought sparked in my mind, like a delayed fuse. Could Edgar possibly be Leonard's son? Did he look like him? I couldn't tell. I kept this thought to myself. If it were true, and Jolene wanted me to know this, she'd tell me. And if this wasn't the case, then asking her would be the dumbest move of the day.

Leonard's never been very good at staying in one place for very long, Jolene said. *I can only imagine where he is right now, somewhere far from here. He never gets as far as he'd like, though. I know that. It's his curse. I'm sure you know about the parties. Oh, God, those parties! I went to one, right in the beginning, and I can't say I was impressed. But I realised the women, the drugs, the craziness . . . it wasn't as simple as I thought it was. It was just another test.*

I thought about the man at the window. Waving. Smiling. Disappearing.

All I said was, *What kind of test?*

That's not easy to explain. I guess, for Leonard, nearly everything's a test. That's the part that interests him. Truth is, Leonard doesn't put much stock in conclusions—which also means there's no such thing as commitment. Or a sense of responsibility. Then she veered: *Do you have any idea when he'll be coming back?*

No, I said. For some reason, this didn't feel like a lie. But it didn't particularly feel like the truth either. It was just two letters. A word. A convenience.

You must have some idea, she said, a trace of impatience in her voice. *How long will you be house-sitting?*

About a year.

You committed to a whole year?

I had an opening.

She laughed; it was toothy and real. *And you're from the city, right?*

That's right.

Do you like it?

The city?

Yes, the city.

Sometimes.

So what brought you two together?

I thought about Leonard at the bar that night, knowing all the while what the grand plan was. A plan all set in his head, missing only a single element: me.

He said he's a fan of the way I play, I said.

The sun dropped behind a hotdog-shaped cloud. A woman grabbed at her hat to stop it from blowing off her head. The corner of a red picnic blanket flapped. An empty chair fell over. Then the sun reappeared and the wind quit its mischief. Jolene didn't look fazed by any of it, slipping her arm through mine as we walked. I allowed myself to pretend we were a couple. I played the game in my head, and went with it more than I probably should have. I even smiled at Edgar as he passed, as if he were my son, and Jolene and I were his married parents, and this was just a day at the park for the three of us. Enjoying some family time. That's what anyone watching us would have thought, I told myself.

But then nobody was watching us, of course.

Nobody's ever watching us.

They're only ever watching themselves.

40.

I walked into the house sometime after six. The fading light of day entered through the windows, washing the walls in burnt orange. I went upstairs to take a shower, and moments came to mind: I thought about the way Jolene's hair had moved and fallen so naturally, and how much more I liked it than at her party. Her sad eyes, full of questions she hadn't asked. The way her arm fitted so well with mine, as if we'd spent our lives as the long separated halves of a whole. It had been a while since I'd been in the company of a woman in this way, nothing sexual, just tender companionship—far rarer than life generally seems to ration.

I stepped out of the shower, stood naked in front of the steamed-up mirror, palmed it clear, and methodically flossed my teeth. I got dressed and went back down the corridor. I couldn't even bring myself to look at Leonard's door as I came into view. It had been too fine and normal a day to think about him. I went so far as to pretend the door was closed up permanently, plastered and wallpapered over—but as I passed by there was a voice from the other side:

You know, they say, hundreds of thousands of years ago, there used to be more than one species of human.

I stopped. I don't know why, but I did. All normalcy bled out of me. Once again, there was Leonard's voice, though weaker than usual, like a battered old boxer, an amputee soldier, a lion with a mortal wound.

Hard to imagine, I know, but some say there were actually around six different human species. Till they all died off, that is, leaving just one surviving line . . . Sapiens. The big swinging dicks. The real question, though, is how we did it, how we Sapiens outlasted the rest. Well, one theory is that it's because we went from walking on four legs to walking on two. Which makes sense. On two legs, we were able to see predators from afar. Not only that, but it freed up our arms, then our hands—and of course our thumbs. Perfect for making tools, right? Sharpening things. Killing things. Not without cost, of course. There's always a cost for our little . . . progressions. You see, becoming bipeds also caused women's birth canal to narrow, which meant they gave birth earlier, when the baby's head was still small. Think about it. A foal stands up just after being born . . . but a baby, well, we all know a human baby is a useless thing. Needs to be cradled for months. Being born weak and useless meant that babies had to be left with the tribe so the moms could forage. Now how's that for a fucking farce 'n a half? We take every short cut we can to get ahead, and then burden everyone with our inadequacies. What a joke. The fuss we make of ourselves, all our proud achievements, and it turns out the two things that define us most as a species are impatience and dependency.

A chuckle.

A hollow, knowing chuckle.

Impatience . . . and dependency.

After leaving food for Leonard, I took the car and fetched Jolene and Edgar. I'd insisted she pick the venue, and it turned out to be an upmarket grill-house. The kind of place where the waiters wore waistcoats and asked how we wanted our burger meat done. Our guy recommended toppings of blue cheese and glazed figs, and suggested we pair our selections with a pinotage. Jolene enthusiastically agreed, and once the waiter had left, she spoke a bit about Edgar. She told me how he'd been struggling at school, and how every now and again he'd wake up in the night after a bad dream about all the rhinos being dead or the ice caps melting. These kinds of things really worried him, she said. Things she couldn't do anything about.

Edgar didn't seem fazed by us talking about him. He didn't even look up from his drawing. The waiter had brought him paper and pens, and it hadn't taken him long to sketch a woman with wings, and a red dragon, and a man in dark sunglasses. The image looked familiar to me but I couldn't recall where I'd seen it before. I didn't bother asking Edgar what it was about; I'd hated those questions as a kid, adults blabbing at me, pretending they were doing me some kind of favour.

Jolene went on to explain how tricky things had been, how she'd had to move from one job to the next. And then—it seemed she couldn't help herself—she brought up Leonard again. I wondered whether she knew how often she spoke about him—not really *about* him but around him, like a spiral turning endlessly towards its own unreachable centre. I went in and out of boredom and jealousy, short bursts, not caring at all and then caring too much.

Jolene ordered another bottle of wine. She changed the topic and asked if I had a girlfriend. When I said I didn't, she asked what kind of women I liked.

I told her, *The kind who like me back.*

That, according to her, made things easy then.

I said I was inclined to disagree.

A Caramel-Banana-Sponge-Daydream was deposited in front of Edgar, and we had two amarettos. The bill arrived and I paid. It was only later that I realised I hadn't checked the total, most unlike me, Mr. Every-Cent-Spent.

I looked up at Jolene. Sweet, sweet Jolene.

As we got up to leave, she said she'd spotted a tan line where the waiter's wedding ring had once been.

Me, I hadn't noticed that.

You're late. I was starting to think you weren't coming back.

The voice drifted into the corridor as I walked past Leonard's door.

Was it a good night? Fun?

He didn't wait for a reply.

I wish I could tell you how late you are, but hey, I don't have the time on me. No time at all. It's a funny story, actually. If you've got a moment in your new busy social life, I'll tell you about it. C'mon. Take off my tie. Kick off my shoes. Relax. You see, I was doing just fine, keeping track of each day. Until the other morning. Couldn't figure out which day it was. It just fell out of my head. And you know what? There's no way to get it back. No clock. No calendar. No nothing. So that's it for me—time's out of my grip. Like it's not a real thing. But I've gotta be honest, chief, not knowing how long I've been in here, not knowing how long I have to go any more, it's the most terrifying feeling. Yeah, Jazz Man. Makes me sweat, gives me the shakes. Makes me wanna gnaw through the wall. Time. Time. Time. Who'd have thought, imagined? It's been cocaine, sugar, nicotine . . . my entire life, not helping at all, just poisoning me.

But, hey, this doesn't change one important little fact, my friend— that tonight . . . you were late.

Next afternoon, I fetched Jolene and we dropped Edgar off with his sitter. We drove to the coast in the Jaguar, top down in the warm sun, to where Leonard docked the *Britomartis*. Jolene's hair danced in the wind as fields of white flowers and lush grasslands rushed by. There was a fixed smile of satisfaction on her lips, as if she'd had a good dream, and it was all somehow happening just as she'd pictured it.

A picture that somehow, miraculously, included me.

The white-walled harbour town turned out to be postcard-pretty, with trendy gourmet pancake houses, art galleries, coffee shops, and bars. Street corners were enlivened by guitar-plucking buskers. It was the kind of place you might fantasise about as a permanent home, instinctively knowing that you'd inevitably get tired of it, and no longer have a place worth fantasising about.

We drove straight to the water. I knew nothing about yachts but it was obvious that the *Britomartis* was a magnificent piece of engineering. We went on board to find a bedroom, a fully equipped galley, and a bar that was half-stocked. Jolene told me how Leonard had taken her out a few times but she'd always get seasick. It was too bad, she said, since she loved being on the boat. Its self-sufficiency gave her a sense of comfort, the idea that the boat had everything it needed to go out on its own. Boats aren't stuck on the land as buildings are, hooked up to grids and bound one to another by a system of pipes and wires.

We left the yacht and walked the narrow streets of the town. Ask me what we spoke about and I couldn't really tell you. We chatted about the things we saw in various shop windows, found handmade satchels and vintage hats we thought were quaint and unusual but couldn't quite bring ourselves to bag. And then, as a plan of sorts, we bought a selection of foods from a patisserie, stopped by a liquor store, and went back to the boat, where we sat on the deck as we ate and polished off a bottle of Moët & Chandon. Later, we crawled below to make drunken love for the first time.

Nice day out?

Yeah, sure it was. I can smell. I know that perfume. You think I don't know it, but I know it. Her favourite. Because I bought it for her. And now, it's all over you. Which can only mean you've met up with her. Right? I don't know how you found her. Or she found you. But that's irrelevant. D'you have a good time? Take her out for a spin? I don't want to pop that big bubble you're bouncing around in, but you think she's with you for you? I mean, does she even know who you are? Does she know about your real life, your miserable moping from one bar to the next? Living in that hole? I'm sure you're doing just great so far—got enough money to keep her interested. But let's not fool ourselves. That's all you've got. You've got nothing substantial to offer her. Nothing real. You know it and she knows it and I know it. But you know what is real? This locked door. *These walls. This empty room. This* nothing. *It's this that is real—and you, my friend, are in a dream. A dream I know well. One in which you're loved—and can love back—when the reality is, you're nothing more than a reflection of a reflection of a stranger.*

You listening to me? I know you're there, I can still smell you. But it's not you I'm smelling, is it? I can smell her—and me. My cologne. And her perfume. And you. In the middle of us.

His voice rose.

Hey. I'm talking to you. You listening to me?

41.

Jolene rolled over on her back and grabbed a cigarette from her bedside table. I'd not seen her smoke before, guessed it was a post-coital thing. The room was warm, though the windows were open. A portable fan oscillated while crickets chirped outside. The moon filtered through gauzy red curtains.

She lit up and took a pull. Calmly and without hurry she exhaled, the smoke twirling to the ceiling from her O-shaped mouth, like the first grey wisps from lit kindling. As my eyes moved down her body, I spotted a small freckle below her breast, which seemed somehow out of place on her smooth olive skin. I felt an odd sense of privilege seeing it there.

She looked up at the ceiling, took a drag, and said, *I have this idea of being happy. Of being totally, deeply happy. It's like, I can imagine how it should feel, but without actually feeling it, if that makes sense. Like when you watch something happen to a character in a movie.* She rolled onto her side and faced me, the curve of her hip haloed by the glow of the bedside lamp. I was thinking I'd never before been with anyone who looked quite this good with her clothes off, when her voice interrupted my train of thought: *But then I think maybe this idea I have of happiness isn't real, that it doesn't exist. That it's something we've just made up, y'know? Some finish line we've convinced ourselves is real, so we don't have to deal with the truth.*

The truth?

That being scared and dissatisfied is unavoidable, programmed into us. A biological survival mechanism—the main reason we've managed to survive so long.

I watched as she blew smoke up at the ceiling.

I dunno, she continued. *Maybe I'm just talking crazy—but maybe not. Take Edgar: I love him more than anything, but I wouldn't say this makes me feel content. I'm a lot of things, but content isn't one of them. Always worried about whether I'm raising him right; concerned whether he'll succeed in life; paranoid he'll get hurt. These are my anxieties. But that's just how it has to be, right? Because if the day ever comes when I'm one hundred per cent happy, free of all those bad feelings, well, that's the day we accidentally walk off a cliff with big smiles on our faces.* She stubbed her cigarette out in a ceramic ashtray shaped like a boot. Another of her cutesy odds and ends. Like the pink vinyl wall clock, and the vase of flowers with their blue-glass petals and wire stems. *I mean, we talk about happiness. We talk about goodness. Fairness. But who're we kidding? These ideas . . . they're just words. Marketing tools. Scams.*

I said, *You don't believe in fairness?*

I wanna believe in it—but that's not quite the same, is it? Fairness is a fairy tale. There's just . . . whatever makes it in one piece— and whatever doesn't. Survival for those with the sharpest claws. You know what I mean?

I think so, I said.

Take you and Leonard.

Leonard. Leonard. Leonard. Dinner for three. King-size bed for three.

I cleared my throat. *What about us?*

She ran her finger lightly up my arm. A pause. A self-conscious smile. *Look, I don't want to cause problems,* she said. *But just because he's paid you to take care of his house doesn't mean it's a fair arrangement. It might feel like an even deal, but it's not. And he knows that. Because he's not paying you or helping you; he's buying you.*

I laughed defensively. *Buying me?*

Hey, man, I'm just saying. That's how people get rich. Not by making fair deals, but by getting people like us to sell our time and freedom for a few bucks they won't even miss. Make no mistake, that's why Leonard's worked to get wealthy. It's not a plan for happiness. Or fairness. Just a plan to stick it out, to endure, to survive—the thing that probably counts most. She paused, then wistfully went on: *Sometimes I wonder what my life might be like if I had the guts to just do what I needed to get ahead, y'know? Really not give a shit, and go for it. To see a picture in my head, zone in on it and say: To hell with everything and everyone, I'm gonna get that! Like that big house you're taking care of. Who knows? With a little not-giving-a-shit, a little brutal self-interest, I might end up with a mansion of my own. The luxury of travelling the world whenever I feel like it—*

She stopped dead, like a car out of petrol. I could tell she wanted to say more, but instead she leant over to kiss me on my lips, as if to say, Hey, sweetheart, forget the whole thing, it's the wine talking, or the sex, or the moon. Or a dirty combination of them all.

But I couldn't forget what she'd said. Her words eddied in my head. I thought about having to go back before the sun came up to feed Leonard his breakfast. And after that, having to get back in time for his lunch, and then his dinner. I thought about doing this day after day after day, under the pretence it presented a valuable opportunity, offering some kind of revelation. A year to do things differently.

It was all a joke, I suddenly felt. And the joke was on me. But not only on me. On Jolene, too. Sweet Jolene, who was trapped by something other than Leonard's money—or his mealtimes. She was trapped by a hope. The hope of being with a man who had the guts and the means to do whatever it takes to survive in the world—a world that lauds survival as the end that legitimises all means, however bloody, however manipulative. In the end, Jolene wasn't drawn to Leonard the Suave as much as Leonard the Survivor. That was the Leonard she wanted—the quality she sought in all men. No more talkers. No more dreamers. Nature favours the doer. We may get the world we deserve, but we *take* the world we want—

And nice guys get finished first.

I thought all of these things as Jolene lay breathing against my neck, her eyes closed. I was thinking these thoughts as she lay a hand on my heart, as she whispered, ever so softly, that she was sorry for being such a downer, and that, you know what, she wasn't sure, but she thought she might even love me.

I bet you even had dreams of your own, once. Not someone else's dreams, but your own. What were they? A concert hall? A record deal? Your name in lights?

Look, I don't wanna nip the hand that feeds, but sometimes I think, maybe I didn't need to lock myself in this room. Maybe all I needed was to move into your shitty apartment. Skulk around at night wasting whatever talent I have on strangers who don't give a crap . . . junkies there for the two-for-one drink special, for the off-chance they'd go home with someone to screw. And since we're on the topic: we both know that Jolene . . . well, Jolene's a very special woman. A woman who deserves good things in this life. She's like me. We're a certain type. Our success is mostly . . . genetic. That's what makes us the same. No offence, Bent. You're a great guy. You probably know how to iron your shirts, cook penne al dente. You might even have got her to sleep with you. But when I get out of here, call her, what do you think she's going to say?

No, thanks . . . I'll take the empty fridge. The damp ceilings, the seedy smoky bars . . . The guy without the guts to give life a real go?

Hmm? When I get out, honestly now—what do you think she's going to say?

42.

M urder is such a strong word.

When I think of murder, it's stabbing someone, shooting someone, or putting poison into a drink. It's pushing a person off a building, or pulling the plug on a life-support machine. Something like that. But that's just the point: murder is a thing that's *done*. An action. It's not inaction. You wouldn't call someone a murderer just for ignoring the starving kids in the world. That might make us ignorers, maybe. Self-absorbed arseholes. But that wouldn't make us murderers. Murder requires a particular type of mind, and I'm not sure I'm that kind of person.

Let's just be clear.

As for a bit of wilful ignoring . . . well, that's something else entirely. I've been doing that all my life. Turning a blind eye. Whistling to myself as I stroll by a world going to shit, as most of us probably do. Which isn't all bad news, if you stop to think about it. Sometimes walking away is exactly what the world needs of us.

You know how they say evil prevails when good men do nothing? Yeah, well, it works the other way too; that evil prevails when good men keep doing things for evil men.

IV.

Thud, thud

43.

I t was easy, really.
One morning, I simply stopped putting food through his door.

I didn't plan it, or think it through.

It just happened.

I'd prepared breakfast at the usual time—Eggs Benedict on an English muffin, Colombian coffee in a plunger, and even some freshly squeezed orange juice—but as I was about to slide it through the door, I hesitated. It was a reluctance that came from nowhere, rushed through me and flooded me. And this instantly became a decision, and the decision was to stand up, tray in hand, and keep walking with the Eggs Benedict.

That was it. That was how I did it.

Or didn't do it.

I returned to the kitchen, put Leonard's meal on the counter, and went outside, as if it were the most ordinary day in the history of days. I laid a table for myself, my cutlery neat on a napkin, and sat down to enjoy my own breakfast in the brilliant morning sun. Slowly and methodically, I bit into my crispy toast, drank my juice, sipped my coffee, and did my piss-poor best not to think about what I'd just done (*hadn't* done). I didn't want to think about Leonard at all, in fact—especially not about him being confused as hell up there, wondering whether I'd be coming back any time soon. No, I just wanted to eat my meal slowly, to savour every taste and texture, and to watch the way the wind moved through the blameless trees, with the sun shimmering on the guiltless lake.

44.

If I was smart, I could make my money work for Jolene and me. For at least another ten months there'd be more money coming into my account through an automatic debit system. Maybe I'd be cut off after then, but maybe I wouldn't. Most importantly, no one knew Leonard was in that room. No one knew when or if he'd ever be back. And no one knew about the task I'd been paid to do. There was that document with the lawyer—only to be opened under my instruction—but that was it. All I had to do was ensure it was never opened, or, if I wanted to be really conscientious, have it destroyed before anyone else could take a look. That way, as with good ol' Schrödinger's Cat, as long as that door stayed locked, Leonard could be just as much there as not there. Just as much writhing in agony in a confined space as milking a yak in Mongolia.

Not that he made it easy for me to write him out of existence. The more time that passed, the more agitated he got. His initial confusion grew quickly to a loud and persistent anger. Then the anger alternated with a sad, pleading fear. To remedy this, I did my best to stay away from the room, out of earshot, but it didn't help; somehow, I could hear him through the entire house. I played piano to help drown the sound of him kicking and screaming and throwing his fists, all the while demanding that I do what I'd promised to do, threatening, *Oh, you fuckin' loser, so help me God, when I get out of here, you're not gonna know what's comin', you're not gonna know . . .*

But this only kept me away, making me skip his dinner without compunction . . . and go to bed that night with a racing heart, as well as a strange and unexpected satisfaction. A satisfaction quite unlike anything I'd ever felt, powerful enough to put him out of sight, out of mind. To take on his broken promises to a mother and son, a bad debt I'd settle with love and loyalty and a family and a future. To play unfair, claim a reward in this shit-accustomed world, and have the apathy of the universe work in my favour, for a change.

To let Leonard Fry starve himself to death.

45.

Jolene was sitting beside me at an outside table of a rustic restaurant. We'd been filling our glasses from a jug of some kind of fresh and fruity cocktail mix. Edgar was playing down by a river that meandered through the grounds. He was leaning over, trying to scoop up some tiny fish with a cup. His mother had warned that he wasn't to harm them—once caught, he'd have to throw them back where they belonged. To be with their fish families.

What would you say if I knew Leonard wouldn't be back, I said to Jolene. *Well, if I knew with absolute certainty that he wouldn't be back in his house for a long while? And that maybe you and Edgar could move in, with me, for as long as you'd like? As a way of making things easier. For the two of you. But also for me—just mulling there, y'know? All by myself.*

I paused, waiting for Jolene's reaction.

Leonard's not coming back?

A needle of jealousy, straight into the main vein.

Not for a very long time, I said.

Oh. Do you know where he is?

I cleared my throat, sipped my drink, and sat back. *He's abroad. On a private island somewhere. Busy with some long-term project. He told me he won't be back for . . . I dunno, five to ten years?*

You spoke to him?

Uh-huh.

When?

I turned to watch Edgar by the river. But I wasn't really watching him. I was staring inward, at the dim images cast on the shady back wall of my mind, as if by a projector whose bulb was about to blow.

A few days ago, but that's irrelevant. I put my drink down. *It's like you said. Sometimes we've just gotta see the chance and take it. Have the guts to go for what we want, right? So what do you say? You wanna take a shot, move in? The two of you?*

She was immobile.

Shit, Bent. When?

My mind flicked back to a long-ago school biology lesson, did a quick calculation. Survival without water: about seven days. Survival without food . . . *Six to eight weeks' time,* I said. *Give or take.*

Silence. A clearing of the throat.

By now a small crowd had come in, placing orders as they chuckled and blabbed and yakked.

And Leonard's okay with all this? She just sat there. Staring at me. And that's when I came up with the clincher, the line of the day, the one I patted myself on the back for before even uttering the words.

Of course, I said, touching her hand. *It was Leonard's idea.*

46.

I'd considered cutting the whole thing short. Making a specially prepared meal—one with fifty crushed sleeping pills stirred into his mayo. But I knew I was incapable of anything like that. There was a line in my mind. To *do* would be to murder. It was easier merely to shut Leonard out. I took solace in the fact he'd entered that room of his own accord. I reminded myself that I hadn't kidnapped him. I hadn't lured him to that house to indulge some sort of torture fantasy (for that, Leonard could count on his orgies with perverted pals). I was simply leaving a careless man to his own devices. Quitting my job. Walking away from a bum deal, like some corporate lackey deserting his cubicle.

But the noise.

The goddamned noise.

There seemed to be no getting away from it, no matter where I was in the house. His voice permeated the walls. He screamed. He whined. Sometimes he even tried to beat the door down.

At other times, he just scratched.

Of all the sounds, that's the one that bothered me most. It was the scratching that kept me up that night. The rest of the sounds were almost symphonic. Crescendos and choruses, or a long breathless solo of *Fuck-you* and *Burn-in-hell* and *Feed-me* and *Please-I'm-begging-you.*

But the scratching at the door.

It went on and on, into the night.

Scratch, scratch, scratch . . .

47

Next evening, I took Jolene to the theatre. The musical we saw was her choice, something she'd remembered from a short but positive review in the paper. I've since forgotten the name of it, but it was about a man who died and made a pact with the devil, then returned to earth, exacting revenge on those who'd murdered him.

The devil didn't look like the devil. He was just a tall old man in a coat, but somehow the stage designers had given him an elongated shadow that followed him across the stage wherever he went. Any character unfortunate enough to encounter his shadow would first burst into verse—part-singing, part-scream-ing—and then disappear into the blackness, becoming part of the devil's shadow, which grew in size as events unfolded. By the close of the final act the old man stood mid-stage, all alone, and delivered a monologue. The joke had been on him, he said: he'd thought it was *his* shadow, to control as he wished—but all along, it was the shadow that had been manipulating *him*. And at the end of everything, there'd be no other option but for the shadow to swallow him too.

I was concerned it was all a little dark for my date, too morose, but Jolene said she'd enjoyed it. As we walked arm in arm through the chattering throng, she mentioned that she liked the fact it didn't have a happy ending.

Do your best. Fuck up. Darkness befalls. The end. It's somehow more satisfying that way, she said. *And isn't that a funny thing? That it can be so terrible and reassuring at the same time? What do you think that means?*

I said I didn't know—and I really didn't.

On our way back to the car, we ambled through a mall, where we happened upon a high-end clothing store. Inside the clothing store, we stepped up to a jewellery counter that was waiting for us hungrily with its gold-toothed maw. That's where the walk came to an abrupt and not-entirely-unexpected halt.

Paris? Jolene replied to the question I'd just asked. She was staring at a gold bracelet under the glass-topped counter. A man loomed on the other side, one smack of the lips short of slobbering on the glass top in anticipation of a big, fat purchase.

Why not? As I said this, I was strangely aware of a row of mannequins, silver hands on silver hips, like aliens from some foodless planet. *I've got plumbers and electricians coming to the house before the two of you move in, and I thought we could get away for a bit in the meantime. All three of us. Have some fun, you know?*

For how long?

A few weeks, maybe. See where things take us.

The man behind the counter played his best card, opened the cabinet and handed her the bracelet. Then he looked at me. I helped Jolene with the clasp, and told her right away that it looked gorgeous on her. I wanted to show her: spontaneous, exciting—a man who didn't just talk, but meant what he said and delivered. A man who needed to get away for a bit, take time out. At which point she turned to me, bracelet on wrist, kissed me in front of the clerk, and said, *Paris, yes, the most marvellous idea, Bent, let's do it.*

I wasted no time, and next day our tickets were booked for exactly a week on. I also did a bit of homework on where we'd be going and what we'd be doing. We'd be staying at La Trémoille Hotel the first three nights. I reserved a rental Mercedes and mapped out a route of the city. A wad of brochures offered colourful pictures and information, though nothing in France looked or sounded real to me. Each building was like something out of a fairy tale. There was the walled city of Carcassonne, its witch's-hat stone turrets pitched as "an unforgettable sight, best beheld at dusk!" A page over, and no less fantastical, was a picture of Mont Saint-Michel, where tides played strange tricks along the shore, making Celts believe that the abbey-island was a sea tomb holding souls of the dead.

I imagined how Jolene, Edgar, and I would spend our days. We'd walk around and explore, and take pictures of ourselves. We'd waltz in and out of bistros, and bouchons in Lyon, and fumble our way around the strange culinary customs. Four weeks would be enough; I needed to ensure that there'd be time for me to air the house when we got back, toss all the crap, and get things in order. There was a home I needed to get ready, and I didn't want as much as a whiff of the past to intrude.

It had to be a clean start for us all.

48.

The blue swimming pool was like a portal to another world—an inverted place where the rain falls up and everything happens with good reason. I stepped to the edge of the water, watched a while as the sun danced on its surface.

Then I held my breath and dived.

The coldness pierced me. Every one of my internal organs seized. My lungs went stiff. The low groan of water pulsed in my ears as a series of images flashed past: Leonard at the bar, sipping his tea with that perma-grin on his face. The locked wooden door, a shadow flickering—Leonard again, big-bearded by now. Leonard hungry. Leonard angry. His fists red and swollen. Jolene's party, the writhing contortion. The dog being eaten by worms, not fifty metres to my left . . .

I resented my clogged mind, wished I could leave it at the bottom of the pool. I couldn't afford to haul my baggage along with me. Not any more. I had a real opportunity here, and I needed to put the shit behind me. Otherwise it would all be for nothing. Sooner or later, she'd see right through me, see that closed door in my eyes. Cos that's the thing; you can hide plenty, but you can't hide a closed door.

My arms and legs wading through the blue, I snorted bubbles that rose to the surface before I burst into the light and warmth. The images in my head evaporated in the sun, and for a rare and exquisite moment, I thought and felt nothing.

And then, the man in the coat.

He stood staring from the shadow of a nearby tree as if he'd grown from it, freshly sprouted like a tall, toxic mushroom. I'd almost forgotten I'd seen him in the rain some weeks before. I'd either convinced myself he was part of a dream, or he hadn't ticked quite enough boxes right then to be banked as a full-on memory.

I blinked twice, like a character in a bad movie.

Still there. Unmoving. His hands deep in the pockets of his coat, his head tipped low beneath a black fedora.

Hey! I yelled, snapping out of a trance. *Hey, you!*

I swam to the edge of the pool, hauled myself out, yanked a towel off a deckchair, and paced towards him. Above his head hung a crooked branch, like the long hand of a puppeteer suspending him with invisible strings. Finally, as if by the will of that same puppeteer, he turned sideways and vanished behind the house.

Wait! Wait a minute! Stop!

As I sprinted, my foot caught the edge of the poolside paving, splitting the skin. The pain hit me, shooting up my leg. My knee gave in and I careened into the outside wall of the house. Blood gushed from my foot, and I hobbled to the corner of the house, hoping to catch at least one last glimpse of the man. But the man in the coat was gone, slipped off somewhere else, to another nook, another shadow, out of sight.

Blood swirled down the bathtub drain. I applied antiseptic ointment, bandaged my foot, popped two pills for the pain, read the insert, and popped another for good measure. Peering out the bathroom window, I thought I'd catch him somewhere. But nothing. Just trees. Hedges. Lawn.

Letting the guy have the run of the estate wasn't going to work. I needed to know who he was, what he wanted, or, at the very least, where he came from. I threw on a t-shirt and trainers, went downstairs, and, in spite of my foot, marched across the front garden, all the way to the boundary.

The estate was bigger than I'd imagined, and its wide circumference took me in and out of so many bushy nooks that the house soon fell out of view. I reached a stream that gurgled through the rotted stem of a tree that had fallen some years before. I crossed a stretch of wild orange and white flowers where a preoccupied swarm of bees hovered and buzzed. Finally, at the furthest end, I found myself in a wooded section on a slope, blanketed in brown leaves. Untended. Forgotten.

The world went dim and grey. Black and fraying trunks of trees shot skywards in all directions while black and fraying birds circled above them, guarding nests that looked like battered wicker baskets. It was another world and another time: the backwoods of Salem, maybe, where conniving Abigail and unsuspecting Tituba may have danced with the devil.

I stopped. Spun round.

I'd been walking for a while, and now I was lost. Every tree looked the same as its neighbour, either dead or dying. All I could do was continue, which I did for another ten or fifteen minutes before reaching a wire fence. The edge of the estate. I continued along the fence, but nary a sign of anyone anywhere.

Who was that man at the pool? At the window, in the rain? Did he know about Leonard and me? Was he part of a greater con? Hell, maybe he was directly in touch with Leonard. I hadn't even looked inside that room—Leonard might have everything he needed in there. A radio. A telephone. A wall of TV monitors, like segments of a fly's eye, each unique angle capturing my every move. And Jolene? What about her? What if I just came out with it and asked, would it turn out she knew the man in the coat? How well did I really know Jolene—

Oh, my God, what are you doing?

A woman's voice, sudden and clear enough to make me yank my head around. I stumbled and gripped the fence. My eyes spun in their sockets, so that I saw every fine detail in the bark of every tree. Every twiggy shadow, each matted lump of leaves.

I waited for someone to introduce herself, or for a gust of wind to emulate a voice, but nothing came. I persuaded myself it was nothing but the wind, brushed the whole thing off, and walked on, despite my aching foot.

I soon realised I was closer to the house than I'd thought. I'd circled the estate and landed alongside the large lake Leonard had shown me. I trudged up the slope, the pain sharpening with every step. All around me, as I looked at the world, the worst of it seemed to seep from its pores. The green, sun-loved lawn rolling out before me looked artificial. The white clouds in the sky were like puffed-up cowards. Their shadows moving across the ground seemed desperate, in a race to be more than merely shadows. And in the distance, between the shadows and the clouds, there was the house—a huge prehistoric animal, its many rectangular eyes watching, without apparent care.

49.

An alternative dream-induced reality: I hadn't met Leonard at the bar. I hadn't gone up to the house at all. I was still sitting at the piano at Ten To Twelve, playing on autopilot as the improbable scenario of being called out to the countryside played out in my head. I could see Coby at the bar, smiling back at me. I could smell the stale smoke on the walls. The oil-soaked baskets of deep-fried snacks. A dozen cheap perfumes at war with one other.

This, I knew, was all real. The rest was bullshit.

How could I have been such an idiot, to think some rich guy had come up with a plan to make me his au pair? On stage now, starkly aware of this revealed reality, I caught sight of Jolene at the back, by the bar. She waved, and gave me a worn-out smile. My heart flooded with love, as well as pity. She'd been my wife for years now. Edgar, our son, was at home. And I no longer lived in some shitty flat in the Crack Radisson—hadn't for years. I now lived in the suburbs. We had a three-bedroomed cottage. A double garage. A coffee machine we fed with pods. A big flat-screen TV. We had insurance. We paid our bills. We went to gym twice a week. We were doing okay, if not a bit bored by the general repetition. We were secretly disappointed by one or two compromises and missed opportunities . . . And as for Coby, leaning on the bar and watching me—well, Coby was just some bargirl I'd been dreaming of sleeping with for months now. Last thing I wanted was to wake up next to her in the morning (I loved my wife, I loved my son), but I did want to screw her just once, and hard, to slay the fantasy for good, mostly just to get on with my life—

I woke up with a gasp.

In Leonard's bedroom, in Leonard's house.

The phone was ringing.

The dream images withdrew into their mental hiding spaces as the morning sun filtered in through the curtains. My mouth was dry, my sheets soaked with sweat, and the phone was still ringing—bleating, really, like a scared, injured animal. I picked it up.

Lord of leisure!

I sat up in bed, cleared my lungs with a cough. Took a few seconds before allowing the world into my unready consciousness. Somehow, I could still feel the pressure of the piano keys on the tips of my fingers. I turned my hand into an upside-down claw to inspect them. There were still purplish splotches under my nails. This time, the harder I pushed down, the more my fingers hurt. But how? From playing too much piano in a goddamned dream?

I asked Jolene where she was.

You just gonna let a lady wait outside all morning, or are you actually gonna invite her in?

Phone in hand, I scrambled out of bed and hobbled to the window, where I slid back a curtain with a bruised finger, and blinked in the bright daylight. Nothing out of the ordinary. No black hole in the sky or car-swallowing crack in the earth. My eyes adjusted and the world took shape, line by line and colour by colour. If Jolene really was out there, I still couldn't make her out.

Hey, Liberace. You there? Her voice floated up from the direction of the distant gate.

My mind scrambled for a quick solution: I couldn't let her stay out there, but no persuasive story was presenting itself. If I let her in . . . well, there was Leonard. He might start his shit.

Banging. Kicking. Yelling. Unwillingly, I buzzed the gate open and went to the bathroom. I splashed cold water on my face, dabbed it with a towel. Then I stepped into Leonard's wardrobe where I pulled on a yellow Polo golf shirt and a pair of cargoes. I ran a matte pomade through my hair, combed it, sprayed cologne across my chest, and returned to the window.

There she was—a small piece of the outside world—entering. Her white VW came into view, bouncing along the gravel road towards the house. I whipped away from the window and walked briskly to Leonard's door. Crouching down on my hands and knees, I peered through the slot but all I saw was a patch of green wall. I considered speaking out, warning him to keep his trap shut (or else, or fuckin' else, you hear me?)—but decided it was better that he didn't know she was there at all.

Pray that the devil sides with the damned.

I hurried away, went downstairs, swung the door open. Jolene was already on the porch, wearing big brown sunglasses and an ink-blue dress. Her smile suggested she'd already got at least six important things done that day. Her lips brushed my cheek and she sashayed in, teasing me again for having left her waiting out there so long. I stuck my head out the door, scanning the garden for my man in the hat and coat. I checked every tree trunk and shadow as if each were a potential conspirator.

. . . did you hear me?

I whipped around. *Sorry?*

I was saying . . . this house—her voice rose, then it dropped—*just when I thought I'd seen the last of it, here I am again. It's as if the house always finds a way to bring me back, to keep me here forever. Like one of its ghosts.*

I feigned a smile. *The house has ghosts?*

Of course it does. She took off her sunglasses and said, *You're one of 'em.*

I closed the door behind me, and focused on my guest. My mind did a quick lap around the dream of Jolene at the bar: my feelings after all those years of marriage, in love with her but looking for something else, something more. She hadn't looked quite as fresh in that dream as she did now, and I wondered whether the discontented dream-me might have tired her out, given her a few sags and lines, dimmed the glow of her smile.

After a second or two, I said, *So, what's news?*

I was in the area and thought I'd stop by, she explained. *Or maybe I just needed to get another look at this place, y'know, to see how it makes me feel now.* Cocking an eyebrow, she said, *You just got up, didn't you? You know it's almost midday, right? Rough night? You haven't started throwing any of those famous parties, have you?*

I could recall nothing of the previous night, incapable of dredging up anything apart from that peculiar dream. But real-world time was a mess. Spilling over and running into itself . . .

. . . what *day* was this?

Jolene turned, scrutinised me from top to bottom, as if I were a large map and she was struggling to find her way. Then she said, *God. The way you wear this house. You look like him. You smell like him. Your hair. Even the way you're standing there.* She came up close and threw her arms around my neck. *But you're not him, are you?*

No, of course not.

You're just the guy who waters the plants.

Twice a week.

You're the reliable one, she said. *A good guy. You want the same things I want.* And then more urgently, *You're safe.*

I couldn't respond to her words, not in any honest and constructive way. They seemed mechanical, rehearsed. As if they'd been said before, used up somewhere else, on someone else. I didn't like it. But I told myself to not make a big deal of it.

I booked our tickets, I said.

Tickets?

For our trip.

Right. The trip. Her arms dropped to her sides.

Next week Tuesday. The three of us. You, me, and Edgar. Paris . . .

A pause. *Why?*

Why what?

She sighed. *Why are you doing all this?*

What d'you mean?

The tickets. The house. It's too much, Bent.

We deserve it.

Do we?

Yes, we do. I felt myself hang there, in mid-air, right in front of her. And then I dropped. *C'mon. How about a drink?*

I needed a moment to myself, to process this clumsy two-minute interaction. Her body language. Her intonation. The way she'd withdrawn her hands from my neck. By now I'd met a couple of versions of Jolene, including Glamorous Host, Dedicated Mom, and Pillow-Talk Philosopher, but this one was new to me—and the least likeable. She was putting on a show, an uninspired repetition of the first night I'd met her—before the park, before the boat, before the bed—back when we were still relative strangers. Right now, she was no longer excited about the trip. But why, all of a sudden? Was it something I'd said or done? *Hadn't* said? *Hadn't* done?

I told her to sit outside while I went downstairs to mix us a couple of morning cocktails. I pointed towards the back door. She said she knew the way. Of course she did. She had a kind of oh-yes-this-old-thing-again attitude, and it got my gut in a green knot. I tried not to let the obvious reason for her familiarity bug me; Leonard was a fading footnote, and this was the beginning of our new life. No more jealousy. No more judgement, I told myself. Jolene and I were starting anew, untouched, unspoilt. If I couldn't wrap my head around *that*, what hope could we possibly have for a future together?

Drinks in hand, I stepped onto the patio. The sun struck out, blinding me. My pupils shrank, I blinked, but Jolene wasn't there. I re-entered through the French doors, my eyes adjusting again to the dark. I sailed through some rooms, the drinks sweating cold against my palms—

Above me, a creak.

A second creak.

A low thud. Another. And a third.

Footsteps. A door opening.

Jolene was on the floor above, somewhere along the only damned corridor I couldn't afford for her to be. I placed the drinks on a nearby writing desk, approached the staircase, rested an elbow on the handrail, and stared upwards—at nothing.

Jolene?

No response.

I climbed the stairs. Each step was its own treacherous mountain. Even the air seemed to thin, the higher I climbed. If she was up there, Leonard would almost certainly hear her. Smell her. Call out to her. At first she'd get a fright, but then she'd recognise his voice and begin to question him—what was he doing in there? She'd try to open the door, but Leonard would explain it was no good, that the door had been locked (perhaps leaving out his own role in this). He'd say he was on the verge of death, that I was to blame, and that—before doing anything else—she should grab the nearest pot plant and smash it on my skull—

Sorry for disappearing on you. Jolene's head popped out over the railing above. Any response I might have offered was stuck in my throat. I could barely muster a smile. Convinced she'd let Leonard out, I told myself her playfulness was a ruse. Any second now, he'd appear behind her, shaking his skeletal skull, cracked lips smirking, rubbing his hands together like a cartoon villain hatching a plan, and glaring at me with murderous, sunken eyes. (*I'm just . . . so disappointed, Bent. So, so disappointed. Me and Jolene both. Maybe somebody needs to be given some alone-time in a room for a year to think about what he's done, hmm?*)

But that didn't happen. Jolene was alone.

What've you been up to? I tried to sound unconcerned.

Looking for something, she said, stroking a salmon-coloured scarf as she held it up.

I see. Where was it?

In Leonard's room. I left it there a while ago.

Of course I knew what that meant. The unabridged version being that she'd left the scarf in the room on one of the occasions she and Leonard had been together, in that bed. It wasn't as if I didn't already know about this, but the fact that she thought it fine to go rummaging for her stuff in his bedroom while I was around stirred up something akin to anger. More anger than outright jealousy, I reckoned.

So, with all the rooms in the house, you're staying in Leonard's? she said, following me down the last few stairs.

Excuse me?

His room. You've been staying in his room. Sleeping in his bed. It hasn't been made. It's pretty obvious, Bent. All your stuff's on the floor.

All I said was yes.

We walked to the patio. She was clearly not amused that I'd taken over Leonard's room—if anything, her face clouded over with disgust. I gave her the drink I'd mixed for her, and she took a sip as she leant her backside against the table.

I should be off, she said suddenly, already heading for the door. *It was just supposed to be a pop-by to say hi.*

See you tonight?

She winced and cast her eyes about, as if looking for some kind of hook, one that might pull her from a scene where she'd forgotten her lines.

Not tonight, she said. *I'm just so tired. I'm thinking of taking it easy and having an early one. You don't mind, do you?*

Of course not, I said.

She opened the front door, letting in the white-hot day, then she turned one last time, pecked me on the cheek, and put on her sunglasses. That was it. She was done. She wasn't going out with quite the enthusiasm she'd displayed coming in, and I wondered if this might have anything to do with her trip upstairs.

Treat yourself, Bent. Do something fun. You need it. The gravel crunched as she walked to her car. Turning, she said, *I'll see you soon. I promise.*

Those last two words. Nobody uses them unless they've at least considered the possibility of not following through. I stepped out onto the porch. Jolene waved her scarf at me, and it fluttered briefly before she got into her car. I watched her pull away and chug down the gravel she'd arrived on just fifteen minutes before. That's how long the visit had lasted, so what had the point of her pop-by been? To fetch her scarf?

I closed the door, went upstairs, past Leonard's locked door, to the bedroom, where I watched Jolene drive to the gate. I was still holding my drink, and I threw back the last of it. I couldn't come to any conclusion regarding Jolene's visit—why she'd turned up like that, unannounced, and why she'd left in such a damn hurry.

I'll see you soon. I promise.

I promise.

With a sigh, I fell into an armchair at the window. My glass slipped from my fingers and hit the floor. It rolled in a semi-circle, drumming a tune till it came to a stop. And that's when the chuckling began.

Chuckle, chuckle, chuckle . . . and then the voice floated into the room.

I do love that woman's perfume. A long, exaggerated inhalation, and then, with a raspy gurgle, he seemed to muster the strength to go on. *So you think you've got it all worked out . . . Bent? Think you know exactly what's going on here, do you? Truth is . . . you have no idea at all. And now you're wondering . . . if Jolene was here, if she was in the corridor, why didn't I take my one chance to get out? Hmm? Well, let me tell you something: Jolene came up here because she knows—she knows more than you think she does— and because it was time she and I had a chat about things . . . about moving forward. So that's what we did. We chatted. I told her what a horrible individual you are. She said she knew . . . and she was sick of pretending to like you. And you know what I said to Jolene? I said, hang on, baby, you hang in there just a little longer. Suck it up. Go to the bedroom and grab that scarf you left behind. Tell him that's the reason you went there. Stick it out a bit . . . because any day now, Bent's gonna get a new visitor at the door. Someone I arranged for months ago. Mr. Phase Two. Someone to help out . . . to put all the pieces in place. Cos honestly now, Bent, you can't possibly think I'd come in here without a plan, hey? You don't really think I'd let you shit all over my life? I mean, don't you find it the least bit strange how Jolene just . . . latched on to you? Why would that be? After all, you aren't the most charming sonofabitch in the world. You're okay-looking, but there's not much else on offer in any other department . . . and from what she tells me, I do mean* any *department, chief.*

I pushed myself up and out of the armchair and moved along the corridor towards Leonard's locked door. I didn't buy any of what he was saying; it was all a trick. One moment he was pissed off that Jolene and I had found each other—and the next he was saying she was part of some grand plan?

Believe me or don't believe me, Bent, but that's what Jolene and I talked about. And I know exactly what you're thinking: if that's all true, why would I tell you? What would be the point? Well, like they used to say in the movies . . . that's for me to know and you to find out. Because, frankly, at this stage . . . you're so deep in your own shit it's not gonna make an iota of difference either way. You're on a one-way trip to the town of Fucked. And you know what my only regret is? That I won't get to see your face when you realise what's coming your way.

50.

There's little that consumes one as much as envy does. Sadness. Disappointment. Regret. They can screw us up, do their worst—but in the end, they all have noble roots. Envy, on the other hand, does not. It eats and eats and shits where it eats. Envy is a tapeworm moving through our bowels, so primal, so efficient, that it's never needed to evolve. Envy doesn't just starve us out. It inhabits us.

I didn't believe Leonard's story, but still I felt envy. The idea that I was on the outside of some secret arrangement between Leonard and Jolene began to consume me. The most likely explanation, I tried to persuade myself, was that Leonard was full of shit. I could tell when I was being had. Leonard, yes. Jolene, no. She'd shared genuine feelings with me. She'd trusted me enough to introduce me to her son. She'd never bring her kid in on a con, would she? No. Leonard was lying. He was desperate. And I wasn't falling for it.

I was still confused about Jolene's sudden arrival and her even more sudden exit, but there were a dozen possible explanations for that. Surely Leonard, figuring I wouldn't be coming by with a casserole any time soon, would have wanted to pull the plug on the plan? Who knew what was going on inside his head? Maybe I'd underestimated his commitment. Maybe he wasn't ready to come out. Maybe he'd be happy for that door to open only after he was a pile of bones. After all, nothing says anti-materialism quite like becoming a goddamned ghost.

As for Jolene, well . . .

If only I'd been able to record her visit with a camera, and pore over each word, each gesture. That might've been helpful. Then I'd fix a whiskey, grab an armchair, play the video on a big screen, study every smile and non-smile and blink and tic and sigh and nod, and I'd take notes, and rewind, and watch again, and take more notes.

That's what I'd do.

Because even though Jolene had suggested we have a quiet night apart, I wasn't convinced that's what she'd meant. She was setting tests of her own, hoping I'd say something to reel her in again. How many times had she gone out of her way to see me? That's what she really wanted from me. That same level of boldness. Guts. Proof I could be just like Leonard . . . the part of him she wanted, anyway. Resilient. Determined. Mr. Take Charge.

But how was I meant to behave to prove I could be the man she wanted me to be?

51.

It was between Bentley for Men Intense and Tom Ford's Neroli Portofino, my two favourite colognes. I'll admit, the regular Bentley for Men is not bad (fragrant wood and leather with black pepper and bergamot) but the Intense is an improvement. It's out with the bergamot and the bay leaves and in with the labdanum and sandalwood. Bold. Powerful. Intimidating. That would have been my first choice, but for the specific purposes of the evening ahead, I went with Tom's Neroli. Casual. Confident. Approachable. Summer-come-early.

I put it aside to shave and floss. I picked out a black Louis Vuitton jacquard button-up and a pair of reverse-pleated khakis. A Rolex Submariner. Tan leather monk straps. Then two spurts of Neroli. After that, I went downstairs, grabbed a bottle of wine from the kitchen, decided on the Mustang, and hit the road. The sun morphed from yellow to late-evening gold as I imagined Jolene throwing her arms around my neck, her *I knew you'd come, been waiting for you!* and the dinner she'd made, and working our way through a few bottles, maybe even some board games with Edgar, and if things got late, her invitation to stay over . . .

By the time I arrived, the sun was gone but a pinkish glow still hung on the horizon. I parked in a quiet cul-de-sac, got out, and walked up a steep slope to her gate. No bell. No intercom.

But I knew to slide my arm over and undo the latch, and the gate obliged.

Her front garden looked different. I couldn't say why, since everything seemed to be in the exact same spot. The pots in the trees. The lumpy couch beside the tabletop made of small triangular shards of mirror. The satyr and the pissing cherub. The untended, throttling vines.

I leapt up the three chipped concrete steps, past the pond with the reeds sticking out and its four lippy fish, and stepped onto the lawn that ran around the old house. It was standing before me now, flaking farmhouse-white, red-roofed, veined with creepers.

Laughter and voices were coming from the house. I couldn't see anyone, but lamplight from the window gilded the garden. Shadows fluttered against an inside wall. Clinking sounds, as cutlery hit crockery. I stood at the blue front door, looked up, saw that the sky was black.

Music. Clearly a recording. Piano. Crooning.

A laugh. Mumble-mumble-mumble. More clinking. And then a chorus: *Cheers!*

I made my way to the dining-room window. Peering in, I could see her—dressed in a black dress, but accessorised with the salmon-coloured scarf—laughing and flirting with a table of strangers who sat in front of their food. I didn't recognise any of them. An old black woman. A tall man in his late forties wearing a beret and tortoiseshell glasses. A blonde. A hotshot kid in his twenties. Good-looking, with gelled-up hair and a leather jacket.

A bearded man beside Jolene dabbed his mouth with a napkin and leant over to say something in her ear. She smiled, slapped him on the wrist, and topped up his wineglass.

Not one of them saw me.

Invisible me, in her front garden, standing beneath a sky that had metamorphosed into night. Who were these people? Why hadn't I been invited? Why had she lied to me about *taking it easy, having an early one*? I began to feel queasy, right in the gut. I didn't understand any of what I was seeing, but the vacuum created by my incapacity to fathom the situation was soon filled with a new and terrible feeling.

No. Not just a *feeling*.

Something else. A gestation. Some oleaginous thing throbbing in my stomach. Something hungry. Something ambitious. Not just Envy the Tapeworm, but something that would keep growing, burst right out of me, abandon the broken husk of my body, get hungrier, eat the world, swallow the sun—until it digested all of time and space.

I stared into the warm and busy house, close enough to the window to fog the glass, losing sight of them all with each burst of white breath, and then seeing them again, and then losing them, and seeing them, and losing them, and seeing them . . .

I arrived back at the mansion totally sopping. The clouds had decided to hold a meeting and concoct a plan to piss the proverbial. I headed to the front door. I flipped the light switch, but the weather had knocked the power out. In the dark, I climbed the stairs. Each step thudded, like a dull faraway knock from inside a buried coffin.

At the top of the landing, I felt my way around until I found another switch. I flicked another dud. The blackness was thicker along those top corridors, despite the drizzle of blue moonlight on the staircase landing. I stroked my hand along the wall, turned a corner, feeling my way until I stood in front of a closed wooden door. My hand slid down to the handle, turned it. Locked. I let go, kept walking. *Pat-pat-pat. Tap-tap-tap.* A second door. Locked. Same with the next three doors.

I was about to turn around, make my way back to the staircase and start again, but I couldn't. I'd taken one too many turns. I was disorientated. Demagnetised. I flung my arms about, grabbing at nothing, until I struck yet another locked door.

And then, at that absurd moment, I heard a lunatic's laughter, a sound that carried along the corridors. If it weren't for my frustration (and my mental image of Jolene's flirty smile and her slap), I'd have been more surprised that Leonard still had the energy to be amused after five days without food. His voice was gravelly and his breath short—but it was him, all right. He'd never be able to keep this up, though. Soon enough, he'd go silent.

Coughing. Raw and rough. *You thought you were special. You thought you were in love. Yeah?* Maniacal laughter. *Okay, here's the truth. You ready for it? Right, let's start with ownership and exclusivity. That's what this is about. The source of all your pain. Not love. Not loyalty. Not some . . . special connection.* A cough collapsed into a laughing fit. *Nope. You thought you had her to yourself. Thought you'd bought her, didn't you? Livestock. Branded with your big hot poker. Ownership and exclusivity—all we ever really want.*

I careered along the darkness of the corridor, trying one door after another. Each doorknob rattled, wouldn't budge—wouldn't offer entrance or escape.

Leonard's voice rasped on: *Hey! We do it every day: it's not yours—it's mine! My sunset! My favourite song! My best friend! My heartache! My home! My woman! My. My. My. Me. Me. Me. Mine. Mine. Mine.*

I surrendered. Slumping to the floor, I decided to stay right there—until the sun came up, or possibly forever, until every clock of the world got wise and parked its hands. I calmed my breathing, closed my eyes, listened to the beating rain, the thunder. And beyond, I could still hear Jolene's laugh, that *Cheers!* as they'd all raised their glasses. Beneath everything, there was the phlegmy cackle of a man who'd long ago left behind his own black, byzantine corridor.

Found his open door in the darkness.

His own way in. His own way out.

52.

The pale light of morning told me I was in Leonard's bed. At some point I must have got up, and in a somnambulist state, sans panic, I'd managed to pilot myself through the darkness with involuntary ease.

The first thing I did was call Jolene. I was still reeling over what I'd witnessed, but the prospect of not seeing her was worse. On the phone, I was brief and polite, said I'd like to meet up with her. I made a bad joke. She didn't laugh, just said I could join her at the supermarket. Grocery shopping wasn't exactly the get-together I'd had in mind, but that was the extent of the offer, so I took it.

The supermarket was a sterile white, the colour of corporate heaven. Shoppers glided around like angels who'd had their wings clipped, trying to make up for it with the crap in their trolleys. The pan-flute rendition of a movie soundtrack was periodically interrupted by a voice reminding us of a washing-powder discount. Jolene steered her trolley along an aisle lined with an absurdly large variety of cereals, where actual fruits were nothing more than the dead and forgotten ancestors of "five fruitilicious flavours," hawked by sunglasses-wearing starfish and giraffes sporting basketball vests.

I hardly knew what to say to Jolene. I walked alongside her as she strolled from aisle to aisle, working her way through a handwritten list. Edgar had his own plan, running from shelf to shelf, pointing out one thing after another to his mother, who mostly turned him down with a sweet smile.

Half the time I don't know what Edgar's showing me, she observed as I ambled beside her. *I don't have to, though. The more fun it looks, the worse it is for his health—that's the general rule.*

I said nothing. Though I'd half looked forward to our little supermarket walk, now that I was there, the anger was back. Minutes ticked by, and still she didn't come clean about the dinner. My resentment bubbled up. Every passing second was a new insult on top of the last. She just kept on pushing her trolley, smiling at Edgar ahead.

So, d'you have a g'night in? I finally said, a syllable or two short.

Excuse me?

Last night. You and Edgar. You had a good night in?

She paused, then, *Yes, thank you.*

That's good.

Yip.

A little mother-son time.

Sure.

She grabbed a carton of soy milk, read the information, or didn't, and put it in with the rest of the stuff.

What did you get up to? I asked. *Movies? Board games?*

Neither, actually. Jolene stopped, turned to me, a dead smile pegged to her lips. *But we're flattered by your interest in how we like to spend our time.*

Edgar ran up to us and told his mother about a new something he'd seen. A chocolate spread. She gently told him she couldn't make any promises. He ran off. We kept walking. Not talking.

And then I said: *I know.*

Know what?

About last night, I pushed on. Held my breath a second or two, then said, *You had one of your dinners.*

She pierced me with her gaze. *How would you know something like that?*

I stopped by.

You came by my house?

Yes.

Last night?

Early evening.

After telling you I wanted a night in?

I thought I'd surprise you. I didn't realise you'd made, well, plans.

A snort, then she glared at me, her forehead creased. *So what if I did?*

I found myself struggling to utter a reasonable response. One that didn't make me sound like a mad idiot. The best I could do was: *You didn't invite me.*

No, I didn't. And so?

And, well, I wanna know why.

You know why.

Tell me.

Strangers. That's what I need sometimes, okay? You know that. I've told you.

What about you and me?

What about you and me?

I thought maybe . . .

You thought what?

That we were in this, you know, together.

In this? In what?

You know what I mean.

Look, maybe we were. But maybe we weren't.

I noted her use of the past tense.

Bent, that doesn't change what I want . . . what I need to do, for myself. For me, you understand? If I want to throw a party, I can invite or not invite anyone I like. Nothing changes that. Nothing will ever change that.

I became aware that we were catching the attention of passing shoppers, so I clamped my lips, nodded, smiled, and kept walking. Jolene couldn't give a shit, just huffed and turned red. Her hair seemed to come undone with her growing annoyance, and she tucked strands back behind her ears. Overhead, the white lights buzzed. The voice crackled into life, announcing a sale on potatoes and mini-pizzas.

So, why did you lie? I asked. We turned into an aisle with a thousand different brands of coffee, tea, and hot chocolate. White sugar. Brown sugar. Caramel sugar. Demarara sugar. Aspartame-based non-nutritive sweeteners.

What? she demanded.

Yesterday morning. At the house, I said. *If you believe what you're saying, and that you've got nothing to hide . . . well, why lie to me? Why not just come out with it and tell me?*

She gave an incredulous laugh. A laugh that said, The-goddamned-nerve-of-you! Then she stopped in her tracks and faced me. I hit my own brakes.

Because I knew you wouldn't handle it, she said. *Because it wouldn't just be an Oh-all-right-have-a-good-time. It'd be exactly this: this pathetic look in your eyes. And I didn't want to explain myself. Not to you—and not to anyone. That's why, Bent.* She huffed in exasperation, *God! And besides, I'm not so sure we should still see each other.*

Her words were a wooden bat to the head.

What d'you mean? I said.

Hands on hips, she looked to her left, her right, and then she glared at me. She'd been working herself up to this, I realised. Long before I'd even picked up the phone to call her.

Bent, I don't know what to say to you. Maybe it's Edgar. Maybe it's confusing for him.

Confusing how?

A sigh. Or a huff. A bit of both, maybe. *That's not it, though.*

No?

God, Bent. Don't make me say it.

I said nothing. I didn't have to.

You . . . you creep me out, she said.

What?

You creep me out! You creep me out! I mean, look at you. She waved her hands up and down, pointing me out to myself. *Who are you? The way you dress. These aren't your clothes. These aren't your shoes. The way you comb your hair. You're . . . him. But you're not him. You make these promises, the perfect life, and all that—the kinds of promises I wish he'd make. But when they come out of your mouth*—her palm flew up to her forehead—*I feel sick. I've tried, Bent, I've tried to reason with myself. To tell myself you're good for me. That you're sweet and you're nice and just what I need. But you're not, because you're not him, and you'll never be him. You're not even you. You're just*—she spat the words out—*this prop! A hologram. Like you don't even have your own shadow. And I don't mean to be cruel, but you need to take this in, so there's no misunderstanding, so I don't ever have to repeat this: you bore me, Bent. You understand? You're boring. You mean well. I believe that. But it's like every word that comes out of your mouth has gone through some kind of process, like a factory line of knock-off responses. And it creeps me out. So, no. I don't want to go to Paris. I don't want to move in with you. I don't want to do any of this.*

Switching from angered to spent, she stopped to catch her breath. She seemed too exhausted to retract any of her words. Then she looked around as if for assistance, for someone to share the load of spelling her thoughts out to me in big bold letters, so that there could be no confusion. But it was okay. I didn't need to hear another thing. Not even a consonant was needed. Nor another filthy vowel. She'd said enough. Until I decided she hadn't.

Who's making you do this? I said.

She spun round. *What?*

Who's making you say this? This isn't you, Jolene.

Listen, Bent. Stop it. You don't know anything about me.

What about Leonard? My final jab.

What about Leonard?

Is there something you want to tell me?

A frown that combined puzzlement and annoyance encouraged me to push on. *I know that you know.*

What? What d'you mean?

I know that you know where he is.

A pause. *What are you talking about? You told me where he is. On some island . . .*

I nodded, playing along. *Okay. On some island.*

That's what you told me! She glanced around, absently shooing Edgar away. Then she said, *Look, I don't know what you're trying to get out of me—*

And the man in the coat?

Bent—

I suppose you don't know anything about him either?

Listen, whatever this is, you have to stop. I'm going to finish my shopping. And you—you go do something else. Somewhere else.

My hand was around her arm.

I didn't remember raising it, let alone taking hold of her, but there they were: my fingers clamped tight above her elbow, my thumb against the bone. Jolene squealed. Her eyes went wide. But I wouldn't let go. Couldn't let go. I wanted to, but there was something else—at the bottom of me, deep inside—that stopped me. My grip tightened. (*Because that's all I needed, you see. One nick. Just one imperfection. And I was free of it . . . isn't that funny? I had to taint the thing to make it mine. I had to fuck it up, to assert myself over it.*)

In a minute her skin would be red. By morning it would be blue. In two days' time it'd be black, and then yellow. The full palette of hate and regret.

Edgar ran up to his mother, held out an orange jar of something or another. She yanked herself free, got on her haunches, and studied the label. I muttered apologies. She pretended not to hear me. Giving Edgar a nod of approval, she kissed him on the forehead and dropped the item in the trolley. He ran off, erasing me from past, present, and future existence in a single, non-reactive instant. I hung back among the tins of jam and pickle jars, watching as a wave of shoppers swelled and sucked her in, consuming her mindlessly, as if she was just another thing off the shelf.

53.

I hit the highway at full speed, then drove the Mustang for what felt like hours. The sun was down. No moon. No stars. All I could make out was the white line under my headlights.

I had no idea where I was going, or whether I was trying to get away from something or head towards it. Not that it mattered. In the end—like at the very start—there was only me. No arseholes expecting this and expecting that. My time. My commitment. My compliance. Fuck all that. Now, I could do what I wanted. Go where I wanted. I wasn't stuck in someone else's place or plan. I wasn't an accomplice, a sideshow, a goddamned curiosity. I was complete. I was free. The one true thing in the lies of other people's lives.

Over a rise in the road, a glowing dome of far-off lights appeared. To my left, balls of flame shot from the tops of a chemical refinery, expelling compounds into the air we breathe, setting secret timers in our bloodstreams, plotting our organ failures and cancers and mutant births.

I entered the city. Trawling the empty streets, I noticed a queue of people outside a nightclub. The huge red-brick building might once have been a fire station, but now bright purple and blue floodlights beamed spacewards from the rooftop. A thumping deep-bass drone permeated the whole place and shook it up. I cruised past the entrance, where clubbers waiting in their half-treasured, half-begrudged positions turned to admire my Mustang. I parked, and a man-shaped rhino immediately waved me to the front of the queue. The interior was a laser-light wonderland, synchronised to computer-generated music. A second bouncer—the fat yet strong type—unhooked a red rope and waved me through to the upstairs bar.

From the top balcony, I observed the masses roll out below, an undulating wave of sweaty flesh facing the DJ, who was up on his platform mesmerising the masses, sermonising with sonic strata. At the black backlit bar, I ordered a drink from a tall guy in a waistcoat.

I saw a woman next to me and ordered a drink for her too. She had long brown hair and wore a gold strapless dress. Even in the low lighting I could see that her lipstick was too red, her eyeshadow too dark—a sick, deliberate attempt at looking smacked around, it seemed.

Battered-chic.

I held my glass up as I glanced at her. It took her no time at all to sidle up to me. Her lips were near my ear, saying something I couldn't make out. But it wasn't words she was offering; it was the tip of her tongue. She pulled back and pointed to a table with a trendy troupe, all waving us over, and I joined them. I ordered three bottles of Bollinger and the table took a speedy liking to me. After that, we did shots. On someone's bid we slid away to a bathroom in pairs and did lines off the cistern lid. I was partnered with the brunette from the bar.

She closed the latch, took the first snort, gripped my face between red-tipped fingers, and pressed me hard against the cubicle wall. Her tongue was long, rummaging in my mouth as if searching for keys in a bag. She tasted of lemon and cigarettes. She pulled out, and it was my turn. A rush of coolness, as my heartbeat synced perfectly with the techno thuds. Each mark on the stall wall sprung to miraculous life.

She led me out of the bathroom, back to the table, where her friends weren't so much in conversation as guffawing all over one another. Big open mouths and big white teeth. Beautiful faces. I ordered another round of shots and they toasted me; I was their new generous pal. Each joke I told, they laughed at. Whatever opinion I had on whatever new subject was met with eager agreement. The brunette kept her hand on my thigh the whole time I sat there, as if in ownership, to ward off the pack.

She suddenly stood up, laughing as she pulled me along past the bar, through a pair of curtains and into a small private room with a turquoise glow. She pushed me down onto a pile of pillows and unzipped my pants. She lifted her skirt, straddling me, and prepped me for entry. I got hard and went in. My mind swirled as she gyrated, leant down, her lips on my neck and chest, taking my ear between her teeth and pulling it hard before she wrenched back. I closed my eyes, and somehow I could see the sounds I was hearing, circular blazes of yellow and pink, exploding and imploding like small stars.

Then I opened my eyes.

Above me, her face was glistening, and behind her, the walls began to bulge, stretch, and lean inwards. My breath rushed as the woman threw her head back, and when I looked again, she was no longer herself—

It was Coby from Ten To Twelve who loomed and bucked. Her face speared with metal, the pixie hair, taut skin. I didn't question any of it. And I didn't fear it. I wanted this, and I went with it. I grabbed her buttocks, pulled her close. She laughed, neither mockingly nor genuinely, and then her face changed—

Jolene—with her hair up, exactly like the first night we met. Her delicious lips, her wide, honest eyes. Jolene. Jolene. Jolene. Smiling at me. Loving me. Or so it seemed. I screwed her hard, put my hands up to her breasts, and as I squeezed, her smile faded. Her attention slipped, as if it were dry sand escaping through my fingers. Sighing, she mechanically went through the motions. Tired of our little pantomime. Her words speared my consciousness, and I thrust harder. *You're a bore. You bore me. And you creep me out.* Lolling on my chest like a floppy doll, she rocked slowly, rhythmically, until—

At first I didn't recognise the figure, which now had short hair and wide shoulders.

And then I saw that the protean person screwing me, was *me.*

The almost-clone engaging in some kind of impossible inter-course with me was a version of myself I'd never before seen or met. Tanned and healthy, with clear whites in his eyes. Straight rows of pristine teeth that had clearly taken no punches. He'd taken every road I hadn't, said a no to each of my yesses and a yes to each of my nos. On top of me.

Bentley Croud.

Screwing me.

Or me screwing him.

I tried to pull away, but with every thrust, at every point of contact, we fused. Our abdomens slapped together, unable to separate. Our bonded skin stretched like kneaded elastic dough. Our chests touched, merged instantly into a trunk with two backs, one sternum, and a single set of ribs. I let out a wail. The other I simply smirked. As Me-Two bent low to touch my forehead, we merged, first the skin and then the skulls. My face dipped into his, as if it were gazing at a reflection in a lake. By now, my scream was screaming into him. But nobody could hear me. I was trapped underwater. The thrusting per-sisted, becoming harder, more punishing—until the moment of ejaculation.

Whether it was *that* me, *this* me, or both of us simulta-neously, I couldn't say. The release was no release at all. No euphoria. No catharsis.

What I did know was this: this other, slicker me consumed me whole.

Or was it the other way round?

In the end, does it matter?

As I tell this to you—or to me, or whoever—does it really matter who was screwing who, or which of us had started this shapeless, snarled mess of ourselves?

V.

. . . take a hint when they hand 'em,
she's dishing him out,
and servin' you first, don't you know?
now i ain't sayin' you blind,
but you're naught but a fool
if you don't know where it's goin' . . .

54.

The sign says BARMAN & WAITRONS NEEDED. Above the sign, I see the name of the establishment, handwritten on a plain black board: Greg's Dregs. There's an outside deck to the left, where tilted chairs lean their backs against wooden tables. Sun-blasted plants sit in clay pots on either side of the entrance, like lazy guards. I walk between them, push the door open, and go inside.

The place is dark. The only lights are the dim bulbs over the bar counter; behind it, crates of beers and wine wait to take up residence—however temporary—in glass-walled refrigerators. There isn't a soul inside the bar. It's a little after four in the afternoon, an hour before the arrival of early dinner patrons and after-work drinkers. The chairs are stacked up on tables, waiting to be pulled down. For now, it's a bit like an indoor cemetery, one that works in reverse: dead and desolate until unseen occupants begin to crawl from their graves, resurrecting as the night advances.

I have no experience as a barman—or even as a waitron—but I've got to start somewhere. I'll figure it out, I tell myself. I'm a quick enough learner. And I need cash; that's the bottom line. The piano lessons mostly dried up as the regular kids moved into extracurricular activities better suited to their own interests than those of their parents. And after my mother hit the giant sofa in the sky, most of what I'd stashed away went into her cremation costs. That, or consumed by the reared-up heads of her secret debts.

I pass between the upturned chairs, call out in a low and feeble voice. No one answers. No one comes. I explore some more, stumble upon a piano—old, black, and dusty—sitting in a corner beneath a Telefunken fixed to a wall bracket. Without thinking too much, I take a seat at the piano and lift the lid. I hit A-flat major, and the sound drones through the darkness. I crack my knuckles, give each of my fingers a tug, lower them to the keys (so that the tips are just about touching), take a breath, and play. Nothing spectacular. Just a time-passer.

After about a minute or so a man appears. It's as if the quickest draw in town has stepped through the doors of a saloon, and instantly I quit playing. The figure is large, and his greased black hair is combed back in a perfect dome. Bushy eyebrows. Olive skin. He's holding some kind of calculator in his hand.

"You don't have to stop," he says. "I was enjoying that."

"Sorry, I was just . . ."

"You play pretty well," he says, descending from the restaurant to the bar area. "You're very good. But you know that already, don't you? Yes, I think you know exactly how good you are. A good thing, that: knowing your worth." Like a human x-ray machine, he scans me. "How old are you?"

"Eighteen."

"What are you doing here?"

I push the stool back and stand up. "You had a sign out front," I say.

He pauses, then asks, "You ever been a waiter or barman before?"

I shake my head.

"But you think you can do it?"

"I learn pretty quickly. I'm good with my hands."

"No kidding," he says. "Where did you learn to play like that?"

I shrug. "My mom taught me when I was a kid. Otherwise I taught myself."

"Your mom must be pretty proud of you."

"She's dead."

"I see. Your dad?"

I shrug again. That's all I've got to give, and he takes it.

"What's your name?" he says.

"Bent."

"You a student, Bent?"

"No."

"You take drugs?"

"No, sir."

"A thief? A troublemaker?"

"No."

"How about a liar? Do you lie?"

"I have lied," I say. His expression seems to soften, and I explain, "But I'm not a liar."

"Me, I'm a giver," he asserts. "My family, we like big dishes on big tables. Mess us around, steal from us even once, and you don't get another seat with us. Ever. You understand?"

"Yes, sir."

"What about having a place to stay?"

"I'm getting kicked out of the flat soon."

"And so you need a job."

"I do."

"To survive."

"Yes, sir."

"Okay. And?"

"And?"

"What else?"

I sort my thoughts. "What else *what*?"

"Well, you're clearly talented. And you're not the ugliest bastard in the world. Or the dumbest. This can't be it, surely? What else do you want out of life?"

I've never been asked this. I jut out my bottom lip and just shake my head.

"Nothing?" he says. "No big dreams? No picture of where you want to be in five, ten years? Anything like that?"

"No. Nothing that comes to mind."

"Okay," says the man, his backside against a table. "Let's try this. What *don't* you want?"

"I don't want to need anyone," I blurt.

"Really?" He smiles. "But at some point you're likely to. I mean, you need someone right now, don't you? You need this job. A bit of cash. That's a need, isn't it?"

I don't have an answer. I wish I could give him one, but I have nothing. I look to the piano as if it's about to help me out, riff a response or two, but it's just a box of strings waiting to be played.

"I tell you what," the man says. "I'm looking for waiters and a barman, but something tells me that schlepping around pints would be a misappropriation of your talents. So let me get to the point." He straightens, leans towards me and slowly says, "I like the way you play." After a brief pause, he continues, "I've got a bit of a farewell party planned this coming weekend, right here, a get-together with a few close friends, and I'd very much like you to stick around and play for them. Friday to Sunday."

"The whole weekend?"

"That's right. You know more than one song, right?"

"I guess," I mutter. "I, well, I improvise."

"Really?" He's clearly impressed. "So you just . . . make it up as you go along?"

I nod.

"And how long can you keep that going?"

"I dunno," I say. "Indefinitely?"

"All right. Let's see what you've got. I'll pay you per hour. Do a decent job and we'll talk about keeping you on. Maybe we get you Mondays and Tuesdays. My quiet nights. Better a gig than pouring drinks and changing ashtrays, yes?"

"Yes, sure."

"One thing, though," he says, assessing my outfit: a baggy brown hoodie and khaki cargoes. Scuffed trainers. Grubby laces. "You'll need a suit. Black. Not navy, not grey, and definitely not beige. Make sure it's black. And a white shirt. No tie, though. We like it casual-ish. Think you can handle that?"

I still have the get-up from my mother's burial. The black jacket and black pants. Black school shoes that need a good polish. I'm not sure about the shirt. I'll have to check.

"I can do that," I say.

"Of course you can."

The big man walks up to me. I take a step or two back as he runs a hand over the piano top. Then he checks his index finger (dust comprises ninety per cent dead skin, I've read), and rubs it away with his thumb. He turns to look at me, stares into my eyes.

"That was a helluva good tune, you know. Been a long time since I heard this old thing played like that. I used to play a bit myself, but nothing as good as you. I have big hands, like Rachmaninov. Thought that might help, but it didn't. Long fingers aren't enough, apparently." He sits down on the piano stool, pokes a couple of the high notes. The sounds have legs in this big empty room, and heels that kick off the walls. "Be honest, though . . . I'll pay you anyway . . . it wasn't really *you*, was it?"

"I'm sorry?"

The man smiles, laying the strip of felt neatly over the keys before closing the lid. "Just saying, chief. The way you played, it sounded a lot more like the devil."

55.

It was the knocks at the door that got me up.

In that space between sleep and wakefulness, however, they weren't knocks at all. They were boulders bouncing down a mountain slope—three, four, five of them—about to wipe out everything. Flatten houses. And people. And parks and schools and coffee shops. Colossal rocks that kept coming, crashing across the earth, demolishing every last thing in their way. Without motive. Without awareness.

When I did eventually open my eyes, the reality of the sound set in: someone beating on a wooden door. My first thought was Leonard—having a final desperate crack at being rescued, perhaps. But no, that'd be impossible. It couldn't be coming from his room. He hadn't made a sound in days.

Leonard was good and well dead.

As a doorknob, they like to say.

And the last few noises hadn't been anything near as emphatic as a fist against wood. Just wheezing and scratching and a long, high-pitched whining, and coughing, and scratching, and mumbling and whimpering, until finally, for the sake of the world over, indifferent to any of it and worn of all patience, the sounds subsided into silence.

I hadn't left the estate in weeks—in fact, I'd barely left the house, mainly to stop a recurrence of my peculiar mental episodes brought on by absences from the house, as if the house itself was refusing to let me leave. They'd been getting stronger. More insistent. Overwhelming, in fact. So it was best to stay put. Shut the windows. Draw the blinds. Lock the doors. Wait it out for a while. And the days and nights that followed the realisation that Leonard had died became one long slithering snake of time. Hisses of dark and light. Uncharmable.

Until the morning of the knocking.

It could only be the groundsman. I tried to ignore the knocking—he could go solve his problem somewhere else—but it went on and on and on, just like the thudding boulders.

I sat up, stepped over my scattered clothing, grabbed a robe hanging over the back of a chair and went downstairs. Everything was in near-darkness, even though the sun was out. For weeks now, night and day, the doors and windows had been locked and the curtains drawn to prevent the gazer in the yard from looking in.

I stood in front of the door. Unlocked, unlatched, and opened up.

The sunlight assaulted me.

So you do exist, said a man's voice, followed by a hatted figure carrying a large bag in his right hand. My vision adjusted, and details came in like the morning news. Early twenties, I guessed. Younger, perhaps. Just a weekly shave needed to stay baby-belly smooth. It was his dark eyes, however, that seemed to betray him: knowing.

Who are you? I asked.

He took off his hat and held it to his chest.

My name is Howard, he said with a smirk. *Howard Fry.*

He waited for me to respond. I didn't. I gave him a once-over. The bulky leather travel bag. The long black coat and the narrow-brimmed fedora. Was this him? The person outside the window, watching from afar, vanishing behind walls? The face hidden by the shadows of trees and hard falling rain?

How did you get in? I asked.

Tipping his head, he put his hat back on. It looked idiotic on him, that hat, beyond anachronistic, as if he'd arrived through some kind of portal linked to the first part of the last century.

The groundsman, he said. *He was on his way out.*

He just let you in?

No reason why he shouldn't. It is my house, after all . . . well, my father's house. But what's a generation or two between proprietors?

Your father? I struggled to control my voice.

Yes. Your employer.

I'd done such a fine job of wiping Leonard from reality that the guy came across as a lunatic claiming to be the relative of some fictitious character. Dracula's nephew. Bastard son of Scrooge McDuck.

You're Leonard's son?

That's me.

And you've just arrived?

That's right.

Right now?

Right now.

Through the front gate?

He didn't answer. The interrogation, he'd decided, was over. He locked his eyes on mine, gave one slow blink. His leer slithered across his cheeks.

I can see, he said, *that this won't be smooth. But it will at least be interesting.*

What will?

You. Me. The house. He tilted his chin and gazed around. *It's a scorcher out here, isn't it? How about we take this all inside?*

I glanced behind me, into the darkness. *Actually, now's not a good time—*

What's your name?

Excuse me?

He waited, refusing to ask again.

I submitted, simply said, *Bent.*

Well, Bent. I'm afraid this'll have to be it—as good a time as any. Didn't my father tell you?

Tell me what?

Man, it was months ago that he called. Said I should fly in and come stay here. Just till he gets back. He told me someone would be waiting—I'm assuming this person is you? I'm not speaking to an intruder, some kind of vagrant, am I? It is you, isn't it?

Me what?

He gave a laugh. Too loud and deliberate, as if he'd gone for laughter lessons at some late stage of his life. Academic instruction after a childhood of having never quite figured it out.

You. The house-sitter, he sniggered.

Listen. He said nothing to me about anyone coming round. I'm not sure about this. He'd have told me.

Yes, well. Though clearly impatient, Howard held on to his smile as if it were the last one left. *Here's what we're going to do. You'll step away from the door. I'll come inside. And then we'll pour ourselves a couple of nice cold drinks. And while you tell me a bit about yourself, I'll smile and nod and do my best to pretend you haven't just kept me waiting on the porch of my own house after a two-hour drive and a twelve-hour flight from Prague. And we'll use that as the new starting point. Because, frankly—Bent, is it?—right now it looks like that's as good as it's likely to get for us.* A chilly pause. *For you.*

His words hit me from nowhere, as if I'd just slammed into a glass door. There was nothing I could say to counter him, or his artful threat. After a good half-minute, I slid over to the side. With a gracious nod, he stepped past me with his bag.

Doesn't seem you were chosen for your housekeeping skills, he said, looking around. *It's so dark. You aren't a vampire, are you?*

What, I began, closing the door, *what can I do for you?*

How about that drink, for starters? Lime and soda, with a twist of lemon. Or real lime—I'll make allowances.

There aren't any lemons.

Pint of blood, then? He cackled. *Virgin.* An uncomfortable silence as he amused his audience-of-one. *Don't bother, Bent. Tap water's fine.*

He flicked a switch and the chandelier shimmered to life. I walked from the hallway to the kitchen, where I grabbed a highball glass and turned on the tap, waiting for the water to run cold. His story had to be a lie. It was him in the rain. He was the guy under the tree by the pool. I was sure of this. Anyway, Prague story or not, he couldn't stay. I had to get him out. I filled the glass, downed it, then refilled and returned to the hallway, spilling along the way.

I handed him the glass, he emptied it and said, *Thank you kindly.*

Adjusting my robe, I began, *Look, I still don't know what you're doing here—*

He held up and hand and said, *Here's an idea, Bent. You let me find my room so I can freshen up, then maybe I'll grab something to eat. And then, after all that, you and I can have one another's full attention. How's that for you?*

It would be no good arguing with him. He was getting his way at each and every turn. I had one main objective, though: to prevent him going upstairs.

That's fine, I said. *But just so you know, the upstairs rooms haven't been done in a while. Downstairs is fine, though.*

He looked at me with a smile of false appreciation.

Well then, he said. *Thanks for letting me know.*

I could tell he wasn't really buying it, but he played along anyway—and right then, that's all that mattered. He grabbed his bag and ambled along the corridor, opening each of the guest rooms, deciding which would suit him best.

Hours later, Howard still hadn't come out of his room. I'd stayed close by, occupying an armchair in the corner of the library that gave me a view of the corridor. I did a bit of reading, but, if questioned, I'd be unable to recall a single word of what I'd read. Mostly, I was doing my best to figure out my new situation with what little info I had.

For one, I remembered Leonard's mention of my unwanted guest. This was after Jolene had come and gone, just short of a million mornings ago. Mr. Phase Two: someone who'd pull all the pieces together, he'd said—or words to that effect. But what did that mean? And why hadn't he mentioned this before? If Howard had been sent to keep an eye on me, then why'd he trusted me in the first place?

But there was a bigger problem.

I had a body upstairs. Locked inside a room. Cooking in the heat—one full day of it after another. I'd been putting off the removal, to the point where I was now faced with a new dilemma: sit it out as the reek of rot worked its way down, or go up and dispose of the body right under Howard's nose.

I stood up, walked along the corridor until I reached Howard's door. It was closed. I put my ear to it, but heard nothing. Then I made my way to the kitchen, where I put the kettle on for a cup of coffee. I hooked a finger into the wooden blinds and spied on the day. From what I could tell, there was nothing out there spying. Not any more.

All eyes were now indoors.

56.

Howard remained in his room for the rest of the day, and all through the night. I considered carting the body into the backyard in the dark, but was convinced Howard would wake up as I hauled the corpse down the stairs. I would never have guessed he'd be in there so long, not having had a thing to eat or a shit to take; he was in his room most of the next day, too.

I was about to think he'd hanged himself in the closet, when, thirty hours on, he suddenly emerged, like a bear from its winter cave. He was wearing a grey shirt, a waistcoat and a tie. His eyes were bright, his face rested. His grin was fresh, too—washed, rinsed, and hung to dry in the sun of his new disposition.

I must have needed that, he said breezily as he came into the kitchen.

He made himself a cup of tea, spent a minute or two dunking the bag, then held a teaspoon under it as he carried it to the bin. Flipping the lid with a press of the foot pedal, he dropped it in. All the while, I watched him from my stool at the counter, sipping at my coffee. He smiled as he brought over his tea cup, pulled up a stool, and sat down opposite me. His movements were so slight and economical, it was as if he had a finite number for the day.

You were here first, he said between sips. *You've settled yourself in, probably had plans for . . . a bit of solitude? Well, I can respect that. Still, I'm sure it'd be helpful to ask a few questions?*

At first I thought this was rhetorical, but he waited for an answer—his body frozen, his stare locked on me. I mumbled something in agreement, and that was enough for him as he immediately loosened up with a smile.

Now, I won't agree to answer all *of them, but would you like to begin anyway?*

Begin? My mind was racing in all directions, mainly along the corridor.

With a question.

My mug was halfway to my lips, but I stopped, held it there a moment, then put it back on the counter.

Right. I took the plunge. Bit the bullet. *So, your father asked you to come here?*

I've already answered that one.

When?

When what?

When did he ask you?

He looked up at the ceiling—a deliberate pose, I thought. And then he said: *Mid-Feb.*

This year?

Correct.

That was a good three months before our agreement.

And it wasn't you? I narrowed my eyes.

Wasn't me what?

That guy in the garden. He stared at me, and I elaborated. *A couple of months ago. I looked out the window, it was a rainy day . . . and then again, that day at the pool . . .*

I stopped, hoping he'd fill in, but his expression was blank. Howard seemed to have no idea what I was talking about. Genuine or not, I couldn't say.

After taking a sip of my coffee, I waited a second or two. Then I switched subjects. *I've heard Prague's a beautiful place.*

It is. One of the few European cities not to be bombed in the war, he said. *It's the architecture—intact, unchanged for centuries. And it's obvious. No matter how well you restore a thing, no matter how close it is to the original, something inevitably gets lost. Even if it's some kind of missing aura.*

I mulled over this a while, rotating my coffee cup on the counter. And then I said, *What were you doing there?*

Last leg of a pretty exhausting tour, he said.

A tour?

I'm a pianist.

For some reason, instead of creating a sense of camaraderie, this disclosure only widened the gulf between us, as if he'd somehow stolen my vocation from me.

Jeez, let me think now. He elaborated, *First, there was Munich, then Berlin. London, Freiburg—and Prague. Five, six gigs in each. In Prague alone there was the Clementinum. And the Rudolfinum . . . with the Czech Philharmonic. The National Theatre. St. George's Basilica. Anyway, you get the point. Like I said, exhausting.*

Was he just being frank, or was he boasting? If the latter, it wasn't tacky or forgivably overt, like the harmless attention-seeking of a child. It was somehow craftier. Underhanded. Foundational.

I asked him what he played, and he replied, *Mostly my own compositions, but of course you need your Schubert. Your Brahms. Your*—he mimed a conductor, waving his fingers like a baton—*Beethoven. And, of course, you can't play Prague without at least a bit of Mozart . . . not that I've ever been the biggest of fans.*

Mozart? Really?

Never much liked his stuff, he said with a sneer.

But you respect him, though . . . as a genius, I mean?

Are you telling me or asking me?

I felt a mental jolt, and said, *Just asking.*

Howard tipped his head back and finished the last of his tea, holding the position, cup to mouth, as if waiting for something. Then with a sigh he put his cup down, and continued.

The man spent sixteen years of his life noodling, and created his first really honest piece of work at the ripe old age of twenty-one. Hardly the stuff of prodigy. He gave a snort as he seemed to reshuffle his thoughts. And then he said, *But that's not even the half of it. Mozart's far too cutesy, much too light. And when he does occasionally attempt a bit of dark, or depth—well, it's phoney. Flat. Forced. His music doesn't take you anywhere.*

After a silence, I volunteered: *I'm a pianist too.*

Is that so?

Unsure how to read his tone, I went on anyway: *Not classical, though. I play jazz.*

And where have you played?

Bars. Clubs. A couple of corporates.

Right.

I waited for another question, but Howard said nothing. Clearly uninterested in the career of a back-alley key-beater, he made himself another cup of tea. He probably didn't even consider jazz to be real music. I switched the topic.

Why d'you think your father wanted you to come? This is a helluva way from Prague. I paused, rather recklessly said, *He's not even here.*

Well, said Howard, *my father and I aren't in the habit of being in the same place at the same time. We've always been close in a like-minded sort of way, but we're also autonomous individuals. He has the life he wants to lead, and I have mine.*

I took advantage of the space he'd opened up, asked about his mother.

They got divorced when I was six. I moved in here, with him. Which was fine. He was a busy man, in and out, but he made sure I got what I needed. I enjoyed piano, so he arranged private lessons with the best in the business. Ernest Gergiev. Charlotte Pavlovna Kantor. Right here, in this house.

I hadn't heard of them, but didn't let on.

He sat me down one night—I was ten or so—asked how far I wanted to take this. I told him I wanted to be the best in the world. And that was enough for him. I had a six-month stint at the Royal

Academy of Music, before being invited to the Berlin Festival, where I gave my debut performance—Chopin's Piano Concerto 1 and 2. And after that, well, I was set. Thirteen years old, and on my way. Me and the big wide world.

He let you go off on your own?

He gave another of his cackles. Whatever had amused him, I wasn't up for it. I drained the last of my coffee, cold and sugary as it was.

You tell me, he then said. *When are we ever not off on our own?*

He got up from the stool and took his tea cup and saucer to the sink. I watched him, this young man, barely an adult, and felt envious of him—his life of privilege, and support, and opportunity. And I realised why he'd made me question him. It was to make sure I knew about it all.

His back turned to me, Howard said: *Another cup?*

No, thank you.

He rinsed his own and placed it on the drying rack, with the saucer slotted in alongside. He grabbed a nearby dish towel.

But you still haven't answered my question, I persisted.

And you have vays of makeeng me talk, I suppose. Mockery in his eyes, he glanced over his shoulder at me. Then he dried his hands and hung the cloth on its hook. *Now, which question would that be?*

Well, I was interested to know why your father wanted you to come down here, so far from Prague?

Taking his seat again, he said, *To decide.*

Decide what?

Whether I'm interested in this house, whether it's something I'd like to keep. Or whether he should get rid of it while he can.

How d'you mean—while he can?

The smile was back. *He didn't tell you, did he?*

I don't know what you're talking about.

Well, Bent, what do you know?

Know about what?

About my father, he said, barely concealing his exasperation.

Not much, apparently.

How long have you been here now?

I shifted in my seat. It was as if a restart button had been pushed, and a tape was running in my head. So much had happened; so little had happened. I couldn't even recall the order of things any more, what I'd done first, last, or in between. Time was a jumble, a knot of moments in my head. My best guess at how long I'd been in the house was three or four months, but I couldn't be sure. For all I knew, five goddamned years had gone by.

I gave an embarrassed shrug.

Howard was immobile as he asked, *Did he at least say when he'd be back? Or did you just commit yourself to staying here, in the dark and the dust, for some indefinite period of time?*

A year, I said. *He said he'd be away for a year.*

And when exactly did he say that?

April seventeenth.

Hey, we're getting somewhere. And did he tell you where he was off to?

I thought about the body upstairs, breaking down cell by rotting cell.

No, he didn't, I said.

Gone to tick some items off the list, most likely.

What list?

Our last list of all. The things we still want to do in the world . . . to get out the way, you know, before we kick it. I felt he was reading my face, closely studying my reactions as he went on. *One year, that's what they gave him. One short and shitty year to indulge in all those fabulous foods, those exotic drinks, to bed a thousand and one wild women, to wake up to drunken sunrises in a hundred strange locations . . . all the while, a big fat tumour in your chest telling you you've got twelve months to wrap it all up— where would you even begin?*

Howard's news affected me in a way I'd least expected: guilt. Until that moment, it felt as if everything that had happened to

Leonard had been his fault. *He'd* chosen to go into the room. *He'd* abandoned the world, though still expecting favours from it. *He'd* been the arrogant, masochistic maker of his own fate.

Somehow, however, the news of his death sentence changed everything.

Perhaps there was no experiment at all. Perhaps Leonard had seen the room as some kind of burrow. A place a dying animal might go—away from the pack and the predators—to keel over in peace.

Or perhaps the room was a way for Leonard to kill time itself—his new enemy. Perhaps without clocks and calendars, there'd be no sense of movement. No advancement. Had he gone in that room with the hope of making his final days seem longer, a slower crawl to the end?

Had he really been that desperate?

So goddamned insane?

I couldn't say. I couldn't say *anything*.

Staring back at his son, sitting across from me, explaining to me how I'd allowed a man to starve himself to death for *nothing*, I didn't say a word. Couldn't.

I listened, but said nothing at all.

57.

Howard had settled into the house like a fresh coat of paint on the walls. The good thing was, he had no need to use the front staircase, since he stuck mostly to his side of the house. It also helped that he had his own daily routine. Not merely predictable, but rigidly regimental.

He had no noticeable vices. He didn't drink. He didn't smoke. He was in bed by ten o'clock, and at around five-thirty each morning he was awake and ready to swim twenty-five lengths in the pool (I, on the other hand, awoke at dawn after agonisingly long and torturous nights). After his swim, Howard took a towel and lay on the lawn, either napping or thumbing his way through a novel. And in the afternoons, after a healthy, meticulously made lunch, he'd do one of two things: take a long solitary stroll around the estate, or head up the back staircase towards the piano room, where he'd flex his fingers for a good hour or two.

Big, bold classical pieces resounded through the house.

I'd recognise a sonata here, a concerto there—mostly from my early days of tuition—but whether Howard was conjuring Brahms or Chopin or playing his own compositions, he was brilliant.

Just as brilliant as I hoped he wouldn't be.

58.

It was on the fourth day of Howard's stay that Leonard came back to haunt. I was in the library at the time, pretending to read a book on World War II fighter planes, watching Howard through the French doors. He was getting his regular noon sun, wearing nothing but board shorts and black sunglasses and reclining on a long white lawn chair. As far as I could tell, he was unaware of me watching him. Or he simply didn't care. He had that confident, languorous attitude of youth—a youth I was all too aware I'd never experienced—the youth of jeans commercials.

I sat wondering as I surreptitiously watched him. Did Howard have friends? Had he told anyone he'd be here? Was there anyone, either here or in Prague, who knew the location of this house? A girlfriend? A boyfriend? If he were suddenly to vanish, I went on to wonder, to poof into thin air, would anyone miss him, notice his absence, come looking for him?

That's when I caught my first whiff.

At first, I tried to convince myself it wasn't what I thought it was, that I'd imagined it. But then a second whiff wafted in the air. I put the book down on the table beside my chair, tilted my head, sniffing left, sniffing right. I juggled dimly hopeful alternatives: a blocked drain in the sink; stagnant water outside in the garden; a refinery down the road . . .

But no.

This smell, it was sickly sweet.

Faintly fruity, but like no fruit I'd ever smelt before. A scent designed to draw flies and necrophagic insects. The stink of some forgotten thing demanding to be remembered again. I got up, opened the windows. I took another sniff. This time, there was nothing.

Was I just smelling the memory of the smell? I couldn't tell. Regardless, I knew it would come back soon enough. Get worse. Become unbearably bad.

Howard rose from his lawn chair, his tanned skin gleaming in the sunlight. He took a long drink from a bottle, grabbed his towel, threw it over his shoulder, and walked towards the house. My eyes swivelled as my head spun round, half expecting to see the smell arrive, walk into the room like a tall man with a terrible secret to tell.

I took one final sniff before Howard sauntered in, eyeing me. I was standing in the centre of the room, gawking at him dumbly. I probably couldn't have looked more suspicious if I'd been crawling on all fours, sniffing at the skirting. He went by without saying anything, flipped his sunglasses up on his head, and stopped at the drinks cabinet. He slid out an ice tray, popped three cubes into a highball. Then he emptied the rest of his bottled water into the glass, looked back at me, and downed his drink.

So, Bent. Things haven't turned out quite the way you expected, have they?

Saying nothing, I picked up my book and sat down.

It's just that . . . Jesus, a whole year in this house? All by yourself? Quite a commitment, that. No wife. No kids. Not much of a career going. You must have really been . . . available, huh? Agreeing to this, I mean.

Your father made me a good offer.

I'm sure he did. Howard sank into an armchair with a sigh, raised his legs, and draped each over an armrest. *I'm sure this was all very alluring. The chance to live the life of a rich man. To wake up and somehow believe it's all yours, that it belongs to you. Guess it'll be tough going back, huh?*

I'll survive, I said.

Hmm. He sank deeper into the armchair. After a long pause, he said, *It's funny that you play jazz.* His legs dropped, both feet in front of him, as he sat upright and looked at me hard. *The fact my father hired a jazz pianist for the job. I was into a bit of jazz myself—when I was younger.* He looked away, seeming to ruminate. *A strange type of music for a kid, don't you think? Anyway, it was only in my teens that I switched to the classics. Maybe it was my choice, maybe it was my father's. He was a jazz fan, after all—loved it, really—he just thought it would be better if I followed a more, well,* lucrative*, line, y'know? Something that would take me places, with better company than a bunch of drunks and dope-heads.* With a wry smile, he went on, *Hey, maybe the old man was getting sentimental in his old age. Maybe having you here was his way of looking back on his life. Some kind of repentance, maybe, for the choices he'd made on my behalf.*

After a short silence, he shot me glance and said, *So, what's your take on it all?*

My only answer was to ask if he regretted it.

Regret what?

His choices, I explained. *The ones he made for you.*

Who knows? I mean, I've played for massive audiences. For royalty. In the most prestigious halls on the planet. It's hard to write it all off. Left to my own devices, I might have gone nowhere. Accomplished nothing. Found myself wandering aimlessly, renting someone else's life for a year. You know, just grabbing at the chance to be in the presence of greatness while wondering where oh where I'd gone so horribly, horribly wrong.

There was nothing subtle about this taunt—he was jabbing head-on. Was it just a rich kid's boredom, with me the new chew-toy? Some dumb unwanted thing brought home by Dad? I got up from the armchair and crossed the room to the cabinet, where I poured myself a whiskey.

Just then, like a cruel playground accomplice, the smell wafted in, a ripe rot reminding me that I couldn't really afford—not at this stage, anyway—to lose my shit, put two to the kid's jaw. Relaxing my fists, I picked up my glass. I looked back at him, but he seemed oblivious to the smell.

I'm just playing with you. You know that, right?

I tossed a smile his way, took a sip of my drink. *A bit of banter. Sure.*

Hey! That's brilliant! You're a real stand-up guy, you know that? In one swift movement, he pushed himself up from his armchair, stepped across to a couch, hopped over the back of it, and came and threw an arm around my shoulder. *I can see why my father likes you, Bent. You've got class, character. Your generation— we can learn a thing or two from you guys.* He let go of my shoulder and began walking in circles in the centre of the room, waving his hands in the air. *I tell you, Bent, some of the people I know—man, they're so fuckin' sensitive! And touchy! You've got to tip-toe around everyone. Politically correct, passive-aggressive sycophants, fibbers, phonies—*

He stopped dead, his chin went up, and he took a big sniff. Howard's eyes flicked to one side of the room, then the other, and then back at me.

I was clutching the glass so tightly I thought I'd crush it. My head raced for excuses as Howard stood motionless in the centre of the room, before whatever spell possessed him vanished, and he cast the last despairing glance of a man marooned in a distant, unreachable world.

That's when Howard turned to look at me, dead in the eyes, and said, *I'm very tired now. I think I'll be going to sleep.*

And then he left the room.

59.

Grey clouds collected, converged, threatening to empty their contents. The wind picked up, seeming to stumble like a drunk at a party as leaves on the lawn whirled and fell and the surface of the lake splintered like broken glass. A wooden lawn chair tipped over. A tiny pink cocktail umbrella tumbled across the patio, like the roof of a small house caught in a tornado twisting off to Oz. On the other side of the pool, a branch was ripped from a tree and made to do an undignified solitary jig.

A loud mess of a day.

Perfect weather for getting rid of a body or two.

I hadn't seen Howard for a while, not since he'd drifted out of the library in some kind of stupor, off to his room, maybe to hibernate. The smell had got worse (it certainly wasn't going to get any better in a hurry), but with a few open windows I managed to halt its spread. I worked out what I'd need: black refuse bags. Duct tape. A pair of scissors. A spade. A carpet. Once I'd slid the body downstairs, it'd all get trickier. I'd have to drag him outside—the back door would be best—and head to the woods, where I'd give Lenny his belated burial. After that I'd return, take a shower, pack my things, climb into my Cressida and hit the road without so much as a squint in the rear-view.

That'd be the sequence.

The exit plan.

Passing Howard's door, I tilted my head, listening for sounds of movement. Nothing. I carried on to the kitchen, opened the cupboard below the sink, pulled out some black bags. I was relieved to see a roll of duct tape—and there was even a can of air freshener. In a drawer I found a pair of heavy-duty scissors. I put it all into a bag before checking the carpet in the library. Wide enough to wrap him in. Perfect for the job.

I was making good progress, I thought, and about to head to the shed for my spade, when I was thwarted by the last person I'd have expected: Beethoven.

His fifth rolled down the corridor, winding its way through the rooms, reverberating off the walls. Soaring. Surging. Collapsing. I hadn't heard the piece in more than twenty years, and I'd either forgotten its mischievous splendour or never heard it played in such a confident, effortless way. It almost made me forget a most important fact: Howard wasn't in his room.

He was upstairs, at the piano.

Then, as suddenly as it had begun, the music stopped.

I cocked my ear to the silence.

As if on cue, the phone rang. I listened as it went on and on, and then I snapped out of it, flew upstairs, flung open the bedroom door, and picked up.

A soft and familiar voice: *Bent?*

The air was sucked right out of my lungs.

Jolene?

I sat on the edge of the bed. It had been weeks since I'd heard her voice. All I could tell was that she was smoking— her lips lifting lightly off the butt, a breathy exhalation—as she said, *I don't even know where to start.*

Unable to say a word, I waited.

God. I'm just so sorry, she said. *So sorry. But I didn't know who else to call, and I needed to call someone. I've been sitting here on the couch, in the dark, for hours now.* Another pause. *Bent, can I talk to you? Would that be okay?*

Voices swirled in my head. One called out forgiveness, wanting to console her, take care of her. Another gloated that she deserved her fate, and that she could just drop her bags on the doorstep of hell, for all I cared. And then there was the one with a word or two on the subject of survival: her problem was irrelevant. Nothing to do with me.

Bent, are you there?

I took a moment, put all my thoughts in a row, slowly flipping them over, one by one, like Tarot cards.

I'm here, I said. *But I've got to go.*

Then I hung up.

60.

I was brought out of sleep by music.
Not the soft, lulling kind.

It was as if there were an immense machine beneath the house—a coal-powered monstrosity, churning, thundering at the core—somehow keeping the whole world going. The clock on the wall said two-forty. I got out of bed, slid my feet into a pair of slippers, and stepped out into the dim corridor.

The booming and blaring was so loud that the pictures were askew on the walls and the windows trembled in their frames. I closed the door behind me, and headed down the corridor. At the staircase landing, a razor blade of moonlight sliced the wall. By now, I was able to put a band and title to the sound, with its doubled-stopped guitar, whimsical baseline, and snatches of whiny, wasted vocals: Television's "Marquee Moon" doubled the darkness.

I stared over the rail into the dark spiral of the staircase below. Still no hint of activity in the house. I even called out, but my voice vanished, like a match flicked into a tornado. I descended, one slow step at a time, and at the bottom of the stairs I heard the giggle of a woman, followed by a man's voice. Then I turned.

Standing in front of me was a tall blonde woman I'd never seen before. She was wearing a man's white shirt, unbuttoned to her belly. Below, her long bare legs stretched to the floor.

Boldly, she ran her eyes over me, from my toes to my head.

So you're him, huh? she said, her eyes level with mine. *Hey, man, you're missing out on all the good stuff.*

I could just about make out what she was saying over Tom Verlaine singing about listening to the rain, but hearing something else . . .

I'm sorry?

She snickered, turned, and disappeared into a room along the corridor, like a ghost through a wall. I looked around—left, right, and over my shoulder—and when I was sure there were no more surprises in the shadows, I headed her way. I got to a doorway, the room where Howard was staying, it turned out, and looked in.

The scene before me was so weird it seemed to have been staged, like some kind of late-night experimental theatre. In the dim blue glow of a bedside light, Howard lay sprawled on his stomach, naked except for the fedora perched on the back of his head. At the opposite end of the room, a woman was sitting in front of a mirror, brushing her long brown hair very slowly, repeating the same stroke over and over and over again. The blonde I'd just met was on her back beside Howard in the bed, her raised legs swinging like two unsynchronised pendulums.

If he'd rented the women for the night I couldn't give a shit. But what did worry me was how easily they'd gained access, and without my knowledge. Where else had they been in the house? What had they seen . . . or smelt?

Howard turned on his side, waved for me to enter, to join in. I gestured for him to turn the music down. He cupped an ear and scrunched his face, pretending not to understand, and waved again. Obliging him, I took a step into the room. It reeked of sweat and sex. I'd evidently arrived after the main event. Then Howard stood up on the bed, stepped over the blonde, hopped off onto the floor, and dropped the volume on a big black sound system in the corner.

How's that? Any better?

I nodded. *Thanks.*

Oh, man! Were we keeping you up? Yes, we were keeping you up! What time is it? He looked at his wrist for longer than it should have taken him to realise he wasn't wearing a watch. He looked to the women. *Girls, what time is it?*

Both mumbled non-responses.

I really am sorry, Bent, he said with a grin. *You see, it's my birthday.*

One of the women chimed that he was a liar.

Okay, he continued. *It's Tina's birthday.*

The other chuckled, saying how full of shit he was.

No, but seriously, Howard laughed. *We've got to keep it down. For my friend Bent here. Bent's got to be up early, right? To do whatever it is he does.* He swung round and said, *What is it you do, Bent? Besides, of course, skulk around. I've noticed you're pretty good at that. Here. There. Like a busy little spider.*

The blonde said she was hungry, but Howard's stare seemed bolted to me, not even a blink.

Eight eyes, eight legs. Skulk. Skulk. Skulk.

He broke into laughter again, sauntered over. With a hand on my shoulder, he said, *I'm kidding, man! Look. We got a little out of hand, but it's a first offence, okay? First verbal, then written. After that, no excuse. You get to lock us up and throw away the key.* With a theatrical sweep of an arm, he turned and said, *Sound reasonable, everyone?*

His hand was back on my shoulder, but this time it was pushing, until I was back in the corridor. Howard tacked a smirk to his lips, joked that his guests should *Hush now, dammit, people are trying to sleep around here.*

And then he shut the door.

61.

The morning after was bright and warm. Not so much as a cloud in the sky, a breeze through the trees, or a ripple on the pool. I had my coffee out there, sometime around ten, but within a few minutes I had to move into the shade. The coffee probably wasn't the best idea, either; I felt dehydrated after a poor night's sleep. I'd tossed about, replaying the surreal scene in my head: those two wacko women, bare-arsed Howard and his dumb hat. That music playing at such an eardrum-ripping volume he could only have done it to irk me, to lure me down.

There was no sign of any of them in the house. I pictured the two women draped over Howard in that bed, all asleep or dead, baking in the hot darkness. Remembering Jolene's guests—melding as they danced, skin into skin, merging into one shapeless mass of flesh—I pictured the three-way: Howard and the two women intertwining, filthily amalgamating. My stomach flipped at the thought, and I went back inside the house.

The bedroom phone rang. It could only be one person, and I was right.

Bent, she said. *I don't know if now's a better time than before, but I was wondering if we could talk a bit. Would that be okay, if we just talked a bit?*

I closed the door, and fell back onto the bed with the phone to my ear. Up on a wall, I saw a big brown spider. I couldn't tell if it was poisonous, and though I knew the larger ones generally weren't, this did nothing to relieve my unease. If it moved, even a little, just one of its hairy legs to the left or right, I decided I'd get up and kill it.

What do you want to talk about? I asked. My voice was cold, colder than I'd wanted.

I don't sleep so well any more, she said. *I'm on these pills. They're supposed to help. But they make me feel so zonked, so out of it.*

I promised myself I'd stay aloof, but I also felt my control slip away. I remembered the smell of the nape of her neck. Her silkiness. The toothy smile. It was as if there were hooks in my guts, and everything was being tugged down.

I have these recurring nightmares, the voice went on, *and I wake up in a sweat. I get these icy cold sweats, and my pillows are soaked through, like I've just got out of a lake. I just don't get it any more.*

Get what? I heard myself say.

This path I'm on, and why I'm on it, and where it's all heading. Like, this thing I have for the company of strangers. I don't know why, but things somehow feel safer, it numbs something inside, keeps it down. And then you—you stopped feeling like a stranger to me. Bent, that scared me. Don't ask, because I wouldn't know what to say. Does any of this make sense? I took some pills . . . ten minutes ago. Or an hour? Maybe longer. Maybe just ten minutes. I can't say . . . but please tell me you're trying—trying to understand.

I am, I said. *Trying, I mean.*

Okay. That's good. That's really good.

I sighed, closed my eyes. An image formed in my head. I saw myself as a child, sitting beside my mother. She was beaming as she held my hand, gently moving it over a piano, guiding me across the keys. She was in the dress she'd worn on my eleventh birthday. Her hair was done up. There was colour in her cheeks, a glint of something alive and well in her eyes. I looked at the ceiling, and as I did so, the picture faded away, like warm breath on cold glass.

The voice again: *Bent, what about you?*

What about me?

How are you?

I hadn't been asked in years. *I could be all right.*

Sure. Okay.

There was nothing else in the world right then but me and Jolene. I didn't want to make any more promises. I didn't want to tell her I could save her, or that she could save me. I just wanted to be there, right there in the room with her, cut off from the chaos of the world. And I didn't ever want to go back.

She laughed nervously, continued: *Y'know. It'd be okay if it was just me to worry about. But there's Edgar too. I jump out of bed after these nightmares, and the first thing I do is go to my son's room, look in on him . . . and he looks so peaceful . . . and I want to wake him up, tell him that no matter how I behave, no matter what I say, or where I go, it's not his fault. None of it is his fault. He should know this as he goes on, and grows up, and becomes his own man. He should be totally free of it. You know what I mean?*

I said nothing, her vulnerability making me ache for her, want her—more than ever. I wanted her next to me. In front of me. All around me. I wanted to drown in the ocean of her.

I'm not expecting everything to be perfect, not right away, but maybe we could just see each other. We don't have to rush anything, just see each other. It was fun. We had fun—didn't we?

Jolene . . .

Would you at least consider it?

I don't know.

What are you thinking right now? she asked, her voice low.

My hand dropped to my side and I stared out the window, into the blue. Then I put the phone to my ear again.

Look, she said. *Let's just give it time . . . and possibly, maybe, one day we could even work our way back to, I dunno, rethinking your offer?*

Wanting reassurance, I asked her to remind me, and she replied, *The offer you made at the restaurant, about Edgar and me coming to stay there with you. And, hey, when Leonard finally gets out, we can make some other plan, go somewhere else.*

I wasn't sure it was such a good idea any more—if we were going to have a new start, we'd need somewhere new. Some place far away from that goddamned house.

Then something clicked in my head. Like a seized cog in a machine: when Leonard finally gets out.

Gets *out.*

The shadow of some terrible, looming thing fell over me. Over the room. Over the house. Over the world. I asked Jolene to repeat what she'd said, just to make sure.

I said we could move in, and when Leonard gets back we could make another plan—

No, I cut her off. *That's not what you said.*

What?

You said: when Leonard gets out.

I don't know what you're on about—

I propped myself up. *Look, I heard what you said. You just said, when Leonard finally gets* out.

I don't know what you think you heard—

I sprang to my feet and demanded, *Jolene, what is this?*

Bent, I—

What the hell are you up to?

Bent—

Stop saying my name! I shouted, my fist tightening on the receiver. *Just tell me. Tell me now.*

Tell you what?

I stomped to the window with the phone in my hand and scanned the garden. I didn't know what I expected to see out there, but my leg began to tremble and I felt a wave of dizziness.

Bent, are you there?

So, this whole time it's been some kind of game?

A game? I don't—

You and him! You and him!

Look, she said, *whatever this is about, just hold on. I'm coming over, okay. We'll talk then—*

I slammed the receiver down, battled to catch my breath as I closed my eyes and put my head between my legs. I needed to think clearly. I wasn't mad. I wasn't imagining this. She'd said it, given herself away. Just as Leonard attested, she didn't actually want me. She'd *never* wanted me. She'd been coaxed into some kind of plan. That's why she'd ditched me at the supermarket; she couldn't take it any more, having to be with me. Smile at me. Sleep with me. But now, something had happened: she was forced to call, make amends, get whatever twisted plan it was back on track.

But she'd fluffed it.

Minutes later, I stood up and walked out the door. The hallway was unnaturally bright, and the ceiling began to bulge like a plastic tarp filled with water, moments from bursting and flooding the house. Not again. No. Not now. I needed to keep it together. I lurched forward to the staircase landing, held the rail, and took another breath. As I hurried down, the light of the day flared through the windows, and I felt a compulsion to get the hell out. Forget the corpse. Forget Howard. Just go.

I went into the kitchen, grabbed a glass of water, quickly drained it, then cupped my hands and splashed my face and the back of my neck.

Anything the matter?

My head almost spun right off my neck.

Howard stood at the counter, his hands behind his back. *Not feeling so well?*

With both palms, I slid the water off my face, then wiped my hands on my shirt.

You gave me a fright, I said. *I was just . . .*

My hands fumbled to complete my non-existent explanation with a series of awkward, meaningless gestures. Unruffled by my theatrics, Howard stuck to his spot (just as he had in the rain, and at the goddamned pool, the bastard).

You know, he said coolly, *the moment you opened the front door on that first day, I knew.*

Knew what?

That something wasn't quite right with you.

I pretended I hadn't heard him. *Look, you're here now,* I said. *You've got things covered. I think I should be off.*

Oh, you're leaving?

Yes. I'm off.

In such a hurry?

This isn't working out.

Oh? Why's that?

I've not been feeling well. I unhooked a tea towel and dabbed the back of my neck. *I think I need to see a doctor or something.*

Yeah, you sure don't look well, Bent. All red and sweaty. Like you're about to have a heart attack. He gave me a funny look. *By the way, before you go—you know what it was, the thing that got me thinking?*

Tell me, I said.

You're not at all how my father described you.

For a moment, Howard inspected his shiny black shoes. Then he pinned his eyes on me again.

I leant against the sink. *How so?*

For one, he said you were charming. And eloquent. Confident. Essentially, he said we'd get on like the proverbial house on fire, lots in common.

Sorry to disappoint.

And then, he began, and paused. *And then, Bent, I started getting this feeling. Because the thing is, I don't see any sign that my father's gone anywhere. You've taken his room, but what really gets me is that everything of his is here. I mean, everything. I even found his travel bags in a cupboard. Together with his passport. Now how do you suppose a man travels the world without a passport?*

He stepped forward—quite clearly, he did not expect a reply. *But there's something else. Something I found, that maybe I wasn't supposed to find. Any guesses?* He tilted his head at an angle. *Hmm? Mr. Charming. Mr. Confident. I asked you a question.*

He pulled his right hand from behind his back, and dangled a bloodstained shirt in my face. The one I'd worn the day I'd hit the dog.

I froze. *Where did you get that?*

It was his turn to ignore the question, and he continued, *This really got me thinking—and you know what I see here, Bent? I see the full picture. A picture of a psycho. A loser. A man who saw an opportunity. Who thought, hey, here I am, out in the middle of nowhere. And here's this rich nut who's just given me the key to his house, to his entire fucking estate, and maybe, just maybe . . .*

He held up the shirt, gave it a shake.

Howard, that's not what you think it is. There was an accident—

An accident! Looks like one hell of an accident. No. You know what? I reckon he's still here. You didn't expect me that morning, and you've been skulking around ever since, trying to clean up the mess. Right? Tell me I'm right? Maybe that's why it stinks in here— hey, look at me—I said that's why it smells so fucking terrible in here.

He glared at me, gave a shake of his head—but this calm was just a prologue. I sensed the rage amassing within him, which he was struggling to hold in, to contain.

Howard, listen to me, I softly said. *That's not your father's blood. I hit a dog. With your father's car . . .*

He began to laugh. In seconds, his facade would be gone, and he'd blow up. My eyes flicked sideways to the door, my exit route if he decided to grab a knife from the counter and come screaming towards me.

Trust me, I said. *That shirt—*

Stop. Just stop. I don't want to hear it.

Instead of coming for me, he stepped briskly away, out of the kitchen and into the corridor. I went after him, stopped at the door, and saw him heading for the hallway. He was muttering that it was all over for me, and he'd make sure I lived out the rest of my days in an endless, inescapable hell of his own devising.

There was a phone just off the hallway, I suddenly clicked— and ran to head him off.

Don't do that! I shouted. *Wait! Put it down. Don't . . .*

Howard dialled, slipped me a side glance, coolly turned to complete his task, and turned his back on me. I yelled for him to just hold on for one minute, to take a second to hear me out—when my eyes landed on a nearby object on the floor. It was a large ceramic pot. Without so much as a thought, I bent down, grabbed it with both hands, raised it above my head, and brought it down squarely on the back of his skull as he stood waiting, the receiver in his hand.

He went down instantly. The pot cracked, spilling soil all over Howard's legs as if his burial had already begun. Blood oozed out the back of his head, running into the world like a living thing escaping a doomed vessel.

Just then, his left leg moved, the knee bent in an attempt to lift himself up. His right hand extended with a shiver, streaking blood across the floor. The sound he made—low, guttural moaning punctuated with a high-pitched squeal—signalled confusion and profound, instinctual fear.

I wouldn't leave him like that.

Of course, if I wanted to, I could have (there was no way he'd last more than a few minutes), but that would be wrong. I hadn't intended for him to suffer. All I'd wanted was to stop him dead in his tracks. To protect myself from the mistake he was about to make.

So, as Howard tried to crawl away, his brain damaged and his blood draining from his skull, I dropped the pot on his head once more, smashing that thing to pieces, and silencing him for good.

It was only after Howard was a corpse lying prostrate on the floor that I remembered his two guests, both of whom could still have been in the house. I peeked through the downstairs doors, called upstairs, but there was no sign of anyone. I went off to the shed for a spade. On my way back, I imagined opening the front door and finding Howard's body gone, his blood mopped up, the pot shards cleared, and the soil swept away.

I pushed open the door.

He was there, all right, all twisted and limp, face down in his own fluids. I stepped over him, then went to open the library doors that led outside. I came back, grabbed Howard by the ankles, and dragged him through the library, leaving a wide, snaking line of red on the wooden boards, before I eventually deposited him on the steps outside. A wheelbarrow stood near the vegetable garden. I went over and wheeled it back across the lawn.

Howard lay propped against a step, his head slumped like a drunk's. I lifted him under his arms in a kind of embrace, and then dumped him in his rusty chariot. His arms and legs, draped over the sides, flopped about as we trundled past the pool, over the slanting lawn, towards the trees farther below. The lawn thinned to dirt, which was strewn with dead leaves as I entered the woods. Between the trees, out of sight of both the house and the perimeter fence, I rested the wheelbarrow and pulled out the spade. The crows had their own opinion on the proceedings, cawing from on high, fluttering their wings, and moulting fine black feathers like snow in hell. I found a clearing where the dirt seemed fairly soft, and got digging.

Leonard's game, whatever it may have been, was over. Christ. I could barely comprehend how quickly things had unravelled, how I'd got myself there at all. I ran through the events, taking one final shot at figuring it all out.

I took myself back to Leonard at the bar, replayed his words, re-examined his intentions. What had he *really* wanted from me? What had been the point of it all? He could have got any-one to do the job, be there to yell at from behind his locked door. I mean, even Carl could have done it. Leonard had clearly trusted the man, more than he could ever have trusted me. So: why me? What special characteristic convinced him I'd be the man for the job?

And Howard—goddamned Howard—why hadn't Leonard mentioned him, told me he'd be arriving? Because Howard, like me (and unlike Jolene), seemed not to be aware of too much. It was almost as if . . .

As I jabbed the dirt with the spade, something else occurred to me. Christ. More than just to shove food through a door, Leonard had brought me (specifically *me*) to the house for one—and only one—important reason: to be the person at the door when his son turned up.

That was it, surely?

It was never about Leonard at all, in fact. He was on his way out, with no plan to exit that room. No. From the get-go I'd been prepped as a pawn in a plan set up for his son—for *Howard*—part of a father's ploy to test allegiance, to provide one final assurance that the kid he'd raised was deserving of his inheritance.

In some deranged, Leonard-style way, it added up. He'd been scoping me out for months before finally inviting me to the house. Of course he had. It was no coincidence that Howard and I were both pianists, both from fractured homes. I'd been invited to role-play ownership of Leonard's estate and possessions, but just as I'd begun to settle in, his son and putative heir, Mr. Part Two, had arrived. The result was competition between a contender raised by his father, and one who'd remained with his abandoned mother. One provided with prospects and opportunities, and one left to trawl the streets on his own. Leonard had squared us off against each other with the aim of answering one final question for himself: which version of his son was the more deserving?

A bit of an insane proposition—but one that was right in line with Leonard's level of nuts. After all, wasn't that also the reason Jolene had been persuaded to be with me? Another of Leonard's tests—a means of making me confront the unsettled shit that for years and years had been stirring in my head: not just a bungling lover, but also a lonely single mother and her abandoned son.

Maybe.

Maybe all of it.

I couldn't say.

Regardless, here I was, knee-deep in dirt, securing a piece of prime subterranean property for Mr. Fry Jr.—

Oh, my God, what are you doing?

My head twisted to face the familiar voice.

Jolene stood immobile between the trees—ten, fifteen metres away—eyes wide, mouth agape. I had no idea how long she'd been there, or how she'd got onto the property at all. Had Howard left the gate open after letting his two female friends out? My thoughts raced, and I tried to assess the scene from her point of view: Howard in the wheelbarrow. The hole I was standing in. The spade in my hand. The blood on my shirt.

Jolene. What are you . . . how did you—

As if a generator suddenly kicked in after a power outage, Jolene's world seemed to snap alive.

It wasn't quite a scream. Not at first.

More of a moan. A wail.

One step back, and another, and then she turned, tripped, and scrabbled up the slope, scooping the leaves from under her. Her legs buried in the leafy mush, she launched herself up and out. Holding on to my spade, I leapt out of the hole. She was running now, and I was running after her. She erupted from the woods into the open, flapping her arms as she crossed the lawn and passed the pool. I dropped the spade and called out her name, again and again and again—but she didn't so much as glance at me. She didn't slow down, as she surrendered to a high, uncontrolled screaming. But the sound was lost to the countryside. There was no one to hear her. No one but me, and the birds, and the eternally indifferent dead.

She rounded the side of the house, and, breathless and spent, opened her car door. By the time I got to her, she'd rolled up the windows and locked herself in. She stared ahead, her face flushed with tears. The car growled to life, and I pummelled the window as it backed away. As she switched to first, the tyres spat gravel, and she was gone. I tried to give chase, but eventually stopped. Then, with my hands on my knees, I watched as her car shrank in the distance.

She'd seen it all. There was nothing left to hide, to drag, to bury. She'd head straight for the police station. I could see her bursting in there. Blubbering. Incoherent. Petrified. Eventually, she'd get it all out—what she'd seen and heard and how she'd had to escape a madman waving a spade in the air. She'd lead them back here. Maybe there'd be one police car. Maybe two. Or an entire squad, sirens whooping, guns ready—depending on how dangerous and deranged she made me out to be.

But was I? Was I really dangerous?

Given what Jolene now knew, there was every possibility that I wasn't the dangerous one at all. Because in an hour's time, or two, or three—however long it took for the sirens to arrive, for Krymeer's many doors to be kicked down, its rooms to be emptied of their secrets—Jolene would be the dangerous one.

62.

I turned on the shower and stepped inside the cubicle. I stood under the pelting water and let my mind go free. Everything and everyone vaporised in the steam. No Leonard. No Howard. No Jolene. Just me, and the wetness, until it all came crashing down.

I turned around under the stream of water, lathering and scrubbing the dead skin, from my back to the soles of my feet. I finished by washing my hair with tea-tree shampoo, then I stepped out, towelled myself. From a cabinet above the basin I took a tube of moisturising self-tanner. A bottle of two-week toner. Rejuvenating eye gel. I examined my profile in the mirror, then brushed my teeth (best done *before* eating, to prevent acidic erosion) and flossed. I gargled with some bright-blue mouthwash for exactly thirty seconds, then spat. I turned, entered the walk-in closet, and picked up a bottle of Emporio Armani deodorant. I went with Shu Uemura pomade, perfect for a single right-to-left comb-through.

Clothes-wise, I had the full picture in my head, and followed through, item by item. Third rack from the wall: the Givenchy Contrast cutaway collar button-cuff shirt. Two rails across: the notched-lapel wool-and-silk-blend jacket. For the bottoms, the straight-leg silk-blend trousers. A reversible leather belt. Tod's Gommino leather driving shoes. The Hublot Classic Fusion wristwatch. I buttoned my cuffs as I stood before the full-length mirror. Then I turned at an angle, and took another look at the man in the mirror, that stranger in a foreign place.

A copy of a copy of a copy.

Next, I went downstairs, past Howard's blood puddle in the hallway, and climbed into the Mustang. I started up, pressed the remote, waited for the door to open, and slid out. The house was in the rear-view mirror as I cruised through the gate. And then I hit the road. Eyes forward, I headed for the highway.

I drove into the burnt-out sun.

I drove towards the city.

VI.

Thud, thud

63.

Coming back to the city after a long period of time is like running into a secretive and sophisticated woman you once made laugh at a party, but who pretends not to know you the next day. It felt as if I hadn't been along those streets in years. Everything was just the way I'd left it, but also different in some way, as if each bench and lamp post had been substituted with a plastic prop.

Nobody seemed to be out and about. It hit me then that I had no idea what night of the week it was. I didn't even know the month. I'd clearly lost more than I knew, out there in the countryside—more than I'd bargained for. The truth was, I regretted having ever said yes to any of it, for having thought it could be so simple. After all, Leonard himself hadn't thought it such a simple thing to leave his inheritance to his son. No. He'd needed to turn the entire process into a test, to pit Howard and me against each other and have one of us come out on top. And that's what had happened, right? I'd come out tops and Howard had come out bottom (of the goddamned woods), which, according to Leonard's logic, meant I'd won it all for myself. The house. The estate. The money.

Of course, I wasn't naive enough to think the police would see it that way, but the next big Q was whether or not Jolene had gone to the cops at all. There was still a chance she hadn't. Maybe she'd be afraid of what that might mean for her. It would lead to a comprehensive investigation, surely, not only into the man with his wheelbarrow-o'-death, but into the entire orbiting subplot, which included Jolene herself. So, was she willing to hand it all over? To sit at the station hour upon hour as the befuddled officers listened to her explain how Leonard had paid her to deceive me, to mess with my head, as they exchanged shifty glances, trying to make sense of it all?

Time would tell.

Either way, my return to the city hadn't been an attempt at escape. I knew they'd find me there if they searched for me. Rather, what I wanted to know was what it'd feel like just to see it again, in all its decrepit splendour. I needed to know if I still belonged there, if the new clothes and car made me feel any different about it—about myself, *in* it. All I wanted at that very moment, entering the city, was to drive through it—to process and absorb each paper bag blowing in the wind and each aimless drunk and each flashing neon sign pointing to the end of the line.

My hands turned the wheel in the direction of the Crack Radisson. I don't know why. In minutes, I was outside my apartment block with its cramped flats above the Korean Mart and the dingy barber and the half-empty hardware store.

I parked the car outside and took the rattling elevator to the top. I'd never realised how strongly it smelt of sweat and copper and old linoleum in there. On the second floor, the doors creaked open and I stepped into the corridor. Door after familiar door stood along the walls. The only open door was the one alongside my flat—belonging to Professor Paedophile. A paramedic was standing just outside, having a cigarette. He shot me a glance, as if I were about to tell him off for puffing indoors, but then he looked away and blew a smoke ring.

Everything okay? I asked.

He didn't say anything, didn't make eye contact. Just studied my outfit, apparently making his own judgements. Then a balding man came out, followed by a short woman pushing a gurney.

I asked what had happened.

"Heart attack," she said. "The whole thing lasted no longer than a few seconds. The best way to go."

The man asked, "Did you know him?"

I told them I'd met him a couple times, that I was a neighbour—but I could tell they struggled to reconcile my fancy get-up with my less-than-humble abode. Then the man pulled back the sheet for me to have a look.

But it wasn't him.

It wasn't the old professor who'd beaten my door down about the mystic numbers that had supposedly come from the radio. This was someone else. Also in his late seventies or early eighties, but unfamiliar to me. My only thought was that Prof. Paedo had moved on, and some other geriatric on his last few ticks had moved in, but it seemed an odd possibility.

I stepped back as the paramedics manoeuvred the corpse into the corridor, and squeezed into the elevator. They'd forgotten to lock the door behind them, and I entered the dead man's apartment. It was exactly how I remembered it, the numbers scrawled on the walls, the brown couch, the filthy bin. It didn't look like anyone else had moved in at all. The more I wandered about, the less sense it seemed to make. I went to the window and looked out. It was an almost identical view to my own in the room next door, just at a minimally different angle.

I left the flat and took the elevator down. Outside, the cold hit me. I needed a drink—something to realign the mind. Shoving my hands in my pockets, I hurried along the pavement. The moon over the tall buildings seemed bigger than it had in the countryside. Bigger, but malnourished.

A bouncer outside a pool hall slid aside to let me in. There were around fifteen, twenty pool tables, each blotted out by smoke. Every table was taken, and I navigated between jutting cues and arses, towards the bar. I pulled up a stool and ordered a whiskey and ginger ale. Without a word, the barman went to get my drink.

I perused the scene. Bland nineties rock music blasted from the speakers, but I could still hear the clack of cues and balls and the drunken guffawing of what looked to be mostly rowdy varsity students and dopey, bearded punks. When I turned around again, my drink was in front me. I paid and took my first cold sip.

Coby.

She was sitting across from me, on the other side of the bar, watching a television screen in the top left-hand corner of the hall. Teenagers on tiny BMXs ramping up absurdly tall half-pipes and doing twists and turns in the air. Coby sat sucking on a cider, her eyes fixed to the screen.

"Hey," I said, as I walked over. She seemed not to hear me, so I said it again, louder. "Hey, you."

"Yes?"

I waited, gave her a moment to acknowledge me, but seconds chugged by and nothing appeared to click.

"It's me," I said.

She looked me over, clearly unimpressed.

"Look, if this is a pick-up line, forget it. Oh, and I don't need you to buy me a drink, either, I've got one."

Throwing her head back, she drank from her bottle as if to prove the point. Her long, slender throat undulated as she swallowed. She banged the drink down on the counter, just hard enough to show what she could do with a fist to the nose, to the throat, to the groin. Then her eyes swivelled back to the television.

"How's your sister?" I asked her. I didn't know what else to say. All I felt I could do was push on.

She turned to me and said, "What?"

"Your sister. The doctor."

She laughed, as if in disbelief of my persistence.

"Sister? That's a new one," she said. "Look, man, I don't have a sister. But I'll play along. You tell me where you think you know me from, and I'll decide how far this goes."

"Ten To Twelve."

She made a half-turn on her stool. "I *do* work at Ten To Twelve." Her head inclined to one side, she gave me a second, protracted look. "I do know you. You're the piano guy. You play . . . uh, jazz, right? You've gigged there a few times, haven't you? Whiskey and ginger ale. That's your drink, right? How're you doing, man?"

Hesitating, I said, "I'm fine."

"This is more than you've ever spoken to me at the bar, you're usually so quiet, just sitting there with your drink, not talking to anyone. I don't even think we've met. I'm Toni."

She stuck a hand out for me to shake.

"Sorry, what did you say your name was?"

"Toni."

"What about Coby?"

"Who's Coby?"

"You are."

She bit her bottom lip. "Nope."

"You're . . . *not* Coby?"

"Sorry, pal."

"You've got a sister who just graduated?"

"This isn't clicking with you, is it?"

"Your cat . . . "

"My *cat*? Ha, definitely not. I'm allergic." She sucked at her cider. "Hey, you all right? You don't look so well."

"I'm just . . . " I looked around, mumbled, "I'm fine."

I didn't want to say another word to her. I retreated a step. All around me, balls were being smacked to and fro and drinks were being downed and carried and spilt and there was laughing and swearing and strutting and smoking and just sitting around, watching, waiting.

"I'm sorry for bothering you," I said. "I . . . I thought you were someone else."

She gave a snort and a laugh. "Okay. Whatever, man. Have a nice life."

She wasted no time shoving me into the back-alley of her mind, and focused on the BMX teenagers. The volume swelled. The lights got brighter. Harsher.

I didn't get it. All those nights at the bar. All our conversations. Toni? Had I heard wrong one night and then run with it? I pushed through the players in the pool hall, staggered downstairs, and flung myself into the dark. I looked left, looked right, then glided along the street like a shadow on the loose. I passed a bookstore, a Mexican grill, an antique shop, a travel agent, until I arrived at a barricaded hole in the wall—the pancake house once owned by the Sicilian, which I'd gone to as a kid. I'd run out of breath. I leant against a wall and retched. Nothing came out. Just a bit of spit.

Groggily, I looked up.

The Bijou, my old haunt, with its sign buzzing in blue cursive.

I wiped my mouth with my sleeve, went inside.

There were only four or five occupied tables out of a good fifteen, twenty. I beelined to the bar and ordered a double whiskey. I downed it, immediately ordered another.

"You okay?" said the barman.

I asked him the exact same question, and again downed my drink. He suggested I follow up with some tea. It was a joke, of course, and I laughed. I told him to run a tab, then took a seat at one of the tables at the back, and undid my top button. How could I have got it all so wrong? That first time, just before I'd met Leonard, had she in fact ignored me, or did she genuinely not know me? How could I have deceived myself so badly, an entire history of conversations and friendship and flirtations that hadn't happened at all? It was scary: I must be full-on brass-band mad to have pulled off something like that. I felt the booze move through me. But I decided I didn't want to be too drunk. I wanted my wits. A waiter approached. For the hell of it, I ordered a pot of camomile.

Why was I still in this city? I could sit there and pretend I was catching up on old times, but there were no old times. Not in that place. Not in any place I'd ever been. Nostalgia is a shitty picture in a shiny frame. And that was the whole point, I saw. I needed to ditch it all and really disappear. Head for the airport. Fly to France, see if La Trémoille had a room for me, rent a car, drive to Carcassonne with its fantastical stone turrets. After that, head to Lyons, walk around a bit, smile at the locals, and have lunch in, what do they call it, a *bouchon?* Maybe even, at some point, I'd pop by Mont Saint-Michel and see where the souls of the dead hung out.

Fresh air. Wide horizons.

A real escape.

My tea arrived.

A man I recognised as the owner of the bar came on stage, thanked everyone for being there, with a reminder of an upcoming motorcycle charity show. After that, he introduced some musician, clapped like a circus seal, and exited stage right. A light beamed over the piano, and a kid I'd never seen before—barely into his twenties—took his seat. The suit he was wearing was a little looser on him than it should have been, and I wasn't certain his pants and jacket were the same colour.

He played, however, like a mad animal. Feverish. Urgent. I sat mesmerised, relishing what I'd always loved about jazz. It was all so unassuming. Just a guy doing what he loved. He was young, and somebody was paying him to do what he did best, which just about meant he'd won the grand lotto of life.

Fifty minutes later, he stopped. He didn't get up—or not straight away. I watched him as he sat there, arched over the keys, sweating, slowly returning to the world. Finally, he rose, moved through the crowd, and hit the bar. My waiter returned, and I told him to order a cup of tea for the talented musician.

Borrowing the waiter's pen, I grabbed an old receipt and wrote *turn around* on the back. I instructed the waiter to leave it on the pianist's saucer. I waited, drinking my own tea, wondering if he'd take me up on my invitation. Ten minutes later, after a few tequilas, the young pianist got his tea, along with the note.

His eyes swept the room, found me in my corner, and then he slowly and cautiously made his way over . . .

64.

I opened my eyes. I was back at Krymeer.

How this had happened, I had no idea. But there I was, in Leonard's crumpled clothes, lying on the top sheet of his bed. The room was hot enough for me to assume it was late in the day. I watched nomadic motes of dust move in a beam of sunlight. I could hear birds outside. The wind against the windows. The soft and benevolent tick of a wall clock.

I sat up and looked around.

Something was different.

I couldn't say what—not right away, at least—but it felt as if I'd been sleeping the entire time, or that I'd been awake the entire time and now I was sleeping. Unreal, or *too* real; I couldn't decide. Had I really gone back to the city, or had I dreamt it? No, that was preposterous. It was all so lucid in my head. My senses were still tingling from the music and the booze. I could smell the cigarette smoke on my clothing—but not on my fingers, significantly. I stretched the muscles in my face as nebulous memories of the night encircled me, begging for confirmation: driving to the Crack Radisson, seeing some dead stranger on a gurney. Then Coby (or was it Toni?) suggesting I'd sat at that bar night after night and only *imagined* I'd chatted with her. And after that, well, I'd gone to The Bijou, where I'd listened to some kid pianist. Bought him tea. Invited him over.

But then what?

Krymeer was more than an hour away from the city, which meant I'd either driven myself back in some weird state of mind or been knocked out and *brought* back. It made no sense. Who'd have carried me inside, up the stairs, tucked me in? Which made me think: since taking up Leonard's offer, had I ever woken anywhere *other* than his bedroom? On the night of Jolene's dinner, hadn't the same thing happened? Blacked out in public, woke up in that bed, in that goddamned house?

The more I thought about it, the more it began to feel as if my trip back to the city hadn't happened the previous night at all. The events of the night seemed to retreat further and further into the past, as if I'd experienced nothing more than a new dream of an old memory. One from years ago—dragged out of the filing cabinet, dusted off, and spruced up with a few fantastical flourishes, if only to fuck with my internal clock.

I shook it off.

I got up, rinsed my face, squeezed toothpaste into my mouth, slapped it around with my tongue, and spat it out. I dabbed my face with a towel and raised my eyes to the mirror. The good news, it was still me there. The bad news, it wasn't anyone else. I was in deeper shit than I was allowing myself to grasp, as it hit me why I'd left the house in the first place.

Howard. Leonard. Jolene.

Had she come back with the police?

Was my face already on a WANTED billboard?

I went downstairs. There was no sign that anyone had been there. No crime-scene tape and no kicked-in front door. I headed for the library, expecting to see blood on the floor.

Nothing.

Not a smudge in sight.

Leonard's cronies must have been waiting in the wings: come in here like some kind of clean-up crew, got rid of every piece of evidence while I was asleep. And as for the smoking gun . . .

The ceramic pot was back in its corner. Perfectly intact. My mind lumbered, labouring to make sense of it. I left the library, my eyes on the tiled floor, right to the back door, tracing the route I'd taken with the corpse. Not so much as a smear in sight—not even on the more porous concrete porch. The wheelbarrow I'd used (or almost certainly used), was sitting next to the vegetable patch, exactly where I'd first found it. Rusty and lined with soil, but nary a drop of blood. I looked around, imagining a dozen or so well-dressed men and women having a good cackle at my mad endeavours, and the dumb, confused look on my face. Of course, I saw no one: I was either completely alone out there— or they were looking on from some unseen spot. I composed myself, refusing to allow them the pleasure of witnessing my bumbling, and went back inside. I was about to take the stairs, when something made me stop at the dining room.

Made me look inside.

On the far wall, beyond the long dining table, hung a painting of a park—the one I'd noticed while sitting with Leonard in that very room many months before. A wide and rolling stretch of lawn, with large evergreen trees and a lake. People picnicking, enjoying the dappled shade, the freshness, the freedom. A girl with a kite. A man in a hat, reading a book under a tree. Two boys with paper boats at the water's edge. And, in the background, a solitary figure in a black coat, standing apart from everyone. Faceless, his hands deep in his pockets—

I'd *been* there—not *to* the actual place portrayed—but rather, I'd been *in* that goddamned painting. With Jolene. And Edgar.

I dismissed it, hurried away. As I hurtled up the stairs, the framed photographs caught my eye: the man on the deck of the *Britomartis*. But no, not just any man; it was *me*, in black sunglasses, and hanging a banner of big white teeth. The man on a Friesian horse—this, too, was me. And among all the well-dressed folk, there I was, yet again, having the time of my other-dimensional life, grinning at the camera—

I was losing my mind. Tripping.

Something.

I didn't pause at the landing, didn't look at Leonard's door, just flew to the room with the sofa and the bar. I poured myself a double and drank it neat. I backed up and sank into the sofa behind me.

Staring at the unlit fireplace, an unearned calm fell over me. There must be some reason for Howard's disappearance, for my face being in the photographs. Maybe the whole thing was a hallucination? Or maybe I *had* been drugged in the city—and if so, how many people were in on Leonard's scheme? The guests at Jolene's party? Had I been drugged that night too? And what about the nightclub? Did Leonard really have such wide influence, an accomplice on every corner? There was still something missing.

A whole other angle I wasn't seeing.

I got up, left the room, and went straight to the bedroom. I grabbed my travel bag and flipped it open on the sheet. I knew neither the reason for my pictures in those frames, nor the reason for the mopped-up floor, but I didn't care. Not any more.

Entering Leonard's walk-in, I swept some shirts off their hangers. Grabbed a few pairs of pants. And shoes. I folded the items neatly and packed them inside my bag. I strapped on my watch and checked the time. If I hurried, I could be at the bank by one, draw the maximum amount of cash, close the account, and turn up at the airport by three. That's what I'd do, I decided. The idea of leaving that house behind, of vanishing into the world, made my heart jog with anticipation. I saw myself standing beneath that big digital board of destinations, before heading off to some exotic place.

I zipped the bag, checked the time again, and stood there. Shafts of light fell onto the bed and floor in bright frame-shaped squares. Just then, as if suddenly teleported into the room, an object on the dressing table caught my attention.

A small, familiar box.

A meticulously made artefact from a far more patient era. The longer I stared, the more certain I became: it was the same box given to me by the attorney. My mind tumbled; I couldn't recall bringing it here. Unable to resist its pull, I stepped up to it, ran the tips of my fingers over the lid, examining the engravings. My eyes followed the line of its charming little tale—an eagle swooping down on a rabbit, which was chasing a carrot, which was being dragged by a bicycle ridden by a boy, chasing a girl ascending into the sky with wings, in pursuit of an eagle.

I flipped the small brass latch and lifted the lid.

A long, rusty key. I took it out and studied it from all angles. The attorney had hinted it might be some kind of symbol, with sentimental value. But I hadn't bought any of that, and I certainly wouldn't be wearing it around my neck.

A thought flew into my head, sudden and without logic.

This was followed by a strange urge, and I felt compelled to turn from the dressing table, key in hand. And so it was that I left the room, entered the corridor, and found myself standing before Leonard's locked door. I took one more look at the key, stuck it in the door, and gave it a turn.

Click.

I held my breath.

No. That wasn't supposed to happen.

This couldn't possibly be.

It wasn't the same goddamned key I'd used to lock the door, the key Leonard had given me that first night, all those weeks and months ago.

Slowly, I pushed the door open.

With a long, whining creak, it swung wide.

65.

Standing at the entrance of the one room in the house that I hadn't yet entered, I wasn't quite sure what to expect. A drab, unadorned cell? Perhaps a few items of clothing folded in a corner? A blanket on the floor? A stack of shitting paper? A partially decomposed body with an odour so strong I'd gag as soon as it hit me?

No. There was none of that.

None of what I was told would be there.

And, most baffling of all, no Leonard Fry.

Instead, what I got was a well-ordered, fully furnished bedroom. Quaintly suburban, entirely unlike any other room in the house. The walls were navy blue. In the corner, a three-quarter bed with a blue-striped duvet and three matching pillows. Beside the bed there was a table with a red lamp. An old-fashioned record player. A shelf of books. Everything clean and shiny. Immaculate. The large windows were framed by pale-grey curtains. On the walls, there was a set of posters—all featuring the same person: a pianist.

I went in and studied the space, taking in each detail, breathing in the trapped scent of linen and wood and old books. I explored the inside of the cupboard and found piles of shirts and t-shirts. The types a trendy teen would wear. The stuff of jeans commercials.

I crossed the room and stood at the bed, where I noticed a white envelope. It had been crudely opened, and was stacked with sheets of paper. I was about to reach inside, when I looked up and caught sight of the poster on the wall above the bed—

I *knew* that man.

I'd seen him before.

But it wasn't his face I picked up on; it was his right leg, which was sticking out of a specially tailored trouser bottom. The leg was bloated, and the skin looked pebbly. I looked around the room: in another poster he was stooped over a grand piano on a stage, sweating under the lights. In a third, he was sitting at a piano in a sound studio, resting his elbow on the lid. Again, his face didn't flick any switches, but that diseased limb couldn't be confused for any other. At the bottom of the poster was a signature, scrawled in blue ink.

Sincerely, L. Fry.

I looked to the next, and the next—

Regards, L. Fry.

Stay true, Lenny.

Yours, Leonard Fry.

I spun away from the wall.

No—

There'd been a mistake.

There *must* have been a mistake.

This man in the poster—he was not the man I'd met in the bar. Nor the man who owned the house, the man I'd made an agreement with. This poster-man—the "Leonard Fry" in these pictures—he was the man I'd met as a boy, sitting alongside my father and drinking warm Fanta in a living room that stank of mothballs and stale food.

I looked at the old record player on the bedside table, saw the lone album with Leonard's face on the cover. Carcassonne. Pointy turrets in the background. *Sea Souls of the Dead: Live in France.* I picked it up, slipped the vinyl out of the sleeve, set it down, and put the stylus in place.

With a crackle, it began.

A few notes in, I recognised the tune.

All those years ago, it had stuck in my head, and here it was again. The tempo picked up. A snare led the way. Bass and sax joined in. The stylus spun in its groove, and Leonard's voice kicked in.

He was singing about a woman.

A woman who threw parties for strangers, who you couldn't help but fall in love with, but who could never love you back, no matter how hard she tried, or even wanted to—or promised she would. It was the ballad of a woman so intensely drawn to the loneliness of others, she was fated to endure her own.

She throws a helluva shindig
Knows jus' how to get the drinks in,
And them all singin',
Til it sudd'nly sinks in,
That we ain't never met her before.

She jabs like she knows us,
Keeps toppin' glasses,
And it's clear to us all,
She throws a helluva shindig
For every stranger she meets, see?
So we 'n she ain't ever alone.

Sweet, sweet Jolene
Sweet, sweet Jolene

Jolene?

My Jolene?

I stumbled backwards, the music diffused, filling my being, and then, like a rogue wave, a memory crashed over me— clearer and more complete than ever before . . .

. . . The attorney is watching as I study the box before me. It's the one with the rusty key inside—courtesy of my recently deceased father.

The fat man weaves his fingers into each other and sits back in his chair. It whimpers under his weight.

"As I've already mentioned," he says, "I don't know the significance of that key, whether it's for an actual door or drawer, or if it's a memento of some kind. Whatever the case, your father made it very clear that you're to have it. He made a big thing of it, too, far more than the, er . . . "—he clears his throat and continues—"the more financially substantial part of his will."

I look up with a frown. "I don't understand," I say.

The attorney chews his bottom lip, and nods.

"What you may or may not know, Mr. Croud, is that your father was a wealthy man. His business affairs have been dealt with by relevant parties, as per his will. That side of things, you don't have to worry about. There is, however, the matter of a house."

I say nothing. Not yet.

The attorney pages through a folder on his desk.

"Well, house is a bit of an understatement," he says with a half-smile. "It's a mansion, really, on a very large estate in the countryside, and it's known as . . . I have it here"—flip, flip, flip—"Krymeer. An hour or so away, off the N1, I believe." He looks up at me. "The point is, it's yours. That, and a kick-start sum of two million rand, to be paid in two instalments. Non-taxable."

My brain doesn't fully register his words. "I'm sorry. I'm getting a house?"

"A mansion. Yes. Along with one hundred and twenty-four hectares of land. The mansion itself has quite a significant history; you can read all about it in this." He pushes a file towards me and I open it. The attorney adds something about a long-standing servant and a groundsman, but it's entirely up to me whether or not they stay.

I slowly turn the pages, sheets of white paper secured with paperclips. There're some photographs, too, in the folder, all showing the mansion from different angles. The last one is different. A Polaroid of a man on a couch, with a boy on his lap. My older self turns it over, and in black ink is written: 7th June 1983. Happy burp-day daddyo!

"That's you and him," the attorney says. "I believe he was fond of that one."

I shake my head, tell him this is all some mistake.

"No mistake," the attorney says. "I assure you. It's yours. All of it. Like I said, do with it what you will. It's in your hands, now."

He pauses, reaches inside a drawer, and continues, "One final thing." He pulls out a long rectangular envelope, and hands it to me. "There's this."

It's got nothing but my name on it, written in cursive.

"It's a letter," he adds. "From your father. I have not read it, and I have no idea what it relates to. But perhaps it has a few answers to questions you may have. What I do know is this. Included in your father's final wishes was a request for a weekend wake, to be held at the mansion, for his friends, relatives, and yourself, from Friday to Sunday, two weeks from now. In addition to that, you should know that your ownership will only come into effect after completion of the weekend proceedings."

When the time comes, I turn up at Krymeer in a white Cressida I've just bought. The sheer size of the estate overwhelms me. And angers me, some. The mansion looks like a stony cross between a parliament building and a cathedral.

There are a number of cars in the parking lot. I lean over for my suit on the back seat, then go up the steps, bracketed with classic columns, and knock on the door. It opens, and an old man is standing there. Tendrils of grey hair are combed over to hide a balding head. He greets me with open arms, smiles, and tells me I look just like my father. The resemblance is unmistakable, he says. He talks about the numbers, oh, the numbers, how they miss the numbers. I figure he's talking about piano songs. I follow him into the house. He turns out to be an uncle I've never met (a former university professor, he says he was, specialising in graph theory). We pass by half-open doors, and I glimpse the occupants, who are dressed in black. The clink of glasses can be heard.

They're all sobbing. Consoling one other. Discussing my father, from what I can tell. I realise there isn't anything I could say to any of them about the man. Everyone else in the world seems to know *him better than I ever did. I sigh at the thought of his wake lasting the entire weekend, but a final wish is a final wish, after all. As for me, I want to stay as far away from everyone else as I can. Upstairs, I find a small room with a tiny television and decide I'll be staying there. The only time I leave is to play a piano I find at the other end of the corridor. I hear people move around, freely making use of the house (my house, I have to start accepting), though I have no idea what they're up to. Eating. Drinking. Crying. Or just gossiping about the aloof son upstairs. I hear them scuttling, way below the floorboards, like rats.*

As Sunday comes to a lazy close, I figure people are leaving, so I exit the room. I go to the window and watch the procession of black cars pull out of the parking area, returning each of my father's relatives, friends, and acquaintances to the pantomimes of their regular lives . . .

I took another look at Leonard's pic on the LP cover before putting it down on the bedside table.

This was my house.

This entire time, the house was mine.

The estate. The money. All of it. But what about the rest of the story? The naked woman at the door that first day I'd arrived? What about Leonard's mad plot for me to lock him up for a year, feed him, ignore him? I stepped backwards, sat down on the bed. As I did so, an image beamed against the wall of my mind, bright and clear as the moon on a cloudless night.

The envelope.

I reached for the letter from my father—as forgotten as the man himself. My stomach cramped at the thought of reading whatever was on those pages.

I turned the envelope over, looked at it front and back. Inside, there were three pages, all handwritten. The paper looked old and tatty, as if it had been pulled out a hundred times by a hundred different persons. I flattened the sheets against the striped duvet, took a breath, and began:

Dear Bentley,

I don't know how to start this & maybe that's always been my problem. Or maybe it's that I don't know how to finish things. I'm not sure. Maybe neither is true. Maybe it's the middle where I really bugger things up. Whatever the case, all I can say is that this letter is probably far too little, far too late. Maybe you've been told a particular story of me & this is the story you've come to believe. Before I proceed, I must say that I have no intention of confusing you or upsetting you or turning anyone against you. All I want is to share my side of the story.

It's true that I wasn't as present as I perhaps should have been. I missed your birth, for one. That was the start of it. I'm also not sure what I'd have contributed by being there, though if I had been there you might not have been named Bentley. I always hoped you'd be named something stronger & more classic, like Howard, or even Edgar, but your mother was adamant you'd be Bentley & of course she was there to have her say, so Bentley it was.

I spent a great deal of time away on business, often for weeks on end. I'm not sure, if I could travel back in time, that I'd do any of it differently, but for all my ambition, for all my accomplishments, I have in these final days found myself overcome by a peculiar sense of regret.

I know people dream of having the things I've got. Doing the things I've done. At one stage of my life, I myself dreamt about wanting all this & so that's why I find myself here. In this big house. Surrounded by my things. There's very little I haven't done, very few places I haven't been. Yes, of course, I could simply have gone on—there are always new toys out there—but after a while I seemed to lose my appetite. I realised that all I've done is pile everything up, endlessly, year after year, without ever stopping to strip away the layers—to discover what kind of man I am beneath it all.

Take away the things we own. The houses. The clothes. The cars. Etcetera. Take away the people. All the jabbering & the dinner dates and the handshakes. The schmoozing. Take away the weekend retreats and the jet-setting & the events and occasions and all the traditions on top of traditions. Take away the things we convince ourselves are important. Our little responsibilities to each other. Our mundane habits. Our rituals. What to wear. What to eat. Where to go next, do next, on & on & on. Take away this entire swirling cyclone of existence & then take away our ability to control any of it—and then ask yourself: what remains of us? Who are we without any of that?

Well, Bentley, here's the thing: I really don't know. I never allowed myself to ever find out, & so in this way I feel I've missed out on the opportunity to be the father I could & should have been to you. Beyond this, I hope you have at least a few good memories of me.

I have one, in particular. It was the day I took you to meet the musician who lived across the street. Leonard Fry. Remember him? Way back, before he was famous. I can still see the look on your face the moment he started playing. You were hooked. His biggest fan, though at the time he didn't have many. You even had your favourite song of his. Remember it? "Sweet Jolene." You'd play it over & over & drive your mother mad. You sang it all the time. I think even at that young age you were kind of in love with the woman in that song.

Anyway, I'm wandering off the point—if there's in fact a point to be made. What's most important for you to know is this: I did not just leave you, abandon you. I did not escape in the night, in spite of what you may have thought or been told. The truth is, I was asked to leave—by your mother. I did try to see you, but she wouldn't let me. I wanted you to live with me. It'd also be fair to add that your mother went through a period of alcoholic indulgence that concerned me greatly. I tried everything to have you come home with me, but she used my earlier absence against me. In the end she won & I was sent away from you.

But I never forgot you. So, little as it may mean to you, I'm leaving you this house, this estate, a payout of R2 million—& on top of that a hefty living allowance which will be deposited into your account every month.

All of this & a key to a room. It's a room I've been wanting to show you for a very long time. A room I've kept prepared for you for many years now. A room I always hoped you'd one day occupy & call your own. Even though it became unlikely you'd ever actually stay in it, I kept it all those years to show you, to prove to you that I never gave up hoping.

I have to admit, though, that I was never sure I could be the parent you needed. And I was never the most open of fathers, as you're aware. But who knows how you might have turned out? Knowing me, I'd probably have encouraged you to play classical rather than jazz, if only to ensure you didn't spend your time in the company of pot-smokers & drunks. I'm joking, of course.

I also can't be sure it's a good idea telling you all this— changing the story you've been carrying around with you all these years. Maybe I should have gone to my grave with my mouth shut. One thing's for certain, though, the cancer in my lung will soon take me. That's what you get when you take in more cigarette smoke than fresh air. The chemotherapy's been useless. I've lost my hair. I'm a frail man who struggles to get out of bed in the morning & I don't imagine I'll last longer than a few more weeks.

So that's that. I'm not sure what else to say. It's a start but also an end.

You probably have questions & I apologise for not being there to answer them for you. I suppose over time you'll have to figure out a few things for yourself. You've got this far on your own & thankfully you've turned out to be the best thing you can be in a world where fairness is a fairy tale & all that matters is who's got the sharpest claws: a survivor.

Regards,
Your father

I dropped the letter on the bed, then wandered to the window. My mind was running over my father's words in the letter.

That letter.

That *letter*—

This wasn't the first time I'd read it. Of course not. I'd read it many, many times before. Without recalling having ever pulled those pages from the envelope, still, I knew this with certainty. Those words. I'd heard them all. The complaint about the burdens of wealth, of endless choice.

I sucked air between my teeth, exhaled. I needed to leave. I felt the first few swells of panic rise in my chest. I needed to get out of that room, out of that house—

The door was shut.

I couldn't recall closing the damned thing.

What was going on?

I clutched the handle with both hands, turned it.

I tried again, and again, and then shook the handle.

"Hey," I called, pulling at it. "Hey!"

No answer. Not a murmur.

"Who's out there?"

I paused, my chest heaving, and stepped back.

I ran at the door, thumping it.

"You hear me out there? Whoever you are, open this door!"

I stopped, my fist suspended in the air as I looked down—

I froze in my spot.

Scratch marks.

Hundreds of them, criss-crossing the lower half of the door, creating a crude carving of wood and flaked paint. I turned my hands over and studied my fingertips: chipped nails with purplish blood underneath, seeping as far as the cuticles. All that blood I'd never been able to get rid of, never managed to scrub away . . .

(*Scratch, scratch, scratch*)

I retreated a step, took a second step back, my eyes flicking from my nails to the door, and back, and then they caught a full-length mirror on the wall—

Me, staring back.

But *not* me.

A withered, shabby version of myself. Pale, bearded, with blue-black pouches under my eyes. Everything else could have been a stunt, a sham of some kind, but not what I was seeing now. This was me. Barefoot, with cheap clothing sagging on my bony frame.

I staggered backwards. As I did, the walls of the room warped and bulged. With a mental flash of flesh and faces, a distant, haunting echo of expired laughter in a heaving house, I remembered everything . . .

. . . *the house has been heaving for months now. It's full of people I don't know, there for the booze and the drugs, for the sex, for the chance to escape their pedestrian little lives. It's no secret. And yet, for a reason I can't place, I want them here, these strangers, all over each other, screwing, partying, using all my stuff. Because I don't give a shit. Because this house is so big.*

So stupidly big.

I'm slouched in my couch beneath a chandelier sailing back and forth, watching these people in front of me, these men and women laughing and drinking and doing lines off any smooth surface in sight. The music blares as if it's coming from an immense machine beneath the house—a coal-powered monstrosity, churning, thundering at the core—somehow keeping the whole world going. I know the song. Television's "Marquee Moon." Tom Verlaine singing about listening to the rain but hearing something else . . .

I grab a bottle of whiskey and step over sprawled strangers. No one notices. I pass by the fireplace, and the tables of fruit, and baskets overflowing with all kinds of furry and leathery and plastic props. Someone swigs a bottle of champagne, and with an ape-like laugh spits it out in a spray. I pass by, leaving behind all that bedlam.

I'm in the empty corridor. I feel relief now that I have some space, but the relief doesn't last longer than a few seconds. I'm drunk or high or both, but that corridor, it just goes on and on. I keep walking, keep swigging. I stop, close my eyes, slam my back against the green wall.

I open my eyes.

I'm facing a door.

Not just any door. It's the door to the room.

I tip the bottle back. The booze runs, burns my throat.

To hell with my father, I think.

And to hell with that letter he left for me—

To hell with it all.

Except for that room. This one little room.

Sealed off from everything.

Waiting for me.

I look to my left, at the entrance to the bar area with all those strangers. Clambering, wallowing, swallowing each other whole. I can still hear them in there. Trashing my place. A woman I don't recognise enters the corridor and heads towards me. She's wearing a man's shirt unbuttoned to her belly. Her legs stretch out from underneath. Her eyelids can barely stay open, but she's dozily eyeing me. I wish she'd leave me alone.

"So you're him, huh?" she says. "Hey, man, you're missing out on all the good stuff."

She blows a kiss, moves on, and I look back at the door. The door, it just sits there. Shut. Fixed in its frame, unperturbed by the chaos of the world.

What did my father have in mind, I wonder, when he set it up for me all those years ago? The bed. The posters on the walls. The record player, Leonard Fry's album (as if that's the only music I'd listened to since the age of seven or so).

That neat, well-ordered room, prepared for a person who doesn't exist—for a possible me, if I'd only gone to live with him. And now that he's given me the house, I'm not sure what he imagined I'd do with that room—apart from possibly sitting in it for a while, pondering some grand, unlived version of my life.

The room doesn't even feel like a real place, at least not in the way anything else is. It feels separate from everything else that exists. There is the world as it is, with whatever's in it—and then there's this room. All that remains of some alternate reality. My own personal limbo on earth, my Hamistagan in the midst of hell, cut off from the mess of my life, and immune to time itself . . .

. . . Groggily, I look up.

The Bijou, my old haunt, with its sign buzzing in blue cursive.

I wipe my mouth with my sleeve, go inside.

. . . Borrowing the waiter's pen, I grab an old receipt, write TURN AROUND on the back. I instruct the waiter to leave it on the pianist's saucer. Ten minutes later, after a few tequilas, the young pianist gets his tea, along with the note. His eyes sweep the room, find me in my corner, and then he slowly, cautiously, makes his way over.

He thanks me for the tea, tells me he's not much of a tea-drinker. I introduce myself, ask him to take a seat.

I clear my throat and smile.

He's a good pianist, I say, adding that he knows that, and it's good to know one's worth. He seems pleased, mumbles something about growing up in a family of pianists, and how his mother wished he'd stuck to playing for the church. That was a long time ago, he says. I ask him then if he has family, and he says no. A wife? No. Girlfriend? Shake of the head. I nod, take a sip of my tea and turn my eyes to the people at the bar. A man chatting up a woman, or the other way around. A barman punching an order into a touchscreen terminal. A guy running a cigarette under his nose for a whiff before putting it back in the box. It reminds me of how my father died— that painful, six-month suffocation—what was it, almost two, three years ago now? Have I really been living at the house that long?

Time's all messed up in my head.

Past, present, and future swirl in a bog.

The kid asks if I'm all right.

I laugh, say I'm fine. Then I compose myself, lean forward, and cut to the chase.

I tell him about a farewell weekend, to be held at my house in the country. I also mention money. That there'll be a lot of it.

But he doesn't play for money, he says, money corrupts—and I laugh then, and tell him only cowards are afraid of money. Cowards and posers. And we're more interesting men than that.

I sell him a chance for the two of us to take a risk, swim out from the islands of our lives. Slowly, he comes around. He seems to get it. I tell him the dress code, the arrival time, the departure time. He says little, seeming to soak it all up. Finally, in the miasma of that dark bar, the young pianist in the cheap suit—who played like the devil up there on the stage and is playing with the devil down here—he smiles. It's a smile like a gash from ear to ear, of agreement and anticipation and utter unknowingness. And I know, after all the searching, the visions of myself spending a year in absolute solitude, that I've finally found the one . . .

No. *No.*

It couldn't be true.

I hurled myself at the door. Gripping the handle with both hands I shook and twisted and threw my shoulder at it.

"Open up! You hear me? Listen, please—there's been a mistake! Open the door!"

At the sound of footsteps, I banged again, yelling, then swiftly, hysterically, ran to the window, and pressed my face against the glass to spot an escape. I looked down. There was no point. Fine metal shavings indicated I'd already tried to file through the bars, though there was no hint of an implement. No balcony, either. No gutter, no piping—

(*. . . But here's the kicker. No release. No shortcuts. No diversions. No channel-hopping my way out of it. There'll be nowhere to go, except straight through the muck and the mist . . .*)

I ran at the door again, bashing it with my fists, ten, twenty, a hundred bruising times, until I closed my eyes and leant my forehead against it. Panting and out of breath, I slumped to the floor. There was no way out.

There'd *never* been a way out.

Precisely what I'd paid for, after all.

My limbo. My Hamistagan in hell.

Cut off from the world.

Immune to time itself.

(*Cos what I really want to know is this: after everything is gone, after everything I've spent my life obsessing over has been taken away, what's left of me? How deep's my rabbit hole? What will I find in the company of nothing and no one but myself and my own thoughts? And if I go in that room and it's madness, if there's nothing in the basement of my stripped mind but eat-my-own-shit madness, well, hell, won't that be a trip . . .*)

I opened my eyes again and saw the loose pages of the worn, years-old letter teeter on the edge of the bed before they fell to the floor and landed in a tatty fan. All those words. Bitter, forgotten memories. Incomplete answers. Mine to stitch to the content of my own mad mind. Christ. That's why I'd gone in at all, wasn't it? To understand the reason I'd been left that vast inheritance in the first place. To work my way through the shit in my head. A lonely, insecure mother and her quiet, fatherless son. A version of *me* who'd got everything I'd ever wanted from the world, from my career (before I'd caved his head in with a pot, the pompous prick). All of that, along with a judgmental voice from behind a closed door, a voice that reminded me I hadn't earned any of what I had—and that I never would, or could.

But then what?

How many times had I told myself this same story already, run through this same charade? How many times had I realised that, all along, I've been *here*, wasting away in this room? And then, how long after knocking and banging and screaming and scratching my fingers raw would it take for me to finally give up, to accept that I wasn't going anywhere, to begin the process of forgetting all of this—the letter, the posters, this room— before slipping back into my convoluted fantasy all over again?

Come on. Spit it out, Jazz Man.

While you still can.

How goddamned long before you imagined yourself walking around in a painting of a park alongside a woman from a song and seeing yourself standing in the rain and down at the pool, before blacking out and waking up and blacking out and waking up on the same big bed of the same big bedroom of the same big inescapable house between the hills—

again . . .

and again . . .

and again . . .

and *again?*

VII.

Don't bother tryin',
I'll save you the trouble,
Love her . . .
But cut it off there.
She ain't up for it too,
It's not 'cos of you,
She just don't see
. . . that you're there.

Hey man . . .
Jolene just don't see
That you're there.

66.

It was a beautiful day.
No one could say otherwise.

The view I had was of a part of the estate I couldn't recall having ever explored—dense woods leading into an immense expanse of countryside, craggy mountains, and, in the distance, the haziest hint of what I knew to be the city. Seeing it from where I was standing made the city feel both farther and closer than it actually was.

From my window, I pictured everyone going about their lives, confined to office cubicles, or having cappuccinos at sidewalk cafés, or listening to the Top 40 in their cars. I pictured a mother and son in a cinema, watching a movie on his eleventh birthday. A woman with face piercings smiling at an unsuspecting man across a bar counter. An over-privileged twenty-year-old playing Brahms in some lavish hall in Prague. A woman throwing dinner parties for strangers. A sensitive boy drawing pictures in a restaurant. A jazz pianist in a nightclub on the corner of Bree and Orphan—the one that sits between a restaurant and a musty old bookstore. And finally, I pictured a bored lunatic in the background, looking on. Clapping. Drinking his tea. Waiting his turn.

I pictured them all and wondered what each one wanted from their ordinary little lives. I wondered whether any of them could declare that they were happy—really, genuinely happy—with the self-told stories of who they were and what they wanted and where they were going. Or whether, as a woman in a song had once said (a woman I loved, as if being in love without being loved in return can ever be enough): there was no such thing.

I also wondered if they were unaware of their own madness, and oblivious to the simple truth that eludes the so-called sanest of us: the wars we have with ourselves become wars we have with others, and the wars we have with others become wars we have with ourselves.

I perched on the edge of the bed, feeling painfully hungry, and tried to remember when last I'd been fed . . .

Whether there'd be a next time.

Sunlight filled the room, and I looked outside. Clouds. Three clouds of different sizes, sailing across a sky as blue as any I'd ever seen before. I watched them for as long as I could, as long as they'd allow me, but they soon scudded beyond the window frame, and were gone.

Out of sight.

But not out of mind.

No, not out of mind just yet.

Scratch, scratch

1.

First things first.
My name is not Bentley Croud.

It's been so long since anyone's called me by my full name that I imagine it belonging to some smiling stranger at some dull party. Someone tanned and healthy and successful. Whites of the eyes admitting to few or no vices. Straight rows of pristine teeth that have taken no punches. Someone who looks like me, has my face, shares my birthday, but who's taken every road I haven't, said a no to each of my yesses and a yes to each of my nos. That would be your Bentley Croud, and that would not be me.

No. The I in the story I'm about to tell you is simply known as Bent.

Bent. The misshapen state.

Now . . .
Where was I?

The Inside Out Man

Acknowledgements

Ideas, like most things, die in isolation.

Brent Strydom, my brother, who finds the time to read my writing between plots for global takeover and pool-dips in Vietnam. Tom Southey, for being there at the start, and periodically reminding me not to fuck it all up. Carl Gough, my new good friend and off-the-record editor, who's due to call in a major favour any day now. My actual editor, Lynda Gilfillan, who made me question every comma and somehow uncovered music allusions I had no idea I'd written in. Manager and muso Ryno Posthumus, who's backed me from book one, but is no doubt thrilled I've traded in rafts and robots for jazz and madness. Aoife Lennon-Ritchie—my agent, mentor, and creative confidante—who grafts harder than anyone I know to get the world on my side. My family, both in my wife's corner and my own, who have continued to offer a level of encouragement and enthusiasm I've never had any right to expect. Once again, my mother, Juliet, and Wytze Voerman, to whom this book has been dedicated. And, ultimately, my courageous and talented wife Bron, and hilarious, handsome-devil-of-a-son Charlie-Max, for ensuring I'll never have to resort to fiction to experience the life I've always dreamed of living.

My love and thanks to you all.

Fred Strydom studied film and media at the University of Cape Town. He has taught English in South Korea and published a number of short stories. He currently works as a television writer and producer in Johannesburg, where he lives with his wife and son, two dogs, cat, and two horses. *The Inside Out Man* is his second novel; his first, *The Raft*, was published by Talos Press in 2015.